37.50

BIRTHDAY

BY THE SAME AUTHOR

ALAN SILLITOE

Birthday

Flamingo
An Imprint of HarperCollins*Publishers*

Flamingo
An Imprint of HarperCollins*Publishers*
77–85 Fulham Palace Road,
Hammersmith, London W6 8JB

Flamingo ® is a registered trademark of
HarperCollins*Publishers*

www.**fire**and**water**.com

Published by Flamingo 2001
1 3 5 7 9 8 6 4 2

Copyright © Alan Sillitoe 2001

A catalogue record for this book
is available from the British Library

ISBN 0 00 710781 1

Typeset in Galliard by Palimpsest Book Production Limited,
Polmont, Stirlingshire

Printed and bound in Great Britain by
Clays Ltd, St Ives plc

IN MEMORIAM

June Sillitoe

Part One

ONE

Arthur dropped gear going downhill. 'Trams clanked through here once upon a time. Then you got tracklesses. Now there's ordinary buses. But it pays to have your own car. Saves hanging around.'

Brian's bedtime reading, set in the smokey-hot olive groves of Greece, was a potent antidote to the sight of his home town. 'I like driving from London in a couple of hours, to call on the family whenever the mood takes me.'

'We're always glad to see you,' Arthur said. Trains at one time grumbled up and down the double line through Basford Crossing, from the main station in town to populous colliery places such as Bulwell and Kirkby and Sutton-in-Ashfield, not to mention Newstead, which Brian had noted long before he knew of the Abbey and Byron.

'Coal smoke used to reek as if it would cure the flu,' Arthur told Avril, out for the first time since her bout of chemotherapy. 'Even when it makes you cough enough to think you'd got TB it was a tonic for us.'

'I'll bet it was,' she said wryly.

Shops selling food and cheap clothes, ironmongery and paraffin, had been packed around the crossroads. A public library gave shelter to a few down and outs in winter while they read the papers, and those with nowhere to lay their heads at night could trudge to a workhouse not too far up the road. A park for sitting in on sunny days had a pond at the centre, and Arthur thought God help the poor bloody fishes, though they seemed lively enough when fingers twirled the water, even if they did have two heads and a split tail from the bleach works nearby.

Children out of school would shout to be heard above the thunder of the unstoppable rhythmical puffer under its whitey grey coils of smoke, eyes showing envy and maybe fear at an engine that didn't care (as if it could) whether they lived or died.

Brian remembered counting the trucks, and marvelling at the load a shining black locomotive could haul, staring as if his soul was struggling to get free from under the heaps of coal so that he could run as far away as his feet would take him. Magic names stencilled in big white letters along their sides flickered in his dreams on hearing wagons rattle through by night as well, unseen places more glamorous than the one he lived in.

'I'm sure it's altered a lot,' Avril said, who had been brought up in London, and could only laugh at their talk of past and difficult times. 'It must have done, by the look of it.'

Arthur recalled standing on the footbridge, which was still there, with its terracotta girders and white grid rail to stop people tumbling over. No more coal trucks laboured under canopies of smoke because there were no collieries for them to go to. 'We never thought it would change like this.' Pubs and pawnshops and bookies had been a part of the place as well. 'There were crowds around here, but it's a desert now. It's half past seven on a Saturday night, and where is everybody?'

Shop doors were boarded up: brambles and dandelions sprouted from doorsteps, strips of paper swayed from a hoarding between two shops like the withered arms of a dead octopus, and a faded notice from way back advertised three-piece suits. 'People are in flats and new houses,' Avril said, 'and good luck to them.'

The lights on stop, Arthur gently braked before a wider road with more traffic on it. He would have gone through on yellow, but there was always a flash bastard coming the other way in a BMW to clip you. 'Some of us didn't mind living like that. We didn't know any other life.'

'I remember telling people at a dinner party in London about my early days,' Brian said, 'and they asked whether I'd been happy growing up in a slum. When I said I didn't remember it like that they thought I was putting it on.'

Arthur pointed out the white stuccoed façade of an old picture house, now an emporium for builders' materials. 'You're right,' he said to Avril. 'It wasn't so good living around here. You just didn't realize until you left.'

Lights flashed permission for Arthur's Peugeot to rumble over the crossing. The Methodist chapel, having lost much of its clientele for Christian worship, had a social security office on the upper floor, while newish houses beginning to replace the grubby dereliction of the old looked as if no one lived in them. His attention didn't deviate from the macadam while nodding to Brian in the back. 'I expect Jenny'll get a shock when she sees your phizog at the party.'

'I suppose she will.' It was another reason for being here, apart from seeing his brothers, and trawling what places of his youth were still upstanding. They mostly weren't, many Stalingrads having come and gone on the old stomping grounds, though he'd never stopped regarding his home town with affection, whatever happened to it, hadn't left with alacrity at eighteen out of dislike for the place as because he wanted to see more of the world. No matter how changed, it was an area in which he had no need of maps. Everything was in the past, but an event could leap to mind with such intensity it might have happened in the last five minutes.

Whatever his age, he contrived not to take in the reality of the staring face during his morning shave, and joking in a pub with his brothers about living forever was a fair reason for drinking to the prospect, while aware that death's blackout could descend any minute. Lucky the man to whom it came quickly, though going to Jenny's seventieth birthday party kept such thoughts at bay.

'It's a good job me and Derek will be with you,' Arthur said. 'We can't have you getting her in the pod again.'

Such jibes called for the expected Seaton laugh, because Jenny Tuxford, after a lifetime of misery endured with unimaginable saintliness, had been freed at last from an anguish which must have seemed eternal while it was going on. She was his first love, never forgotten, so he had been invited to the party. 'I never did get her pregnant. Some other swine had to do that.'

They had gone at it every weekend on the settee in her parents' house like rabbits in a thunderstorm or, to use another local phrase, had many helpings of hearthrug pie in front of the fire. Her father, a miner at Cinderhill, got a good allowance of coal to heat the council house, as if such juvenile passion needed it.

He had never seen her with no clothes on, nor had she witnessed him 'bare' – as they would have put it. In those days a man's shirt wouldn't come off except over the head, and he might have to pull it back on at the click of a gate latch. It was bad enough undoing braces to get your trousers down, though there was never a man smarter at yanking them up.

Jenny was armoured in roll-on, heavy duty brassiere, lisle stockings and suspenders, though the advance guard of his fingers always closed on the vital spot, which led to the soaking of camiknickers in love juice (the embarrassing term came back to him) until he learned enough from a mate in the factory to call at the chemist's once a week and provide himself with an adequate supply of french letters. No lack of sex education for him, and with such memories who needed pornography?

Arthur broke in: 'A woman can have a baby at whatever age she likes, or so I read in the paper. Maybe Jenny will make you use a contraceptive this time, and put your spunk in her deep freeze. She'll have the kid in five years' time, and let one of her great granddaughters bring it up. It's hard to say, with a deep one like her. But if she does have a kid you'll just have to keep sweating your bollocks off writing them television scripts to pay the maintenance. She might even have quads.'

'You are a devil,' Avril laughed, 'talking like that about a respectable woman.'

'You never know how respectable anyone is,' Arthur said, 'till they're dead.' He crossed the dual carriageway going left to the city centre and right to the M1, over on the free lights to go through the estate of Broxtowe.

A tranquil evening, the blaze of late sun caught the roofs as if to set them on fire. Nearly every council dwelling had its car, sometimes a caravan for whoever hadn't been able to get far enough from Basford Crossing but liked a look at the Lincolnshire coast now and again. And if they were too dead-alive to go that far a satellite dish pulled in four hundred channels of boring television.

'This is an area of high crime and vandalism,' Arthur said. 'In the old days the houses were a lot closer together, so people policed themselves. They had to, if they wanted to live in peace. Anybody thieving or making trouble would get a good thumping, and if your parents didn't do it, one of the neighbours would. If anything went missing from a house in our street all we had to do was find Billy Jones, who lived a few doors away. Somebody would put a fist under his nose, and make him give back what he'd nicked. If Billy said it wasn't him you showed him the other fist and then he'd tell you who it was. I think thieving was in his blood. A woman spotted him taking a meat grinder from under his coat at the pawnshop one Monday morning, and knew it belonged to Mrs Greatton, so she gave him a terrible pasting, and took it back to her.'

Brian laughed. 'It nearly always was him' – though you might also say Poor Old Billy, who had even more scars inside than out, and almost from birth had never known where his next meal was coming from. He belonged, if that was the word, to parents who fought all the time, when they weren't boozed up on dole money, or on the proceeds of whatever their children earned or stole.

'They had eight kids and a grandma in that family,' Arthur said, 'and I'll never know how all eleven fitted into one little house. I expect they slept in a row on the floor. I went in one day to call for one of the kids, and I nearly got gassed. Nowadays I expect they'd all be in care.'

'Most families managed better than that,' Brian said, knowing that not a few of his mates, including Billy Jones, had been packed off to Borstal and then to prison. It was easier to get sent down, because the police looked into every small crime, if they got to know about it.

'I'll keep an eye on you at the party,' Arthur told him, after a silence. 'You were lucky Jenny's daughter invited the whole Seaton mob and not just you.'

Maybe he wouldn't recognize her after all this time. She would certainly look different, and so would he. Mutually

8

knowing each other on the street would be impossible. At sixteen she'd been robust and full of hope, lived only for the passing day, earned her living and had nothing to fear from anybody. If she imagined the future it was only to picture the man who would fall in love with her generosity and treat her as she deserved. SCUM would have his bollocks for thinking so, but in those days it was true, and in any case Jenny would have laughed at such notions.

On days when they walked out, a freshly ironed blouse covered her bosom, and an open brown cardigan (which she had knitted) draped over that, the brown skirt not so low that he couldn't see her legs. Hair cut in a fringe across her pale forehead fell long and dark over her shoulders.

As a self-absorbed sixteen-year-old youth he had stood on a winter's evening by the arched redbricked gateway of a clothing factory with Pete Welbeck who was waiting for his sweetheart Lottie. She came out arm in arm with Jenny, among scores of other women who worked eight hours a day among the noise and dust of sewing machines, long rows in a vast room, three floors of women running up pieces of khaki serge to make uniforms, hair hidden from speeding belts by turbans which outlined their features like bathing caps, some worn to show the colour of hair underneath. The only males to be teased and flirted with were lads below the age of eighteen who shifted enormous bundles, or acted as rudimentary toolsetters, tutored by one or two chargehands over military age.

The vitality in Jenny's gait, even after a day's work, illuminated her good nature beneath which, nevertheless, a calculated stoicism blandly assessed whoever she looked at. Pete told him next morning that she had been curious about him as well, wanting to know his age, where he worked, and what street he lived in.

9

They had no photographs from those days, not even separate ones to exchange. Camcorders were ten a penny now, but few people had cameras during the war or for a long time afterwards. Yet the memory was so much richer for dragging scenes back through the haze, whereas clear photographs would do nothing for the reality he and Jenny had known.

Walking the streets, they were said to be courting, but he had never thought the responsibility applied to him, a feckless workman of seventeen (by the time they had split) and nowhere near as staid as Jenny expected. She was too proud, or lackadaisical, or too imbued with a paralysing infusion of both, to broach the fact, only wanting him to speak the homely promise and sooner rather than later.

He knew well enough what she wanted but, in his juvenile slyness, let her wait, caring only that their weekends of love would go on for as long as forever might be. You didn't think about getting older, or making up your mind on anything as deadly as wedlock, which locked you up and no mistake, having only to recall the past miseries of his parents to know that such a state was not for him.

The parting was sudden, though he had known for some time that she wouldn't for much longer endure his wilful indecisiveness. He lacked direction in the world as it was, lived in a dream he couldn't let her share, because even not knowing exactly what it was, he wanted it for himself alone. On the other hand his sensibility, not entirely blunted by selfishness, knew all too well what was in her mind.

Meeting one evening on the street as arranged, she told him she was fed up and didn't want to see him anymore, but was going for a walk with a couple of girls a few yards away laughing, as if they had put her up to it, he thought. The three of them would sit in the pictures and see what lads they could pick up. He was surprised at a firmness she had given no sign of before, knowing from her tone it was no use arguing, that such determination to pack him in was a kindness that saved him pleading for her not to do so.

In any case he didn't want to, and his self-esteem suffered no bruising because he went out with another girl too soon afterwards to wonder whether Jenny had chucked him or he had chucked her. There were all the boys for the asking and all the girls for the taking, always had been and always would be plenty more pebbles on the beach, so you had to make hay while the sun still shone.

The same pure breeze from the Derbyshire hills came through the car window on its way to the middle of Nottingham. In winter it was cold enough to work through the thickest jacket, but the benediction of sweet air at the moment brought back all youth's hopes and expectations.

'We'll be a bit early,' Arthur said, 'but I expect they'll let us in at The Crossbow. Jenny's daughter's booked the upstairs room from eight o'clock.' A mile away to the right the M1 crossed the old bucolic courting grounds of Trowel Moor, slicing a wood and a few fields out of existence to make room for a service station. 'Something else gone forever.'

So will we be soon enough, but Brian didn't say so because Avril had cancer, and in any case they were going to a celebration. Jenny's daughter had written to him in London that she and the other grown-ups were arranging a surprise birthday party, and would he come up for it? 'She talks about you now and again, so I know she would love you to be there.'

You can't say no to a request which might give some meaning to your life. Why otherwise had he said yes? His existence couldn't have been more different from Jenny's,

11

and that of the man she went on to meet. At nineteen she'd got pregnant, and the baby was now the woman of fifty who had organized the surprise party for her mother. After having the daughter Jenny got married and bore six more kids from a man who was to wish many times he had never been born.

'She used to come up to the house now and again, and have a cup of tea with mam,' Arthur called out. 'I suppose she had to talk about her troubles, or she would have gone off her head. She used to reminisce about when she'd gone out with you, which cheered her up a bit. Mam liked her a lot.' He aimed for a black cat, knowing it would get out of the way, which it did, just, so that they all laughed. 'You brought Jenny home for tea once, do you remember? But mam knew her parents already, because everybody knew everybody in those days.'

Brian nodded. 'Jenny's old man was a cheerful bloke, though I expect he knew what I was getting up to with his daughter. Luckily, he was fond of his ale, and went out with his wife to the pub every Friday and Saturday night.'

'You had it made,' Arthur laughed. 'And you fucked her blind on the sofa.'

'Well, who wouldn't?'

'Men!' Avril gave her usual dry laugh. 'That's all you can talk about.'

'It was the same,' Arthur retorted, 'when Sarah called on you a couple of years ago. You thought I'd gone out, but I was in the living room with my ear stuck to the wall. I looked in the mirror, and my face had gone like a beetroot.'

'I'd have known if you had been there,' she said. 'Even when I'm in bed and you go out into the garden I can tell you're not in the house.'

'Anyway,' he said to Brian, 'I'd have fucked Jenny blind as well. You should have stayed with her.'

'I ought to have done a lot of things, but they'd have been just as wrong as what I did do.' His many mistakes in life had only been useful for counting over and over when he couldn't get to sleep.

'She'd have had a better life,' Arthur said, 'though I don't suppose somebody like you would have stayed with her for long.' He nodded towards the mass of clean slate roofs going down the hill. 'Do you remember all them blocks of flats they built there twenty years ago? They had to demolish 'em after ten years because the partition walls turned into wet cardboard when it rained. A fortune was lost over that, which must have gone into somebody's pocket. Nobody got sent down for it, and I expect a lot of people are still living in Spain on the proceeds. I'd have stood 'em against a wall and shot the lot. Some made even more money when they built new houses in their place.'

'It provided work,' Avril reasonably suggested, 'and saved a lot of dole money.'

A pool of sunlight flowed into the car, and Arthur put the visor down. 'In them days there was always work. It was just a shame Jenny's husband took a job at that iron foundry. The best luck he ever had was when he married Jenny, even though she already had another bloke's kid.'

'A lot of men wouldn't have taken it on,' Avril said.

Arthur flicked the visor back when cloud hit the sun. 'Yeh, but she made up for it a million times.'

TWO

After the early days of being in love Brian hadn't seen Jenny for fifteen years, until a letter came from Nottingham to say his father was dying. He'd seen little of the old man in the previous decade, during which the binding of love and detestation had turned into tolerated indifference. Still, his imminent death meant something, as he stood on the platform thinking it strange that he always had to search for the station exit, never an automatic walk up the steps and across the booking hall onto the street, as if the roots of his instinct were cut on the day he left.

From the crowd around the train his name was spoken clearly enough to startle, and for a few moments he wondered what this half familiar face had to do with him. The express would leave in a few minutes. 'Hello! Don't you know me?' As if the likelihood of his not doing so would devastate her, though the distress in her features wasn't due to his changed appearance. 'It's me, Jenny.'

The more he looked the less altered was she from the girl he had known. He supposed he had mumbled the right words: 'What are you doing here? Why are you getting on the train? Are you here to meet someone? Or are you going to the seaside?' He must have said something like all those things, his smile covering the love and curiosity he should have felt, her signals indicating a catastrophe he lacked the nobility of soul to comprehend, and in any case the past they shared was far too far away to be of any help. Eyes filmed by heartache, she held back tears, as if trying to say something with a silence to which he could not respond since he had no silence of his own to give, his heart a ball of string that would need a lifetime to disentangle because he had become another person, and so had she.

Without luggage, she looked too unhappy to be travelling for pleasure. He noted the usual kind of blouse, and one coat button done up unevenly as if she had put it on in a state of shock. 'I'm going to the hospital in Sheffield.'

Train doors clacked like rifle shots, shouts and whistles normal to him but a grief to her who only wanted to be on her way. He tried to remember whether she had relations in Sheffield. 'What are you going there for?'

'My husband's had an accident in the foundry where he works.' She gave a mad woman's smile. 'I've got to run, though, or I'll miss my train.'

'I'm sorry. Is he badly hurt?'

'I don't know. They telephoned the corner shop. But I'm sure he must be.'

'Perhaps it's not as bad as you think.' He held her warm and vibrant hand while wanting only to get away, yet they were drawn close for a kiss, as if it might reduce the bad news. She wasn't altogether there, but who would be? He hoped she would remember the meeting as he pulled open a door the guard had just closed, to make sure she wasn't left behind, being already with her husband as the train went into the tunnel of its own smoke.

He had cut so many people out of his life in order to make a different world for himself, couldn't connect any more to a woman whose husband had been smashed up in a foundry. The death of his father seemed a formality by comparison.

16

He found the exit easily, as if instinct had come back at the sight of her, marvelling at the chance meeting while walking up the steps.

George, paralysed from the waist down, had to be cared for night and day, lifted and carried, taken and fetched, wiped and fed and humoured and honoured, and no doubt loved, Jenny's subtly harassed expression the most she would allow herself to show. She did everything, and would have done more had it been demanded or possible. She could have fled – others had been known to – left him in a hospital or convalescent home on the coast, but abandoning your husband wasn't what you did when he'd stood by you until the time of the accident. In any case, you had sworn to care for each other until one or the other died.

He was never surprised when his brothers' thoughts ran on the same lines as his own, often so close as those between husbands and wives. 'By the time George had his accident he and Jenny already had seven kids,' Arthur said, 'so maybe it was just as well he did, or he might have given her half a dozen more.'

Brian's laugh took him away from the tragic aspect of Jenny on the station platform. 'I should be glad I didn't stay with her then. I might have had the same number pulling at my turn-ups.'

'She would have dragged a rabbity bastard like you on every night,' Arthur said, 'and in your dinner hour as well, if there'd been no canteen where you worked.'

If he'd got her pregnant he would still have escaped, because the dynamo of curiosity had been busy in him from birth. His departure was both as if swimming out of a vat of treacle, and wandering away like a somnambulist, hard to know which because too far back and they hadn't

17

been logged at the time. Circumstances had carried him, and those situations met with as if to make him pay for his new life had their own compensations. Being novelties, they were an anodyne against what loss was left behind.

Another question was that if he'd asked Jenny to marry him she might have laughed in his face, because no person can avoid what the future has in store, though you may not know it (he'd certainly had no suspicion) giving the illusion that freedom of choice is possible for everyone. Having a baby already by another man, she had no option but to marry George, whether she loved him or not. George didn't know how much of a bargain he'd got until her devotion became vital for his existence, though in the years and decades of his catastrophic misfortune he was to wish he had never set eyes on her, thinking it would have been better if the falling block of iron had killed him outright. He certainly never imagined in those early days that under Jenny's care he would live more than thirty years.

George had been called up in 1940, and taken prisoner at Tobruk in Libya. He'd already lived forever on coming home from Germany in the long belly of a Halifax bomber. A young soldier in his early twenties, he queued to be measured for his demob suit, a thin man after three years' imprisonment, hoping to find a country more to his liking than the one he had left and, if not, at least to get the job of his choice.

He was promised work as a van driver, but couldn't start for a month – a long time at that age – so he walked into a nearby iron foundry and was set on straightaway. The job was more strenuous, and altogether satisfying in putting him among the sort of blokes he had fought with in the army. You had to be alert in such an occupation, but as long as you looked out for yourself and for others, and if others looked out for themselves and for you, life seemed less dangerous than driving a van.

The chain slipped: no time or place to run, a million lights turning brighter and brighter at his scream. Even if you weren't killed the number chalked on the side of the iron was plainer than on any shell fragments around Tobruk. One of his mates who called at the hospital said he could have been as badly injured driving a van, but George knew there was something more final about a fall of iron in the dismal light than there could be from any crump of tin in the street. He had got unblemished from the battlefield, had survived the boat trip across the Mediterranean, not to mention the journey by cattle truck to Germany – and now this.

A new house was provided out of the compensation, and appliances installed to make staying alive the slowest form of torment, though as easy as possible for Jenny. There was nothing more they could want, but wanting for nothing at such a price was no bargain to George. He couldn't believe it. 'Me! Why me?' he said a million times, to himself but to Jenny as well often enough. 'I'd have been better off wounded as a soldier. There'd be some pride in that. But in a foundry! That's what I can't understand.'

The more quickly his thoughts returned to the point from which they had set out, without having made him wiser or more content, the darker his anguish became and went on for months before he reconciled himself to the fact that any good reason for being on earth had been taken away. The short change of mental torture turned up no meaning to his fate, and the nightmare was that he would live as a cripple for the rest of his life.

Jenny's skin blistered with tears as she sat by him. She loved him. Everything would be all right. At least he was still alive. But so deep was her misery that she sometimes thought how good it would be if they could be struck dead together.

Walking through a bookshop to get a present of coloured pencils for Eunice's birthday she saw something on the table with Tobruk in the title. During the week it occupied George he wasn't in such despair, so from then on she took everything from the library connected with that place during the war, so that he could relive his days and stop regretting he hadn't died in the foundry.

His experience of artillery and machine guns helped his expertise with a wheelchair and orthopaedic bed. When a telephone was installed he smiled that it was like having his own headquarters in a dugout, able to call up friends and family whenever he liked. She suspected that he never left off secretly wanting to die, but knew it was a comfort for him to go even further back in time before he met her, and live again in the world of Tobruk. Dangerous though it had been, he'd at least had the use of his limbs.

Brian first saw George when he'd been twenty-five years in a wheelchair. His mother persuaded him to call: 'Sometimes Jenny comes and sits with me. If I'd been in her place I'd have gone mad now, but she always asks after you, so it would be nice if you'd pop in and say hello.'

Sunlight through the gaps of a high-clouded day gave amplitude to the spirit. He slowed along the tree-lined dual carriageway, reading each street sign so as not to overshoot the drive on which Jenny's house stood. He found a dwelling anyone should be happy to live in, the roof as if someone got up to scrub it every morning, windows as clean as if without glass, nothing too old to be unpointed or shabby, immaculate paintwork on doors and window frames, the house behind an area of sloping well cut lawn.

When setting out on his travels he hadn't wanted to live in either the cosy but decrepit houses of Basford Crossing nor a place like this, but he was happy for Jenny that she had such a pristine house. He had thought only of getting away, even if to be a homeless figure stricken by rain and bitten into by the cold, for whom any house would be paradise.

To be well fed and shod, to be out of the rain and have clothes on his back, was all he needed. A one-roomed dwelling in the middle of a wood had figured in his childhood dreams, but by craving the romantic he had achieved far more. A house like Jenny's had seemed an unattainable luxury, but as soon as he had money enough to get one he despised it. The fee for a single script could buy a dozen huts in a wood, as well as the wood and surrounding fields.

Believing that this life was the only one, that there was no God to help you (and he was intellectually incapable of believing He was other than dead and buried) meant that safety and contentment didn't exist, an ever-likely and interesting state in which there was no class, nation, or religion to capture his allegiance or give comfort. If you allowed yourself to conceive of immortality you were no longer free.

An inane Strauss jingle brought her to the door. 'Brian Seaton!'

The emphasis on his surname hid her pleasure. Well, he couldn't be sure about that, but he enjoyed hearing she would know him anywhere, though it didn't bring back the old shine in her eyes. He should have telephoned first, but wanted to surprise her. In London you never called on anyone without warning, but he had acted as if Jenny was inferior, or out of familiarity, in his usual off-hand way, an attitude which over the years had become a habit. I suppose that's how they live in London, she might tell herself, just dropping in without any notice at all. Even in the old days she often hadn't known he'd be where he said he would be.

'Your mam phoned, to tell me you were on your way.'

'And here I am. It's good to see you again.' He made up a script about a man knocking at the wrong door, then starting a conversation with the woman who answered. She asked him in for a cup of tea, which led to a new life for them that neither had thought possible when they had got out of bed that morning, but which made sense when it happened. The change in their existences was so passionate that when they went away together the relationship turned into a disaster.

He had made no such mistake with Jenny, for she had known all about him, gave him that special weighing up which now showed much of the old self in her features. Her shorter hair was a mix of grey and dark, curling around the head instead of a long and vigorous band of black, making the face seem smaller, fragile and more vulnerable. She was pale, almost sallow, lines scored for a woman in her fifties, perhaps more so than on women of similar age he met in London who hadn't been through half as much. She was slim and middling in height from what he used to think of as tallish and more robust, though she could hardly be shapely after having had seven kids. 'I was passing, and thought I'd call.'

'I'm glad you have. Come on in.'

Everything you did was wrong, even more so when you thought well and long before doing it, but she seemed happy at him standing before her, the only sign a tremble of hands as he followed her in. 'An old friend's come to see us.'

George had been forewarned perhaps, so as to hide the importance of what they had been to each other, though he didn't see why she should be diffident about it. George must have known of her life before they met, since she'd had a kid already, but the hint that they had been more than acquaintances made Brian smile. Maybe she thought that the old adolescent intensity might even now flame up between them. At least the lifetime of suffering under George's misfortune hadn't broken her.

They entered the brightly lit living room. 'Brian's an old friend. He used to know mam and dad.'

Large windows showed a well trimmed garden, an umbrageous laurel tree in the far corner beyond a newly creosoted tool shed. In the room blue and white plaster birds were fixed in attitudes of purposeful flight along the wall opposite the fireplace, on the wing to a place George might well mull on in his despairing hours, glazed eyes following the direction of their long necks. With such wings, and being heavier than air, they would fly neither far nor easily, kept from a real sky by the ceiling.

He looked away as they came into the room, the open book face down, on knees kept together by his all-tech wheelchair. A palish glow on his face suggested that movement was hard labour, as if eternally sitting with the useless lower part of himself sapped his energy, took far more of his attention than in the days when he had walked with his shovel from mould to mould around the foundry thinking of the ale he would put down in the pub after knocking-off time.

The shine of his intensely blue eyes, out of a broad face in which the bones were nevertheless visible, hinted that the accident happened last month instead of twenty-five years ago. His expression was of living by the minute, as if things hadn't changed nor time moved from the moment he had come out of the hospital. Nothing to look forward to, and little enough to think back on the longer his incapacity lasted, kept him separate and aloof, king of each moment on his wheelchair throne, only able to reign since he could no longer hope.

The furnishings of a three-piece suite on the thick piled carpets gave a temporary aspect to the room, as if George hoped to be moving out in the next week or two. Maybe Jenny had created it that way out of a restless nature now that she too was imprisoned.

The floral pattern of wallpaper was broken by pictures and framed photographs of children on a climbing frame, a youth straddling a motorbike, two young wide-smiling girls in Goose Fair hats. He was never alone with so many children and grandchildren, a living theatre to vicariously take part in. He sometimes stared at the photographs as if he hardly knew the people in them, though he did right enough, because who else was there for such as him to acknowledge?

His blue shirt was open at the neck, grey hairs below the throat, pudgy white veined hands resting on a tartan blanket covering his withered knees. Order had been arranged around him by Jenny, as much for her benefit as his, because without the routine of a twenty-four hour job such a life would have been insupportable. She had to make sure he was fed, get him into and out of bed, wash him and dress him and see to his toilet requirements, knowing it would go on into old age, never a thought of giving in, of saying it was too much, that it was breaking her back and would one day burst her heart. Maybe she wanted to shout: 'For God's sake take him to a nursing home, this is killing me, I can no longer cope,' but she'd never say it because George was king, and she the country he ruled over, a pact which enabled her to go on living.

He took Brian's hand between cool fingers as if the rite was foreign but he wanted to pass the test nevertheless. 'She's told me about you a time or two.'

24

He wondered what she had said, though anything would be of interest to George, for whom the past, no matter how far off, was only yesterday. The face-down paperback on the arm of his chair was about the siege of Tobruk. 'Are you reading that?'

His smile indicated eternal worry, self-pity the desert of his affliction, sandstorms depriving him of visibility on long passages through and back and through again. When able to rest from the irritation he was amazed that the small distance had taken such gruelling effort, which showed on the part of his mouth to which the smile was hinged. 'I was there, once upon a time.'

'It looks interesting.'

'I find it so.'

'Thanks, duck!' Brian used the old lingo for Jenny when she came with tea and a plate of biscuits, the cup rattling against its saucer like a garbled telegraph message. 'You were in the army, then?' he said to George.

'Yeh, when I was young. And after the war ended I never thought I'd look back and say how wonderful life had been in a German prison camp, though maybe it would have been the same even if I wasn't in this contraption.'

Jenny's smile showed relief at George talking with such liveliness. In trying to read more from her expression, Brian got as far into nowhere as he always had. Her back was straighter than when she had met him at the door, a stance showing more alertness, though why it should be necessary he couldn't tell, unless on kneeling by the chair to rework the blanket over his legs, or wipe the tea his shaking hands had spilled, she was fearful of his fist, powered by an inboiling irritation from a mind demented by uselessness, snaking out at her face. He wouldn't do it before a guest, but was easy to imagine in the quiet and seemingly endless afternoons when they were alone. He sensed something and wished he hadn't, wanted to go, sorry he had come, such scenes of domestic knockabout familiar from childhood when the old man battered his mother and the rest of the family out of despair at being unemployed, or at not being able to read or write.

'The only break I get these days,' George went on, 'is a fortnight every year at Ingoldmells. Still, it gets me away from this place.'

'My brother Arthur and his wife go fishing near Skegness,' Brian said. 'I stay with them overnight when they hire a caravan.'

'He fishes in the sea?'

Brian laughed, for no reason except that it was about time somebody did. 'No, it's a mile inland, at a big pond in the middle of a field. But it's good sport.' He had bought Arthur *The Compleat Angler* and he had read it more than once. 'The caravan's parked by the water, so they stagger out in their dressing gowns for an hour's fishing before breakfast. They chuck everything back, naturally.' He didn't want to dwell too long on such a pastime with a man who wasn't able to take part in it, though maybe he could if someone pushed him to the water's edge. 'If Jenny gave you a rod and some bait you could try your luck. You'd probably catch buckets.'

George laughed, for the first time. 'Not on your life. She might push me in.'

'Don't talk so daft,' Jenny said.

'Well, I'm not serious, am I? When I was a kid' – he smiled, as if he might still be one, and have life to live over again – 'I went after tiddlers, scooped 'em up in a jam jar with a bit of string around the neck. It wasn't easy, but I always got some. We lived in Basford Crossing, and the Leen was our

26

favourite stream. There were eight of us kids in the family, and when we went out as a tribe nobody could harm us. We often stayed by the water all day, rain or shine. Mam would wrap us up sandwiches in greaseproof paper, and fill bottles of cold tea left over from breakfast. There was always something interesting to look at, as long as the stream kept running, and it always did. Never stopped, did it? Well, it couldn't, could it?' The idea of the stream ceasing to flow seemed to alarm him. 'It could no more stop than the Trent could stop. Or any river, come to that, though the Leen's only a piddling little brook.' He smiled again. 'It was cold, though, if you fell in, and I did a time or two. It's a wonder one of us didn't drown, but kids had charmed lives in those days.'

Old times meant more to him than anybody else, but they were important to everybody the older or more physically difficult life became. With Arthur and Derek he often made fun of them, because if you didn't the reality of so-called halcyon days didn't bear thinking about, and there was too much happening in the present to have their weight as well on your back. Even so, it would be cruel to scoff at such times in front of George, who dropped a host of sugars into his tea: 'Jenny tells me you've done very well for yourself in London.'

'You could say I've made a living.' George's tone implied that he must have done so out of trickery and skiving. 'But I like to come up and see my brothers, who are always glad to see me. In any case, I'm still fond of the old place.'

'Why did you leave it, then?'

'I lived here till I was eighteen, then thought I'd take off.' Enough of the apologetic tone for having made use of his legs. 'We called at the White Horse for a pint or two last night.'

'Sometimes we get in the car,' Jenny said, 'and go for a drink, don't we, duck?'

'Aye, and a right bleddy ta-tar it is, lifting me in and out of this thing.' He looked at Brian, ignoring Jenny. 'I ain't been in the White Horse for years. Not that I could put much back if I did. Apart from having to watch my weight, I've got too many pills inside to swill ale down as well. Still, I can let myself go a bit when I'm in Ingoldmells. When I'm away from home, if you see what I mean. I don't have Jenny fussing over me every second of the day and night. It's the only time we get a rest from each other, and I'm sure she deserves it. I know I do.'

She kissed him on the forehead. 'It makes a change. You like to have young nurses pushing you up and down the seafront, don't you? And all that sea air! You do look a lot better when you get back.'

'Jenny takes me, and then she fetches me. Anyway,' George said to him, 'you manage to get around a bit?'

Brian set his empty cup on the table. 'When I can. I drove through Yugoslavia to Greece last year, and put the car on a ship to Israel. It was a treat, steaming through the islands.'

'Did you look in on Libya? Or Crete, where we changed ships as prisoners of bloody war.'

'It wasn't on our way. We stopped an hour or two at Cyprus, but there wasn't time to get off.'

'I'd like to go back and see Tobruk.' He gazed at the window. 'On the other hand, I wouldn't. You can't go back, can you? Not if you don't want to you can't. Or you can't if you're knackered like this. It would be funny if I did, though. Still, wanting to satisfies me. As long as you can dream you can tell yourself you're still alive.'

He was sorry for George, because who wouldn't be? But you couldn't tell him so to his face. George was well aware of what everybody felt when they looked at him, knew they had to feel sorry, nothing else they could do. George would feel the same for somebody like himself if he was all fit and full of beans, or even if he was all fit and full of sludge. He'd much rather be the one who was feeling sorry, and if it happened that he was such a person he wouldn't say he felt sorry for fear of being told to fuck off, though he'd still be over the moon at feeling it.

So the projection bounced back at Brian, to inform him that there was no need to feel sorry for George, or feel bad because you weren't a cripple as well. George was done for, and comments of sympathy would be no help. He too had a roof over his head, all the food he could get into himself, any clothes he thought of wearing and, under the circumstances, the finest care in the world. He was all right for as long as Jenny stayed by his side, so it was her you should feel sorry for, and how could he not, heart bleeding drop by drop into his liver at her fate, and though it was proof that he could still feel pity for somebody he much preferred dealing with the emotional turmoil that came from himself, always useful for channelling into his work.

She stroked her husband's pale hand. 'Maybe one day we'll win a lottery, then we'll hire a private plane and go to Tobruk.'

'Don't be daft.' He pushed the hand away, smiling at Brian as if to apologize, though not to Jenny, for his abruptness.

She didn't have much of a life, shackled to his side and waiting for any little request that might pop into his circumscribed brain, but she was glad at hearing Brian tell of his drive through the Balkans, the description of a squalid night-stop in Macedonia exaggerated into as much of a narrative as would interest George and amuse Jenny. Set apart from the world, no such talk could lift them out of their imprisonment. By now he had taken in all he could, and had to leave, Jenny offering to show him out because she wanted to see what sort of a car someone drove who wrote scripts for television.

He had never been a flash lad for posh motors, he told them, not caring to impress anybody when he was on the road. A dependable estate served for whatever he wanted in the way of transport, no need of a blood-red underslung tin lizzie with the power of a Spitfire flashing up and down the motorway at a hundred and twenty till he was nicked for the third time and lost his ticket.

They smiled at his admission that the car wasn't changed every three years, though his accountant said it should be for self-employed income tax. Maybe she was disappointed that he didn't live up to his image, though why should she care? 'It's nothing to show off about, but come and look. Nice meeting you,' he said to George, once being enough. 'I'll call again sometime, if that's all right.'

'You're always welcome.' He told Jenny to put on her mac, the first to notice a drop at the window.

She stood outside with Brian. 'I didn't really want to look at your car.'

'I know.'

'Sometimes he dozes off in the afternoon and wakes up with tears on his cheeks, but what can I do? He used to scream because the iron was falling on him in his dreams, but he doesn't do that anymore, which is a blessing.'

He took her in his arms and kissed her. Because he wanted to? Because she expected it? To give her a treat in her miserable life? Whatever, he pressed her to him, his and her tears meeting after so much time. 'I'm sorry, love.'

'Don't be,' she said. 'It's my bed, and I've got used to lying on it.'

He let her go, whether or not she hoped he might hold

on to her forever and release her from the life she had been pitched into. He saw the light glow again in those melting brown eyes that he recalled after making love so many times in the old days, knew her as she was then, the momentary resurrection of the past suddenly blown away like so much smoke, the poignancy that you couldn't go back setting him as close to a broken heart as he would ever get.

Pain pulled them away, a fire that burned all memories. 'Call again,' she breathed into his ear. 'Anytime you like. I'll always be here.'

George's room faced onto the garden, but he would wonder, all the same, why his departure was taking so long. The neighbours would also be looking through their curtains, but he couldn't care less about that, and neither could Jenny. 'I will.'

If you could dispute the number of angels able to dance on the tip of a pin he wondered how much emotion could be packed into a split second as he drove back through Basford Crossing. A message from a new chapel not noticed before said: 'Turn your cares into prayers.' Only a quick reader wouldn't smash into the crossing gates, cursing a prayer that had done no good at all. The exhortation couldn't concern him, though did suggest that there might be life in the old district yet.

The new estate on which his mother lived was such a tangle of ways and drives and crescents and closes and cul-de-sacs and gardens and walks and rises that all but a madman would get lost, no distinguishing features to indicate one turning from another. Only a pull-in and unremitting attention to the town plan ever got him to her ground-floor flat. Ask someone who lived there how to find a certain address and nine times out of ten you'd get a blank stare and the statement that they didn't know, though the regret was plain at not being able to tell you. The planners had created a nightmarish labyrinth rather than a civilized layout of houses; the street plan of Radford in his younger days had been simple by comparison.

'I'm glad you went to see her.' A Senior Service smouldered in one hand, and a mug of strong tea steamed in the other. 'She told me she'd love to see you, and it makes a change for the poor woman, with that bleddy miserable husband she's got to look after. A right bleddy burden he is. If I was her I'd pack him off into a home. He can be a nasty bogger, as well. She came here once with a black eye, and I said: "You want to bogger off, duck. Don't put up with it. He don't appreciate anything you've done for him." But she said: "I just couldn't do a thing like that. I daren't even let myself think about it."'

'It would be hard to leave a bloke in that condition,' he said.

'Yes, I suppose it would. I don't expect I'd do it, either. When I think of what I had to put up with from Harold all those years, it makes me marvel. Every morning I used to think of packing him in. It's twenty-five years since he died, and I haven't been unhappy a single day since. Before that I was never in peace for a minute.'

The old man had led her such a dance that she let no tears fall at his funeral, though put a hand to her face as if some were there while going through a group of neighbours to the hearse. She cut bread and laid out smoked ham and fresh tomatoes for his tea, fuel for his drive to London. He recalled sitting on her knees and reading when he was six, the air warm at the end of a summer's evening, and she still a young woman (he realized now) resting on the doorstep before going inside to make Harold's supper. He put together one sentence after another, a miracle to them both, from a book about people

32

going fancy free over the countryside in a gypsy caravan – and how she must have wished she was with them!

Doing an effortless ninety after the Leicester turn-off, a car ahead had for some reason stopped on the inside lane, no hazards flashing, or brake lights redly blazoning. There was barely time to notice in the dusk, and who but a murderer or a mindless suicide would stall at such a place and give no warning? By the splittest of seconds he swung the wheel and missed the car's bumper by inches, realizing that in all his years of driving he had never been so close to annihilation. Instinct had saved him, no other way to explain it.

He pushed in a tape of the Messiah. If he had survived as a basket case there would have been no one like Jenny to look after him, because what generous actions had he performed to be paid back for? Scorning to admit that the nearest of misses had scared him, he slowed to seventy and thought of Jenny getting the shit out of George twice a day and emptying it, the eighth baby she was never to get off her hands. His pitiful existence was her dead-end from which there was neither escape nor relief, no matter how often he was shunted off to Ingoldmells. Her placid and uncomplaining aspect didn't mean she wasn't suffering. He knew she was. She had to be, and giving no sign made him as angry as if she was betraying their former love.

The music wiped out her face, kept the mind blank to stay fixed on the road and not get killed. The turmoil of his two marriages and the bother of three children as recalcitrant as himself had taught him at least to be calm. They were grown up, and no longer needed his money (they'd had plenty, willingly given) and rarely telephoned because they didn't approve of his feckless ways. He only knew that no longer being married stopped him inflicting misery on those who had the misfortune to get too close.

To complain about his own life would be self-indulgence compared to Jenny's fate, but she at least had a solid reason for existence, and in any case all lives were at some time pitiable, otherwise there would be nothing for scriptwriters to do except a day's real work.

He hated the dazzle of driving at night, the lack of horizon and uncertain borders, so with half the run gone he forked into a service station. The coffee was like whitewash and the wedge of sweet cake hard to swallow. He lit a cigar, and readied himself for the road again, reflecting as he headlighted towards the exit going south that he had come a long way from Basford Crossing, which couldn't be anything but good.

THREE

Passing Basford Crossing was as if you were going to be hanged, because your whole life went by during the time it took to bump over the cobbles and between the railway gates. Like bumps in your life they passed up the spine and into the brain, and Arthur, mulling on how much had changed in his time, couldn't decide whether it was due to circumstance, or because he was the way he was. He'd often talked about it with Avril, with Derek and Brian and Eileen but, ever suspicious, knew there had to be more to it than a shuffling of cards by blind fate.

As regards housing, the giant ball and chain mechanisms of the council had gone through one area after another, smashing up dwellings that had been lived in for generations, when bathrooms could have been installed above the scullery and made them comfortable for another fifty years. People had been miserable in them only for lack of money when they were out of work, but bulldozing whole districts and throwing up high-rise hencoops was ordained by those who made enough money from the business never to have to live in them.

Jenny and her family had a pre-war council house at Broxtowe, and Arthur remembered going there with Brian because her father had given him the unexpected bonus of sixpence, the equivalent of a pound coin in those days.

Jenny's two sisters had the same long dark hair, and even the mother looked like them, though she must have been older. No wonder the father was self-satisfied and full of energy, being surrounded by women.

Arthur even at thirteen could tell Brian was getting plenty of crumpet, and Jenny's parents didn't put a spoke in the wheel as long as she wasn't knocked up. If he had knocked her up he would have married her, and that would have been that, which was fair enough, if you were daft enough to do it.

Cousin Bert got a girl in the family way. He'd had dozens of girls so should have known better, but the girl's fat brute of a father collared him on his way out of work and threatened to squash him like an orange if he didn't do the right thing. Arthur, who knew he would get out of a similar situation if he didn't love the woman, told Bert to do a runner, but Bert over his pint in the Peach Tree said that if it wasn't Maureen it would be somebody else, a surrender to circumstance so bizarre that Arthur could only suggest that they drink up and go for another in the Royal Children. Thus Bert got married, and lived much like everyone else, happily and unhappily ever after.

When Jenny and Brian stopped going out together, somebody else put a bun in her oven, and her father wasn't big enough, or fat enough, or maybe even fit enough, or not caring enough, or perhaps she kept it from him until it was too late (he wouldn't put it past her) but that was no excuse for not chasing the bastard up and kicking the guts out of him. More likely Jenny hadn't let on as to who the man was, luckily for him, because her father was, after all, a dab hand with pick and shovel at the coal seam.

Brian would never have got her preggers, and that was a fact, because he cared about such things, and hadn't fancied living out his time in a Nottingham council house. He got away because he had the brains to do it, and the guts to live for years in a London bedsitter before earning any money. I sometimes wonder though whether he wouldn't have been happier staying where he had been brought up.

Basford Crossing as he had known it was a far-off country, and he sometimes found it hard to decide whether he'd actually lived there, or had dreamed it in his working time at the machine, as if lost in the early mist of a summer's day that lasted till night time, clearing only at moments to let him see the old buildings and crossing gates.

Reality behind the eyes showed scenery almost too good to be true, yet the ruins of the place were now like those of Pompeii in Italy he had seen on a coach tour with Avril, wrecked, flyblown, empty, resentful at being abandoned, a sudden pull out from the prime of life, as if the RAF had done a thorough job back in the war.

He hadn't seen the area for years and then, passing through one day on his way to somewhere else, he noted that death had already taken place, as if a gigantic fist had picked up the locality and given it a good pasting, people fleeing in all directions as they must have done from Pompeii when fire and ash came down, while those who survived the upshake were rattled to the core, had only enough spirit to pick up their tranklements and form their columns of refugees.

Nowadays there was nobody, no footsteps, no laughter, no joshing voices, no shrieking kids to wave the next train through. A few people walking by in a hurry looked as shifty and guilty as if they'd been responsible for the area getting ruined. Cars going somewhere else were driven by those who in the old days would have walked or taken a tram, and he supposed they hated to be reminded of the place because they'd had no car or television or fridge or washing machine or a mobile phone, maybe only a wireless or radiogram. Far from being happy with all they'd got now, they were dead from the neck up.

He recalled the girls he had taken to the fields around Top Valley Farm, an area now covered with houses and old folks' bungalows, in one of which his mother had lived. The girls were fourteen or fifteen (maybe younger: they didn't tell him and he didn't ask) but when snuggled up to in a hedge bottom they melted softly into the warmth of each other's bodies, hardly knowing it would end in going all the way, unable to tell at that age the difference between spunk and cuckoo spit as they strolled lovingly hand in hand back to Basford Crossing. He knew where in the bedroom Brian hid french letters, and helped himself, until Brian twigged some were missing and told him to get his own, since he was already bringing in money from the bike factory.

He supposed all the girls he had shagged – good looking, passionate, and knowing what they wanted – had got married and had kids, some of them divorced and living as single mothers in flats provided by the council – and good luck to them. Nearly everybody he knew had been divorced, as had he, after Doreen put the kibosh on their ten-year marriage.

He got home from the factory, knackered after an eight-hour stint, the sweat barely dried, and she came out with it before he was halfway through the doorway: 'I'm leaving you. I've had enough. I can't stand any more. The life we lead is no good. I'm too fed up for it to go on.'

Of what she was fed up he didn't know, because at times he felt a lot more fed up than she could ever know about. He was fed up now, and had been for a long time, though why she suddenly wanted her life to change he couldn't think, blinded by her unexpected decision. She hadn't caught him with another woman, because he worked too hard to find time chasing them, much as he might like to.

But now that she'd spoken he knew that he wanted to split up as well, and though he couldn't come out with what enough was, it certainly seemed to be so when they went on to argue about why they hadn't said enough was enough years ago, and wondered why they'd ever got married.

Smoking a cigarette, he stood by the door, watching her face thinned by the firmness of her stand, though the colour was coming back because she had found it easier to tell him than expected, and to get his agreement. It felt as if the boat was sinking under him, water already soaking his boots, on her saying she needed three days to move out so as to have time to make arrangements and clear things up.

She'd been thinking about it, and that was a fact, while his fantasies at the machine hadn't included this one. Maybe she had a boyfriend, a bit of you know what going on with a neighbour or the window-cleaner, but if so he had no interest in finding out. He wasn't one for trying to save a marriage, deciding to get shut of her and the house as soon as possible in case she changed her mind. 'You can have all the time you like to pack up,' he said, unwilling to put up with three days of hatred, 'because I'll be going instead. Keep everything. I don't want any of it.'

At the beginning of their marriage they had shared a house with her deaf mother, and her boyfriend from India whom they always called Chumley, a middle-aged man who spoke so little it was impossible to tell what was in his mind, which was all right as far as Arthur was concerned because Mrs Greatton loved him, and had no time to interfere with him and Doreen.

'You don't say a word to Chumley,' Doreen said to him

more than once. 'He's only human, you know. He wouldn't mind if you said hello now and again.'

'When did you notice the last time he opened his mouth and said hello to me?'

'It's the way you look at him. I can tell you don't like him.'

'It ain't true. We don't have anything in common to talk about. I offered him a fag the other day but he refused it because he didn't smoke my sort. He didn't even want to try it. And when I asked him out to the pub he said he didn't drink alcohol. What can you do with a bloke like that?'

'You're only making excuses,' she said. 'You're lying like you've always done.'

Then one day Chumley packed his bags (one of which, Arthur joked, must be full of hard earned money) and told them with a smile that put life into his face for the first time, that he was going to Wolverhampton. Tears and ructions from Doreen's mother, but he went on smiling and backed out of the door, a taxi waiting on the crescent.

Arthur and Doreen got a council house not long afterwards, and when they called on Mrs Greatton one day found her dead at the kitchen table, a cup of cold Ovaltine by her hand. From then on Doreen said that her mother had died of a broken heart because of Chumley having gone due to Arthur being so rotten. 'He couldn't stand it any more.'

Well, he didn't know about that. He had respected Chumley for never missing a day in the factory, and assumed he had only slung his hook to get married to one of his own people. Mrs Greatton knew it, and if she had died of a broken heart that was her lookout. Nobody could have done anything about it, though he was sorry, all the same.

And now the split had come for them as well, though maybe she was getting rid of him before he could do the same to her. He slept on the couch, and in the morning collected money due to him from the factory, then walked out of the house with two suitcases and a kitbag, and the clothes on his back. After a few days at his mother's he rented a room in a house owned by a Polish man, as far from Doreen as he could get yet still in the same city.

He hadn't seen her since, nor wanted to, and if he refused to blame her for the break-up it was only because he had no intention of blaming himself. But whenever he thought of her, which was more often than he cared to, he saw that she hadn't been happy, and that neither had he much of the time, but it was no crime to be unhappy, in fact lucky that both had been because when the break came there was a better chance of improvement for both. His only pain was that letters to Melanie and Harold went unanswered, and his feelings were not friendly on knowing Doreen had poisoned his children against him. Life was long, and there was nothing to do but endure, though the virulent wound from not seeing his son and daughter closed slowly.

Twenty years later Melanie recognized him on the street. He wondered who this nice young woman with the big smile was, reaching for his arm. She was married, with two kids, and was as glad as all get out to see him. 'Hello, dad! Fancy meeting you. I didn't think you were living in Nottingham anymore.'

He stood, near to tears but holding back all sign while they talked in a café. The kids wanted Melanie to take them home, but she encouraged them to kiss Arthur and call him grandad, trying mischievously to embarrass him, but he enjoyed it, kissed them back and gave each a pound coin. Doreen had been married again, Melanie told him, but the husband died last year, and she was running a pub with a woman in Bedford.

41

Melanie and her husband Barry were buying a house on a new estate less than a mile from Arthur and Avril. Barry was a cabinet-maker never out of work, and when they called with the two kids he wanted Arthur to tell him what it had been like living in the sixties. Arthur didn't think the decade had been anything special, yet gave a lively account of his non-attendance at a Beatles concert, and did his best to dredge up whatever else might interest his new found son-in-law.

Harold, a year older than Melanie, had taken the trouble to locate Arthur when he was twenty-one, calling to say that Doreen had kicked him out, and he hadn't a penny to his name. As tall as Arthur, he stood dead scruffy in sweatshirt and jeans, wore a ponytail, and sported an earring, only a parrot missing to complete the appearance of a pirate. Arthur gave him a fiver, and said he could have another after he had cleaned himself up and found a job – when of course he wouldn't need it, as Harold bitingly reminded him.

Arthur and Avril married not long after their divorces came through. At the same time he also found a better job and, standing at his bench one day, he couldn't help thinking that the death of Doreen's second husband had served her right. He knew it to be unjust, because sooner or later something gets its claws into you or, even worse, he was to realize years afterwards, into the person you love most, though Avril between bouts of chemotherapy carried on with courage and dignity as if life was normal, saying she would fight it, would never give in, wouldn't go easily.

His father and two sisters had been taken by the same malign illness. He secretly admired Jane, who kept it from everyone until she lay on the sofa one Friday night after work saying she wouldn't be going back on Monday morning, dying ten days later. A scarf around her throat had hidden

42

the swelling, and no pleading could get her to a doctor. She told her husband to mind his own business. 'I'm just not feeling well. Leave me alone. I'll get better when I'm ready. It's a sore throat. One of these days it'll go as suddenly as it came, though I don't suppose before it's good and ready. It's only a cold that won't go away.' She was in her forties, and hadn't seen a doctor because she was too frightened to find out what was the matter, or maybe too fed up to care whether she lived or died, which was another story.

Avril, who at the first twinge in her left shoulder called at the doctor's, was told it was a touch of rheumatism. X-rayed nevertheless, still nothing showed, but when the pain persisted deeper X-rays indicated something was definitely not right.

Arthur heard that if cancer was caught soon enough you had an even chance of beating it, but how soon is soon? And how can you know? Cancer can be nibbling away for months before there's any sign of pain, like a sly snake that finds its billet, and the gnawing goes on till it's too late to do anything, by which time you're dead.

Cancer seemed to be everywhere. His sister Margaret had died of it thirty years ago, and might still be alive if the doctor hadn't told her it was only backache. 'It's nothing,' he said. 'Pull yourself together, and take these tablets.' When she could stand the months of pain no longer he sent her for an X-ray. She didn't have a chance. You aren't grown-up if you think doctors know anything.

Jenny's husband lived donkey's years after having the guts crushed out of him by a slab of iron, and couldn't even die when it was the only thing he wanted, while other people fight every inch of the way, and it gets them just the same. Maybe Jane had been right to thumb her nose at the cancer. What he would have done in her place he didn't know, nor in

Avril's now that she had got it, though he wanted her to beat it more than anything in the world. If it did get him he would take Jane's way out and say fuck you to God, let the disease do as it liked, the sooner the better, it would be quicker that way, because even though the doctors knew you were going to die they still had you tortured with chemotherapy.

Thank God Avril wasn't like Jane. He would stand by her whatever happened, because she didn't seem too bad at the moment and might well come through in the end. She looked more or less the same as anybody else on the street, making it hard to believe that she had such a thing, though doctors don't lie, with X-ray machines to prove what they see. She had it right enough, and it was no use thinking otherwise.

Basford Crossing went bump-bump under his wheels, but he didn't need to be reminded about the nightmare that had them by the throat. Everybody had their troubles, and we all have to die, tramps as well as emperors, but we want to put it off as long as we can. Even if we're old we don't want to say goodbye to all that we've sweated for.

Women live longer than men, so it was puzzling why Avril had got cancer and not him, though if he had any say in the matter he would gladly take it on himself. Cancer was eating her, and worry was eating him. She didn't worry, and he hadn't got cancer, which was strange if you weighed it up. Worry wasn't fatal but cancer nearly always was, though worry could lead to cancer if it went on for long and got too deep inside.

It was like roulette: as you crossed a busy road a double-decker missed you by inches, but while you were laughing at the fact that you were still alive cancer had dug its claws into your tripes when you were halfway over, and you hadn't noticed. Some illness or other was always lurking to get at you.

He wondered whether Avril pined after Fulham where she'd lived till she was eighteen, but she told him, and he had to believe her (because she was the sort who knew her own mind and would always speak the truth), that she was happy anywhere providing she loved the person she was with.

She had managed a factory canteen for over ten years, then got laid off when the place closed. Maybe that hadn't helped, but she knew the healthiest things to eat, planned all the meals for taste and goodness, so you couldn't say eating the wrong food had caused the cancer, otherwise why hadn't he got it as well? When you were young there either weren't mysteries or you were too busy living to let them matter, but as you got older they wouldn't be kept in place, and plagued your life.

A daughter from Avril's first marriage lived in London, and her son worked as a heating engineer at a brewery in Nottingham. The only other relation was her cousin Paul, the indispensable chief fitter at a factory, who kept all sorts of ailing machines going, a skilled job that paid good money. He'd been married to a woman called Adelaide, who had three kids from a previous marriage. After they'd had one of their own she went to work in the office of a place making bedspreads, and that was where the trouble started.

Paul was tall and thin, and as strong as an ox. He wore a little sandy coloured beard, and Arthur often wanted to reach out and pull the crumbs away, but didn't, as much for the crumbs' sake as Paul's, not wanting to deprive the refugee bread of its hiding place, or see Paul eat it when he handed it back to him.

Though Adelaide had married Paul for love, or so you had to suppose, she would never stop telling him that he was too rough in his ways ever to make her happy. Paul worshipped her, would do anything she asked, except remove his beard, or cotton on to the extent of looking more presentable. Maybe

45

he had a screw loose, though he was clever with his hands and must have had a brain because of the job he did. Adelaide was a beautiful and personable woman, who told Paul time and time again that he just wasn't good enough for her; for which, Arthur thought, I would either have smacked her in the chops or sent her packing, probably both.

Paul only ever stopped working to sleep. He would come home in the evening from the factory, stuff a sandwich into his lantern jawed face (without washing his hands, Arthur supposed) then put in a few hours at a building site fixing machinery till midnight, all to coin extra money so that Adelaide could buy more pots of make-up and have something to spend at the hairdressers'. Arthur once called at the site to have a chat, and Paul was so tired he didn't notice him walking out with a bag of nuts and bolts, which he took back a few nights later, minus a dozen to fix some bookshelves.

Disaster to Paul's marriage happened when one of Arthur's workmates' wives, who had a job at the same place as Adelaide, told her husband she was being fucked stupid by one of the chief embroiderer's. Arthur's mate informed Arthur, who passed the information on to Avril who, Paul being her cousin, had to tell him about Adelaide's fling, thinking it only right that he should know, and that it was better to be honest because he could then sort out his marriage and go on living amicably with Adelaide, for the children's sake at least. Arthur had always said, even before learning about the affair, that sooner or later Adelaide would start doing it on her cousin. 'And so would I,' he went on, 'because he won't tidy himself up. A man's got to look good now and again in front of his wife, like I do for you.'

Avril laughed, but rewarded him with a kiss. 'I know. You were always a smart dresser.'

46

Arthur couldn't understand why Paul's fingernails were rarely as clean as they should be, even when he wore a suit on Sundays. Personal cleanliness didn't cost anything, needed only ten minutes with soap, comb, nailbrush and flannel at the sink every evening. Even when Paul was dressed up as if he was going to Buckingham Palace to get a medal he looked grubby. He sniffed every few seconds as if an invisible turd swung back and forth under his nose. No wonder he'd never had another woman except Adelaide. No other woman would take him on, and Arthur couldn't understand why Adelaide had, unless she knew she'd be able to shit on him and get away with it more than with any other bloke. She wouldn't even have him in the same room, never mind in the same bed, after their first kid was born.

Paul was so turned over backwards when he learned about the affair that he could hardly speak to Adelaide. His face was the picture of dangerous humiliation. Arthur hoped he would never have to go through such trouble, had advised Avril not to tell him, but the matter was finally sorted out in their kitchen. Paul leaned against the sink, eyes more and more bloodshot as he tried to hold in his anger, cigarette ash spilling into his beard. Arthur, who had just made some tea, could see it coming, and it did.

Paul let rip, but kept his hands firmly together, calling her a treacherous slimy whore not fit to live with anybody. She was a bag of the first water who thought only about herself. She cared nothing for the kids and even less for him, who had been working like a slave to keep the ship afloat for the last five years. He said the same thing in different ways, over and over, on and on for a good ten minutes, till Adelaide went white because she hadn't heard so much talk from him, and certainly not of that sort, all the time they'd been together. She had been standing up during his silence, as if ready for a quick getaway should he try to smash her one, but now that he was talking, and wouldn't become violent, she felt able to sit down. She had to, though Arthur admired her coolness at asking Paul for a fag, which he gave her, and which got them talking with no more bad language or threat of murder. She promised to give up her boyfriend, though Arthur told Avril after they had gone out arm in arm that he didn't think she would.

He regretted his part as the bringer of bad tidings, because Paul, learning who they had come from, disliked him from then on. 'He should have seen it as a favour,' Arthur said, 'because what man wants to be kept in the dark when his wife's knocking on with somebody else? Still, I suppose it's the worst thing, to be a messenger who brings bad news, even if it's good news. They used to kill messengers in the olden days. I can just picture it. You see this bloke on a horse galloping over the horizon. He's got a spear waving from his side, and a couple of arrows in his back. He's in rags, he's covered in mud and shit, his arse is red raw from riding through deserts and swamps and mountains. After he hands his message to the king, who's sitting on a chair outside a big coloured tent, he can hardly stand up. The king knocks off a goblet of wine, then reads the message, which is probably about fuck-all. The messenger looks at him like a dog waiting for a pat on the head, but the king gives a nod to his favourite poncy thug, who's drinking a bottle of four star perfume, and when he finishes it, and after a good belch, he pushes a sword into the messenger's guts, and finishes the poor fucker off for all his trouble. Well, I wish I hadn't opened my trap now. I'll know better next time.'

Not long after the set-to in Avril's kitchen Adelaide dropped in on her moped at half past eight. It was pissing down, Arthur recalled, and she didn't say much, only stopped long

48

enough for a cup of tea. As soon as she'd gone he turned to Avril: 'You know what all that was about?'

'I don't. What's your idea?'

'Well, she didn't come to see us because she loves us, but so's she could have an alibi. She was spread out like a cushion on the chief embroiderer's table longer than she should have been.'

'You think so?'

'I know so. Now she can tell Paul she was with us instead of having it off in the office.'

'I expect you're right. You usually are, you dirty-minded devil.'

'He was fucking her arse off, you can bet. She's a right one, she is. She'd skin your prick like a banana.'

The embroiderer had a wife and two kids, so both families were broken up when they began living together. Adelaide left the kids with Paul, hoping, Arthur supposed, that they wouldn't grow up to be fitters in a factory. 'It was probably the best thing she ever did for them,' Avril said.

'Maybe, but I'd have tracked her down and dumped her three on the doorstep.'

From then on Paul worked his backbone to a string of conkers, double shifting as much as he could, to make sure the children wanted for nothing. In the end, seeing how he'd worked for them year after year, they respected him more than if he had been mother and father together.

'The best part of it was,' Arthur told Brian, 'that one of the kids was so smart at school he passed enough O-Levels and A-Levels (and probably every other level as well) to get through all the hurdles and qualify as a solicitor. He's got his own firm now, and you couldn't do better than that if you think of where he started. It must have been Adelaide's brains and Paul's example of hard work that got him there.'

49

Paul encouraged and rewarded his talented son every stage of the way, at the same time getting what help he could from the system. He wasn't dim at all, only put on by a wife who thought she was too good for him. It must be a sign of the times that with brains you can get wherever you like, but the joke is that the solicitor son is now invited to all Adelaide's dinner parties, after Avril told her about his success when she saw her getting out of a big flash Volvo in Slab Square. Though Adelaide shows him off to her friends, she'll never include Paul in her list of guests. When I asked him what he thought about it, after we started talking to each other again, he said: 'Why should I mind? It's got nothing to do with me. I don't want to know my ex-wife's friends. If I did go there, and met the one she ran off with, I'd murder him on the spot. I'm happy that my solicitor-son comes to see me now and again. We get on very well together.'

Arthur considered Paul to be one of the best, even though you rarely knew what was in his mind. No reason why you should, it was always best to keep your trap shut, only let people know what you wanted them to know, which was how he thought it should be for himself and everyone, if there was to be any peace in the world.

All the same, it would be hard to believe Paul didn't think any further than what he said or what he did, because everybody had something going through their heads. With most people you don't care one way or the other what it might be, since it can't be very interesting, and has nothing to do with you if it is, and if everybody told you what was in their minds you wouldn't be able to make up your own idea of what it was, which was half the fun of being alive.

Paul obviously thought more than most people, you'd be daft not to realize it, because he'd worked harder and done so much good in his life. If a wicked remark came into Paul's mind he would think long and good before letting it go, by which time he'd decide it wasn't worth saying, and would hold it in. But he was bound to have such thoughts, there being times when you can see the mechanism working. I couldn't have done half the good he's done, though certain it is that the more you talk the more you circle back to the start line, so it's best to say no more than you've got to, and keep any thoughts to yourself.

As for Basford Crossing, you can stuff the place, because the only thing that matters is that Avril's got cancer.

FOUR

When Brian parked his car some time ago he noticed that one of the streets he had grown up in had been wiped off the face of the earth. Served him right. That was the way it was. What else did you expect? When God said let there be light he painted it in, and then he painted it out. The same with the surface of cities. They needed clearing off and doing up every few decades.

A glimpse of old places set him reviewing the course of his life, though he didn't like doing so, there being so much to anger and shame him. Such recollections should have been pushed out of harm's way by now but weren't. However long he lived it would be the same, otherwise he wouldn't have left the place of his birth.

Arthur told him never to leave his car in such an area, either in daylight or in the dark, so he hoped it wouldn't get robbed (not much to nick), vandalized for devilment, or set on fire out of malice. 'Nothing is safe anymore,' Arthur said, when they were settled in a snug pub on Prospect Street and could talk without music howling in their ears. 'Nottingham's got the worst crime rate in the country, and the worst murder rate. If you stroll through town on Saturday night you risk a cleaver in your guts. When we were kids we walked anywhere, day and night, and nothing would happen. Nowadays, if I wanted to leave my car on the street for a few minutes I'd put a nice looking hip flask on the back seat, but it would have poison inside so that whoever broke in and took a sip would die in agony.'

'Which would serve 'em right,' he went on. 'Cars are owned mostly by people who need them to get to work, but thieves and muggers who break into 'em only do so to get money for drugs, or so they won't be bored by being too idle to work. It's the poor who suffer most from crime. The rich have got burglar alarms and guard dogs, and when they drive through areas where druggies live they wind the windows up and put their foot on the accelerator. They could stop crime right away if they wanted, but they don't because it keeps the poor in their place.'

'What would you do, though?'

Arthur's graveyard laugh signified he could think of plenty. 'It's unlikely I'll get the appointment, because I'm too old for the job. But I'd be ruthless. Anybody caught for murder I'd execute in Slab Square, and show it on television. Those who say it wouldn't make any difference if you did hang 'em, don't think they're ever going to get murdered. I'd train a special night force looking like old-age pensioners, but they'd know unarmed combat and carry guns, and if they found any trouble they could pull anybody in and ask 'em what they was up to.

'I've worked all my life and don't want to live in a place where some snipe-nosed fuckface is going to point a knife at my guts when I go out at night. If I carried a knife and ripped somebody apart who threatened me I'd get sent down for ten years. It's civil war, and though I'm sixty I wouldn't mind having a go, because I'm still stronger than most of them. It used to be pleasant living in this town, but some areas are no-go now. I was in town the other week, and when a young bloke said something I thought he only wanted to know the time. He was nearly as tall as me, and had an earring hanging from his left tab hole, and a shaved head that made him look like an Aids victim. He asked me for a quid for a cup of tea, so I told him to fuck off. He shouted after me, but I didn't want to turn back and smash his face in because there were too many people about. He looked as if he'd never been hungry in his life, nor done a stroke of work either.'

Brian knew he was thinking of his son, Harold, who rarely had a job – a heartbreak father if ever there was one. 'There isn't much work these days.'

'There is if you try hard enough.' He stared into his pint. 'You don't have to beg. Nobody starves, and I wouldn't want 'em to either. We was brought up on the dole, but we didn't beg.'

Brian finished his drink. 'Have another?'

He would. Both did. Brian went for them. Such views as Arthur's would be in no way agreeable to the people he partied with in London, though after a lifetime away they remained very much his as well, always had been, and he felt no shame having them, though he softened their harshness when with his friends, unless releasing their uncensored force for the pleasure of shocking them, and to let them know there was another side to him. He unpeeled an Antico Toscano bought in Italy, as strong as all get out but tasting like honey when supping a pint of Nottingham ale. 'I suppose the police do all they can to keep the place under control.'

Arthur blanched at the smell of the cigar. 'I was wondering where my socks went to when I slung 'em out of bed last night. It stinks like a damp haystack on fire. Well, I expect they're doing all they can, but I never thought I'd live to say the Nottingham force was too soft. Blokes in prison ought to know they're banged up. There shouldn't be any television, no drugs, no sex magazines, no visits, and they'd be locked in dungeons day and night, the walls running with moisture, with only a crust to eat now and again. Anyway, let's drink up, and see what's going on at the White Horse.'

The next morning they decided on Matlock, asked Avril to come, but she needed time to run up a dress on her Singer, and in any case could have a meal ready for when they got back.

'We used to bike this way for fresh air and exercise at the weekends,' Brian said when they were crossing the motorway. 'Toiling up and down through the hill towns to open country.' He had set out for Matlock with Jenny, who hadn't biked that far before, and was soon worn out with pedalling.

'It's only another ten miles,' Brian said to her in the market place at Ripley. 'And there aren't any hills.' Except a big one on the way back which he didn't mention. 'It's downhill to Ambergate, and flat along the valley the rest of the way. We'll go slow. You'll be all right.'

'I know when I'm done in,' she had said, and promised to wait in Ripley.

Sharp winds blew from the west, metal blue clouds charging over the livid green hills. Matlock felt dead, the line of dismal shop fronts full of artefacts he didn't want or couldn't afford. Hiking parties toiled up a footpath out of the valley, and he envied their freedom and companionship. He didn't feel like queuing for a boat on the river, or shinning up the Heights of Abraham, but stood bemused by the pavement, not knowing what to do.

He turned the bike around, and every mile to where Jenny would be waiting seemed like ten, all strength necessary to pedal four miles up the hill to Ripley. The wish to see her bolstered him during the struggle, mulling on how good life would be if he could spend it with her, imagining a future of mutual comfort and support in that rhythmical pushing forward of his toecaps against the ever ascending road. In Ripley he would take her to a café for tea and cake and, by the steam of the urn, tell her he wanted them to be engaged. After military service he would say, words she had been waiting for since their first meeting, we can get married. We love each other and will be together for good, the only way to go through life. I'll find a better job than in the factory, so there'll be no worry about us having money to live on.

Beyond the houses of Ambergate and into open land towards the summit, trees with their spring shoots wished him well, still no view of the crest for which he was heading. A following wind laid chill hands at the small of his back but helped him to where Jenny would be waiting to greet him in Ripley market place with a kiss of relief and welcome. They would ride home side by side, the ups and downs of the road not so onerous when they were together, talking about how they were made for each other and what a marvellous life they would have.

Drizzle settled on his jacket as he did three turns anti-clockwise around the square. He looked into every shop, pub and café. A stray dog followed and tried to bite his back tyre. He kicked it away, landing a good one at its second attempt, thwarting the mongrel's bid for friendship. Then he cycled three times clockwise around the square, but she had gone home and who could blame her? He should have had more sense than to abandon her. It had been the biggest mistake of his life, and even then he'd thought so. Matlock could have waited, such a place there forever, so what had driven him to go on alone?

As more rain came he only hoped, though it was hardly a help, that she had set off home a few minutes after he had left. Working hard on piece work at the clothing factory, the fourteen miles to Ripley had worn her out. It was a marvel she had got even that far. He should have put his arms around her on hearing she couldn't go on: 'I can't stand the thought of biking all that way, either. Let's go back together.' He ought to have cared for her as he liked to be looked after when exhausted and miserable – though he couldn't remember a time when he had been. They should have cycled happily homewards, stopping at a café in Eastwood for something to eat so that she would have enough energy to go on pedalling.

Forlorn and alone, she would think he had failed her, that he wasn't a young man worth having, and it wouldn't be anybody's fault but his if she did. If you didn't blame yourself for what went wrong you never learned anything, a lesson best taken in sooner than later which, now that it was too late, didn't do much for his spirit as he upped and downed the long road back, rain penetrating to his skin. Jenny's mother and sisters would say: 'Why are you home so early? What's happened to Brian?'

'I got tired. He left me in Ripley to go off on his own.'

They would look at her gone out, as if to say (and they very likely did say it) 'Well, he would, wouldn't he? That's just like him. I can't think why you bother with somebody who does a thing like that.'

How right they would have been. It wasn't the first cold-blooded act of his life, though regret was futile. Similar situations had often been turned against him, and though everyone received only as much as they gave, his treatment of Jenny was one of the first, though when a few days later she didn't complain he felt that maybe his mistake hadn't been so bad after all. 'There wasn't much use waiting in cold old Ripley,' she said. 'I knew you wouldn't come back for at least a couple of hours.'

'I'm sorry I left you all the same.'

'Oh, it didn't matter.'

'I shan't do a thing like that again.'

'Won't you?' She looked as if certain he was only waiting to do something so painful it would part them forever. She couldn't trust him. He couldn't trust himself, and that was worse.

Arthur cut into his thoughts. 'Do we go through Eastwood?'

'No. A bypass skirts it along the line of the old railway.' Every mile brought back Jenny's clear and all-knowing face. 'You shoot up to Ripley, and down into Ambergate. It used to be a real slog on the old push-bike. I didn't even have a three-speed, if I remember.' He clocked seventy along the bypass. 'There's a D. H. Lawrence museum in Eastwood. I'll take you some day.'

'I tried to read *Lady Chatterley's Lover*,' Arthur said, 'but I couldn't get into it. I liked the one you sent the other week, though.'

'Which was that?' He'd recommended so many: *The Woman in White*, *The Autobiography of a Super Tramp*, *The Worst Journey in the World*, *Goodbye to All That*, among many others.

'*Clayhanger*, and it was marvellous. He knew what he was doing, Arnold Bennett did. But I bought *Lady Chatterley's Lover* at a car boot sale for twenty pee, and it didn't interest me, so I gave it to a bloke at work.'

Books brought them closer, if that was possible, but Arthur would have read whether or not they had been brothers. 'He's a great writer, though.'

'Well, I liked *Sons and Lovers*, but not that one.' Into Derbyshire, the narrowing road went through Langley Mill, Aldercar and Codnor. 'In the old days these places were full of life.' He wondered how people occupied themselves now that the mines were closed, mills forsaken, and factories boarded up. 'The pavements used to be crowded, but the area's dead to what it was. They didn't get paid much, but at least they had work.'

Arthur went on to say how, motoring around the coalfields during the great Scargill strike, he had sided with the colliers every bit of the way, yet knew they couldn't win, because not only had the strike started in the summer, when fuel stocks were huge, but the Nottinghamshire men hadn't been balloted, as if their views didn't matter and they could be ordered about like the poor bloody infantry. Maybe Scargill knew they wouldn't vote for the strike but hoped to shame them in when the action began. The Notts miners had their own ideas, and worked on full pelt, so it was only a matter of time before the strike collapsed, though Scargill said that if the Yorkshire men lost everybody would lose. They did. Ten years later even the Notts miners, who thought it could never happen to them, had been paid off.

Brian noted the placid Derwent coiling its way to Derby, and fields bordered by greystone walls, land uprising to either side. Rage against the fate by which people lived dissolved in such scenery, even the diminishing years of life not worth thinking about. He could remember as far back as if he had lived forever, but an existence far easier than Arthur's long stint in heavy industry.

He parked by the chalet style railway station at Matlock Bath and bought tickets for the aerial ropeway. Neither had taken it before, but Arthur agreed they should give it a try: 'As long as the ropes weren't made on a Monday.'

The valley seemed more gorge like from above, the main road winding along by the Derwent, choice houses among clumps of green uphill to the right. 'If I win the lottery I'll buy one, then you can stay in it to write your scripts.'

The cableway stopped half way, over the highest point of the crossing, Brian noting with binoculars the hotel he had stayed at with a girlfriend, while his wife went off on one of her affairs. They had laughed at the system, which he called 'mutual indemnity', but back in London she made a fuss as if her tryst hadn't gone as well as expected. She created a morally indefensible screen to stop him seeing his girlfriend again, perhaps out of revenge, or in the belief that control was sweeter than loyalty or love. Such miserable quarrels didn't go on too long before, discovering that she hadn't stopped his affair, they separated and were divorced.

Such a memorable experience taught him never to get married to, or have an affair with, someone who had been psychoanalysed or taken LSD, and she had done both. Her soul hadn't been her own, so how could she lovingly share her life? From then on, dealing with other women had been like swimming through calm water after dogpaddling in the Sargasso Sea.

His divorce had just been made final when he saw Jenny getting on the train to visit her damaged husband in Sheffield. There had been enough of the young woman in her features for him to pull her close and say: 'Forget your husband. They'll take care of him in hospital. Come away with me to a new life, just as you are. Leave your kids as well. Don't even go home. Let's save ourselves by doing what we should have done all those years ago. We have a right to happiness before it's too late, so don't get on this train. We'll take the next one south.'

The screed of a madman, because he wouldn't have been sincere, never had been, didn't know what the word meant (he did, but it couldn't get a look in) he was all impulse, fell in love with every woman going by in the street, burning with madness, a fire that never went out.

Jenny would have been appalled and enraged. She would have told him not to be a bastard, to stop tormenting her at such a time, to be his age, and maybe pushed him on to the rails as he deserved, if an express had been speeding out of the tunnel. On the other hand she might have laughed, in spite of her tragic errand, as when he used to amuse her with impossible propositions in bygone days. It could have been just what she needed, to judge by her anguished face. And what if she had said yes, take me, let's go, it's the only thing left for me to do, would he have ditched her in London? The question nagged him for years, though he knew she would have got on to the train for Sheffield thinking that at least once in her life she'd shown good judgement in not tying herself to someone like him.

The Georgian façade of the hotel he'd taken his girlfriend to overlooked the main road, and he recognized the window of their room. Her name was Penelope, neither the first nor the last of that name, amazing how many had been christened it, as if scores of those coming back from distant battlefronts at the end of the war had picked up a copy of *The Odyssey* at Victoria Station, and hoped their wives had been unknitting the khaki jersey they had been making for them for the last five years, so that the lodgers wouldn't get at her bloomers.

At the Heights of Abraham station they stayed in the little bug-like cabin and waited for the ride back. 'I suppose every bloke of our age remembers the days when he biked to Matlock with his sweetheart,' Arthur said. 'I did it first with Helen Dukes, who lived a few doors down from us. She was as hot as a cat, and pretty. It was sunny and warm, and we finished our bottles of Tizer at Eastwood, and couldn't find a place to sell us a drop of anything till we got to Matlock and had a drink of tea. We scrambled up that hill over there and bedded down in some bushes. I didn't think I'd get it off her, but I did. It was my first time, and I was fifteen. It was marvellous. She was dying for it, and so was I. I don't know why, but she called fucking "nursing". "Will you nurse me?" she asked, when I'd got her knickers off. "I fucking well will," I said. She was dark and lovely, but I never knew why she called it nursing, unless it was a secret code word between her mam and dad, and she'd heard 'em at it one day.'

The incline was steeper going back, Arthur gripping the railbar as if the little truck might race for the ground, but it levelled out and floated gently over the valley of their dreams, grey clouds bleeding a steady drizzle which obscured the houses like curtains at a theatre. Meteorological phenomena of the valley turned the day magical: to get out of traffic needed only a short climb into the well moistened air of nostalgia.

The ruins of Riber Castle on its hill were still in sunlight, cloud moving across gaps in the masonry: 'Like Frankenstein's residence,' Arthur said. 'After being burned down in the Carpathians.'

'There's a café in Matlock Town where we can have some coffee.'

Showing Arthur so many different places reminded him of the Penelope he should have married but couldn't because, knowing what was good for her, she refused the jump. 'Have you seen anything of cousin Dave lately?'

Arthur had a slab of chocolate cake with his coffee. 'Didn't I tell you? He snuffed it, from cancer of the throat. He was seventy-three, but the same old Dave to the end. I phoned him a week before he died. He couldn't say much, and it was painful to laugh, but he liked hearing me talk about the thieving him and Donnie did when they deserted from the army in the war. He was always as hard as nails, Dave was, and I didn't much like him, but because he was dying I asked whether it had been him who gave our Margaret's husband that big pasting all those years ago. Do you remember? Albert could hardly crawl back in the house because somebody had punched the crap out of him. I was in the army, or I'd have done it myself. Dave had always had a soft spot for Margaret, but she was his cousin so he couldn't try anything, and when mother told him that Albert was knocking her about, Dave waited for him to come out of the pub one night with his usual skinful. Albert probably looked forward to taking it out on Margaret when he got home, but Dave put both boots in. He told me when I asked about it. "Who else did you think did it?" he wheezed. "With every kick I told him to leave Margaret alone, and when he shouted he'd get the police if I didn't stop, I started all over again." Then a week later Gladys phoned to tell me Dave had died. The older you get the more people around you kick the bucket. God used to have a musket to try picking you off with, so at least you had a chance, and when you were young it didn't matter, but now the old bastard's got his hands on a machine gun.' He pushed his plate aside. 'I've heard there's an Industrial Museum near here. I wouldn't mind having a look.'

Parking by the white domed pavilion, Brian saw half a dozen hikers heading across the road on their way into the hills, all rucksacked up and looking like figures on Ordnance Survey map covers of the thirties. He felt a yen to follow, witness landscape with seventeen-year-old eyes, except that in those days he had seen only so much height and so much green, one line folding into the other, little beyond tarmac in front of the handlebars, too controlled by adolescent thoughts to see much else.

Arthur walked among the displays of two thousand years

of mining, quietly studying the giant water pressure engine made out of wood and iron during the industrial revolution, while Brian, though familiar with machinery from his time in factories, knew little about it. He did a ten minute recce, then stood by the information counter to buy postcards he wouldn't look at till sending one to Arthur in a year or two as a reminder of today.

Whitening clouds skimming from the west turned flimsy, larger areas of blue left behind. 'We'll go to Cromford for lunch. It's a nice place.'

Arthur buttoned his overcoat against the wind. 'You know your way around here better than I do.'

'I used to shoot up from London for a day or two whenever I was bored.'

'Yeh, I'll bet you did.'

'I was a dirty young man then, and now I'm a dirty old man.' He swung right into Cromford. 'I think I love this area more than any other.'

He was glad to hear it, as Brian led him into the beamed lounge of the Boat Inn, and sat him at a table, while he went to the bar to get their pints and order two lunches of roast beef, Yorkshire pudding, boiled and roast potatoes, cabbage, carrots and peas.

The enormous platters came and Arthur unwrapped his irons from the paper napkin. 'You wouldn't get anything like this in London, not at this price anyway. Nor in Nottingham, either, as far as I know. It's real fucker's grub.'

Brian relished his use of the old lingo, recalling how he put on his cap to go out with his brothers and sup pints in familiar pubs, and no one thinking him a foreigner who didn't belong.

'You can eat better here than down south,' Arthur said. 'So why don't you come and live this way?'

65

Sell his flat? Find a lace-manufacturer's bolt hole in the Park? See the Castle glowering when he went for his morning paper? Wander moribund more than alive around the middle of town? It was a great city, with concerts to go to and plays worth seeing at the theatre, radio and television stations. The magnet of the East Midlands had a self confidence no one could fault, a cosmopolitan go-ahead conurbation whose unique pulse animated young and old alike, the capital of his heart with a long history.

The garden of Derbyshire was close to its back door, and out of the front it wasn't far to the paddling pool of the North Sea at Skegness. What more could anybody want? Wherever he was, he felt the dynamo power of his life always pulling, and right from the fifties had considered ending his days where they started. 'I'm settled in London. Maybe I live there to have the pleasure of spending a few days here now and again.'

'You've got your room. And you're always welcome.'

Only the clatter of knives and forks disturbed the silence. 'We'll take a drive up the Via Gellia,' Brian said, when the hot roll and custard came.

'We seem to be on a mystery trip.'

'It's a two mile run to Grangemill. A bloke called Gell from Wirksworth laid it out in the last century and gave it a Latin name, but it only means Gell Road. Vyella gets its trade name from it, because a mill up there used to make the stuff. Are you going to want coffee?'

'Better not, or I'll be looking for a piss-house every five minutes.'

'Same here. Fit, then?'

A weaving tunnel of green, steep banks with nothing but trees to see, limestone sides turning the road into a ravine. He sensed Arthur thinking there wasn't much to it, so they were

66

soon up and down and driving back through Cromford. The day had to end with something better so he said: 'We'll have a look at Crich Memorial.'

'I used to like going up there, though the wind's always fresh, and it'll probably blow me away. Turn left at Whatstandwell.'

Not much likelihood of that with Arthur, who was a solid figure, no longer a six foot pit-prop as in the old days, yet not looking anywhere near his age, either. The workshop built on the back of his house was a mechanic's paradise, tools and equipment neatly compartmented. Brian had often seen him with shirt sleeves rolled up, fashioning an artefact for home or garden, his stance like that of their grandfather at similar work.

The lights turned orange, and he was halfway across before the green came up. 'I've never known anybody as quick as you at getting away from the lights,' Arthur said.

'I don't lose much time.'

'Be careful, though. Every road's a battlefield.'

The tower stood, stark and phallic on its hill as he drove through the open gate and along an unpaved track by the lodge. His girlfriend had found the situation bleak, the giant structure too crude a pepperpot cock perhaps. Eight columns supported a domed roof at the top. 'In good visibility you can see Nottingham Castle, sixteen miles away.'

'I don't think I'll go up,' Arthur said. 'I'm feeling idle after that dinner.'

A thousand feet above sea level on the platform, the previous towers served as signal stations, now an impressive memorial to eleven thousand four hundred men of the Sherwood Foresters killed in the Great War, and fifteen hundred in the second.

'And God knows how many were wounded,' Arthur said, 'or who died still young a few years later. It makes you wonder what it was all for, though I suppose it was to stop the Germans walking all over us. They'd have killed you and me for sure, when you think what they did in the last war. I remember that book you sent me, with this photograph of a little terrified kid in the Warsaw Ghetto holding his hands up, and the bastard of a German standing behind him with a gun.'

He had sent the book because the picture reminded him of Arthur in the only snapshot they had of him as a child, with its expression of bewilderment and deprivation. The old man, who took against him from the moment he was born, thought nothing of booting him across the kitchen in order to terrify the rest of them. Margaret, who protested, got a black eye, though he didn't hit anyone for a while after she swore to run out for the police if he did.

Arthur grew into a strong youth, with more and better food to eat after the war began, and when he went to work in a factory the old man became reconciled to his being part of the family. He had no option, because Arthur was taller and stronger. A lot to be said for his good nature was that he never held anything against his father.

'I often think of that kid in Warsaw,' Arthur said. 'It haunts me. I don't suppose he lived to grow up, and as I get older it gets even worse to think about. They did that to millions of others. Why? I'll never understand.'

Brian stood at the railings of the quadrangle. 'The two of us would have been daft enough to enlist in 1914.'

'You're right, and we might have been killed, though three of dad's brothers went, and they came out all right.'

'Maybe it was a pity the old man was too young to go.'

Arthur smiled. 'Then we wouldn't have been born. I don't think I'd have liked that. All these swaddies, though, and from one regiment. It don't bear thinking about. Still, there were times when I wondered why I came out of the army after I'd done my National Service.'

'You thought of staying in?'

'I was a corporal, don't forget. You get a stripe straightaway in the military police, and they made me one of them because I was tall, though I never put anybody on a charge. By the end I'd got two stripes, and my pay was nearly eight bob a day.'

'You used to say you hated it.'

'That was because everybody else did, but before I was demobbed the company CO got me standing to attention in front of him and asked if I'd like to sign on. He just barked the question at me as if I was a dog, so I had to say no. But if a sergeant-major had sat me down with a pint and talked to me for a few minutes like a human being I'd probably have said yes. It wouldn't have been a bad life as an NCO. I'd have got a pension by the time I was in my forties.'

'You might have been killed at Suez.'

'You take the chance. That's what being a soldier is. Still, I didn't stay in, and I'm not complaining. It's just that sometimes I think it might have been better for me.'

'We only see the mistakes we've made on looking back, and we only have one life.'

'I know,' Arthur said. 'I'd like to think otherwise, but I can't. All of them Sherwood Foresters only had one life as well, and that's a fact.'

In the filling station forecourt Arthur said: 'When did you last put oil in your car?'

'I don't remember.'

'Get in and open the bonnet.' He held the dipstick to the light. 'It's bone-dry. Something told me it was. I'll go and get a couple of litres.'

Arthur looked on him as a mechanical numbskull who

didn't realize that a car needed tending now and again, and it was true that he was often lazy, or unable to think of the engine as long as it kept running.

'It wants feeding,' Arthur said, with as contemptuous a look as could be given to a brother. He gurgled most of the oil in, and checked the dipstick again. 'I'd better see to it whenever you come up, otherwise you'll lose your engine, and that'll be a thousand quid up your shirt. Now let's look at the water.' Not perilously low, he insisted in topping it up, and filling the windscreen reservoir. 'We'll check the tyres now.' The pressure being down, he went from one to the other and squirted in the required amount of air. 'Now you won't break down on the motorway.'

Avril brought tea into the sitting room. Brian had never seen her otherwise than smartly dressed. She wore a white blouse with a string of pearls over her bosom, a pale brown skirt and a cashmere cardigan. 'And what have you two old devils been up to today?'

'You won't like it if I tell you.' Arthur turned to Brian: 'Shall I tell her?'

'We had a pleasant day in Matlock.'

'Happen so, but the truth never hurts.' He looked at Avril. 'I don't know how to say this, but he got into a spot of bother.'

'You're lying again.' She sat close to hear. 'Or you're going to. I can see by your face.'

'No, I'm not. We went to a pub to have some dinner, and a young woman sat at the next table. Brian gave her the eye, and they got talking. He told her about all the pop stars he knows in London, and how he's written speeches for famous people, and done films for television. He laid it on with a spatula.'

'Now I know you're lying,' she said, 'using a word like that.'

'She gobbled his lies up, and half way through the meal they went out to the back. Ten minutes later I went to see what was happening, and caught them having a knee trembler by the dustbins. I was shocked, but what could I do? I ran back inside to finish my dinner, but no sooner was the fork in my mouth than I heard shouting and screaming. I ran out, and the girl was sobbing her socks off. Her beefy boyfriend was getting ready to thump Brian, but I told him to back away or he'd get one from me. He walked off with the girl, who was still crying. Our dinners were cold by now, but Brian didn't care. I didn't know where to put my face. Something like that happens every time we go out.'

Avril laughed. 'What a rigmarole!'

'You can't expect him to admit it. I'd have been ashamed for the rest of my life if it had been me.'

'I don't think I would have married you if you hadn't been a liar.' She turned to Brian. 'He made me laugh so much the first time we met I knew I had to marry him. I just made sure we lived together for a few months to see if he could keep it up.'

'Keep what up?' Arthur laughed.

'Then one morning he shook me awake and said: "I've got a surprise for you today." I thought: "Oh, is he going to take me somewhere special?" He was, to the registry office. He'd made all the arrangements without telling me. He even bought a ring. You should have seen the grin all over his face. He only came out with it when we were half way there.'

'You didn't mind, did you?'

'I didn't have much option, did I? I suppose it was the only way you could do it, though it was a good thing I wanted to as well. What would you have done if I hadn't?'

71

He looked forlorn. 'I'd have cut my throat, darling!'

They were well mated, however long their lifetime together would be. Kids from previous marriages had long since grown up, and they'd none from each other. She came in with more tea. 'So you went to Matlock for the day?'

'We did,' Arthur said, 'and had a marvellous time. I like it when me big bruvver teks me out! The best part was when he drove us up and down the Via Jelly-belly. I haven't seen a prettier stretch of road in all my days.'

FIVE

Brian left the car on the street, and if it was nicked, or kicked in, or set on fire, or tipped upside down and danced on with bovver boots (or the latest trainers) then that would be the way things were, so don't moan about it. After a chat with the police he'd go back by train, fill in insurance forms, and wait for the advent of a powder blue chocolate box courtesy car to run about in till his own was written off or fixed.

Yet in his well worn vehicle there were only a few cardboard boxes of supplies for the day when he would set out on a freedom run through Europe to Asia, a stack of old newspapers on the back seat, and an empty plastic container of Evian water, so vandals would merely look in then scout on for better pickings.

If you were too fearful of what nihilistic drug-raddled kids would do to your serviceable vehicle you were only conniving at their habits. He knew the rag-tag-and-bob-tailed bastards well, certainly more than they knew themselves, because as a kid he had done his stint of mischief and half-inching, though never to the extent of wrecking a poor man's push-bike, the equivalent of today's car and just as precious.

He walked through newish houses built in the twenties, then to half a street of older redbricked and probably listed dwellings, whose front rooms opened onto the pavement, good enough to live in, façades neat and clean, but the doorsteps no longer scrubbed. A couple of pubs he and Jenny had sat in were also intact – a shandy for her and a pint of bitter for him, before the long walk back to the real pleasure of the evening.

That she intruded was only to be expected during such perambulations. In those days he'd had an ineradicable itch in the heel, instep, ball and under the toes of both feet, an irritation of surplus blood prompting him to light off since first being conscious of where he was. Not that he had gone far, but twenty or a hundred miles in England was enough to deracinate you forever.

Jenny had nothing to do with his departure. He would have abandoned whatever woman he had known. Unique idiosyncrasies stayed from cradle to coffin, and would have parted them even if he'd lived only a few streets away for the rest of his life. If he roamed Nottingham now and again it was because he had grown up there, and being in thrall to the past only meant that so little of the future was left.

The area used to be a familiar maze of streets and dead-end terraces and double entries, at night a redbricked zone of gaslit cosiness miles in extent, an almost endless playground of freedom and safe adventure for the children who lived there. People long dead inhabited the warrens of memory, and he recalled suddenly and for some reason how sixty years ago everyone was singing 'San Francisco' because the film with Spencer Tracy was showing at the neighbourhood picture house. All knew the tune inside a week, and though his pal Bernard Griffin claimed he'd seen the film already, Brian didn't believe him, knowing he'd heard his mother whistling it after either husband or fancyman had taken her to the pictures.

Dorothy Griffin always had a fancyman because every few

months she separated from her husband. Nobody could make up their minds whether Mrs Griffin left Mr Griffin because he could no longer put up with her carryings on, or whether Mr Griffin left Mrs Griffin because she couldn't endure his carryings on at the way she carried on, and in any case he absolutely couldn't stand the way she carried on. They had a hard time living together, but could never stand being apart for long.

Soon enough after Herbert Griffin left, he would meet his wife Dorothy by accident, in the White Horse or the Dover Castle (or maybe even the Plough) and after some talk and a bit of shouting (the publican telling them to go outside and settle their differences on the pavement if they couldn't behave and keep quiet) they came home hand in hand so that any fancyman who had been in the offing for her, or any fancywoman who had been on the cards for him, were one and both left out in the cold, or sent packing to their wife or husband, for all anybody knew.

Dorothy Griffin never carried on with any man who lived in her own area, because as soon as Herbert Griffin went sneaking off to meet his fancywoman she would get on a bus to calm herself, sitting on the top deck with a fag on the go, and didn't get off till the conductor told her they'd reached the terminus on the other side of the city a good five miles away. Her first call would be to the nearest pub for a few consoling drinks, because the air in the bus had made her thirsty, and after two or three gin-fizzes she would become amiable and talk to someone who might turn into another of her fancymen.

Dorothy Griffin was pretty, always neatly and carefully dressed, even when going to work at the cigarette factory up the street; and Herbert Griffin, who was handsome and smart, was employed at the bike factory down the street. Both were small and slim, though sometimes not as well disposed towards each other as they should have been. Only when together after a suitable break would they be seen walking arm in arm to pub or pictures, or back to the house which, so Brian's mother said, looked like a pigsty.

Their son Bernard was privileged (all the other kids thought) in having both parents at work, and being so taken up with themselves, or with their fancymen or fancywomen, that he hardly ever saw them for more than an hour at a time, though they provided him with a back door key and money for food. He would never let Brian into the house when he called, while he was in the kitchen helping himself to a slice of bread and potted meat after school, so it was never possible to verify whether the place looked like a pigsty.

He walked along the shop fronts of the main road, noting the cosmopolitan scene: The Golden Fish Bar, Sauna and Massage, Mahmood Brothers Halal Store, Nahal's Off-licence, Twenty-Four Hour Taxi Service, Goodyear Chinese Restaurant, Honda Motorbike Franchise, Cellnet Communications, Car Sales Forecourt, and then the White Horse pub, which looked as if it would never change.

His car hadn't been scratched or dented, the windscreen not even a scattering of perspex cobbles across the bonnet, disappointing because the old place hadn't lived up to its reputation, and provided him with a wreck that he could have turned in for something better.

He drove by disused Radford Station towards the bungalow zone of Wollaton. Sitting at his desk in London, coaxing situations from his pen to amuse people, or at least the script editors, he often felt flu-bound or uninspired, but as soon as he got hold of a car wheel and heard the engine purring like a cat at feeding time – cruising up the Great North

76

Road, or drifting around Nottingham – energy and clarity of mind would come back, the contaminations of a fluish cold forgotten.

Window down, a shaft of clean air came in and, turning from the main road, he felt the customary excitement at seeing the towers and balustrades of Wollaton Hall, its three-tiered array of elongated windows, the chimneys and cupolas and stone terracing inspiring against any sort of sky, though when the sun fired its windows into molten copper, it seemed as if its precious insides would only cool when the entire pile was a heap of grey ash.

On his first day at school a bag of variously shaped wooden bricks was emptied over the floor and, reaching what he could into his orbit, or prise from the hands of others, he structured a crude imitation of Wollaton Hall out of a prescient and waking dream long before seeing the place. So taken by the vision, he felt no grief at the sombre bell sounding for a change of classroom, the collapsing bricks scooped away by the teacher, as if knowing he would one day see the real version of his construction.

Coming off the motorway in summer his first stop was always Wollaton Park. He glanced beyond the windscreen to make sure the Hall was still on its hill, as if it had not only been the centre of his world from an early age but had also pointed out the stepping stones of his life towards Rome, Athens and Jerusalem, a quest begun on first shaping that crude replica as an infant.

Lord Willoughby employed Smithson to build the place in 1588, and the cost of eighty thousand pounds – almost incalculable in today's money – was culled from the profits of nearby coal pits. Quarrelling with his family, Willoughby died a demented pauper in London, frying penny pork scraps over a wood fire in his attic room. Nottingham rioters in 1832, after gleefully torching the Castle (what a night that must have been!), were stopped by a troop of yeomanry and a few cannon from doing the same to Wollaton Hall.

He enjoyed seeing the gentle and curious deer over the railings by the parking space, and cattle among pastures under the trees. On waking from an hour's sleep he would broach the flask of tea and split open a packet of biscuits, before the first stage of his walk around the lake.

He passed the conspicuous red telephone box on his walk up the sloping bank of grass to the wide steps before the main doors, as if going to wait for Jenny on the terrace. She wore a brown pleated skirt, white blouse, lisle stockings, laced-up shoes, but no headscarf, on the day he recalled. He had on his one alternative to overalls and boots, a navy-blue utility suit and white shirt, and tie with a pin half hidden by the waistcoat, jacket unbuttoned and shoes well shining.

The Brylcreem quiff stood out as shapely as King George's, and he smoked a Senior Service while leaning on the balustrade to watch Jenny coming up the steps. The green landscape was a balm of ointment after all week looking at mounting coils of brass and steel shavings around his capstan lathe. 'Do you like the view?'

The land undulated as far as Misk Hill seven miles away, a few houses here and there. 'I do like it,' she said, as if to pass the test.

'So do I. I have done since I first saw it. Would you like to live somewhere out there?'

'I already do. If you turn your head a bit to the right you can see Aspley. What you mean, though, is would I like to live somewhere out there with you, don't you?'

'I'm not sure what I meant.' The possibility was bedded in his soul but, for no reason he cared to explain, or even could, he was glad to see the back of such a thought.

Her elbow jabbed playfully at what meat there was below his ribs. 'You're never sure of anything. But you must have meant something. I usually do when I open my mouth.'

'I only asked if you liked the view.'

'Of course I do. I'm not deaf, am I? Nor blind, either.'

'That's all right, then.'

'I want to go in the museum,' she said, 'and look at the stuffed animals' – intimating that she might find them more alive than he seemed to be.

'I want to stand here a bit. I can see a long way, and I like that.'

'You can do it from a lot of other places.'

'I know,' he said.

'So why here, then?'

'Because this is special. And here I am, aren't I?' Her question was a way of trying to find out what was in his mind, as if he knew, or wanted to know. It was a matter of pride not to know, which might be stupid but he didn't care. 'It's got something to do with the scenery, and having the Hall behind me at the same time.'

'I came to the museum the year before leaving school,' she said. 'The teacher brought us for the day. We all had jotters to write down what we saw, but my pencil wouldn't move. All I could do was look at the birds and animals, and what clothes people used to wear in the olden days. I couldn't take my eyes off so many lovely things. The next week at school we were told to write a composition about our time in the museum, using the notes we'd made, and I'd got nothing in my jotter. I didn't know what to do. "Why aren't you writing, Jenny?" the teacher asked me. "I can't, Miss," I told her. "Write," she said, "and be quick about it." So I did. I just wrote and wrote, and when the teacher read it she said it was the best composition in the class. She made me stand up in front and read it out to everybody else. I was trembling like a leaf, but I did it.'

She looked for some response, till he was glad the sun caught her eyes and she had to turn away. Life-changing moments, carelessly passed over, hid what the heart profoundly wanted. Whatever was yet to come which you couldn't know about was more fundamentally what you wanted to happen. 'We'll go in, if you like, and you can tell me about it.'

She turned to take his arm. 'I love you. You know that, don't you?'

'I love you, as well. I always shall.' What an outrageous liar. He always was, and always had been. He could love no one but himself, and knew the truth as he stood looking at how the old trees and fields had been painted by the rooftops of new houses, in one of which they would have been happy, though for how long? She had relinquished him but he had driven her to it. He hadn't argued. Words of reconciliation would have been easy. She had wanted him to put a ring on her finger as proof that he loved her, even though marriage had to wait a few years. He had let go a kind of heaven in exchange for one disaster after another as if that was the only way someone like him could learn, though where such learning had got him he couldn't say.

In the days that mattered he had wanted no tie-ups, no domestic servitude, no obligations, no acquiescing to the call of the times, no giving in to the mindless drive of nature – shameful to fall into line like all his friends. Whatever was expected had to be against your deepest nature, until death did us kill being no state to live in, the black hole too close even then to tolerate, and so the irreversible step was taken, and he ran from the living death of marrying the girl he loved. He opted for liberty, of looking for a refuge from himself and never finding anything he could recognize as a final haven.

The turmoil of fleeing was the only reality, self-defeating, but always exciting, but if you spoil a person's life make sure you know what you do, otherwise your own soul could die. On the other hand he refused to believe he had ruined Jenny's life, any more than he had wrecked his own. You could never be sure of what effect you had had as long as there was a future to look forward to. Jenny was alive and healthy, and since he had been asked to her seventieth birthday party all might yet be well.

At the foot of the hill a mother, father, and three children on their rainbow coloured bikes went between the greenswards like a shoal of tropical fish. Through the brick archway a young woman in the stable was grooming a horse. She swabbed the snot off its nose with a grey rag that looked as if it had done the same service for a posse of others, a tail of ginger hair shifting to and fro down her back. The placid animal royally accepted her care, but she was accustomed to people noting her activity. 'You look after the horse well.'

She turned, but kept a hand on the animal's mouth, her pale worried face not losing its concern for the horse. 'I've got to, haven't I?'

He imagined the shape under her clothes. A funny old chap, she must have thought, though personable young women sometimes fell in love with older men, who would surely be daft if they questioned what sinister undercurrents led them to it. It wasn't the women he fell in love with ten times a day who would improve his existence but the one he laid siege to on deciding to make her his girlfriend, which had now and again succeeded. When one is dying in a desert of your own making, and finally gets to water, thirst kills whatever microbes are hidden in it.

81

His usual quick walk took him by the industrial museum and out to the large area of grass descending from the rear of the Hall. Heading towards the lake, he thought maybe he would call on his first wife when he got back to London, to see if he could persuade her to live with him again. He would surprise her by being suave, humorous, kindly and understanding, a much reformed man in fact, telling so many amusing anecdotes (he would write a list, and rehearse them) about what had happened to him since their divorce, that she would have no opportunity to bring out the big guns of sarcastic disbelief. He would take an armful of flowers, escort her to a good restaurant (with anti-salmonella pills in his pocket) and if he got as far as being invited back to her flat, he would praise her exquisite cooking (it had always been god-awful, when she bothered to cook at all), offer to wash the dishes, and maybe dry them, and even put them away, as well as sweep the kitchen. He would say how much he loved her, that he couldn't live without her (as indeed, how could any man? he would add) and admit that all the troubles of their previous marriage had been due to him (they hadn't, by any means) and would never be repeated.

Which would be absolutely the wrong way to go about it, supposing he cared to try, which he didn't. She knew him too well to trust him, and if he did win her again the same fiasco would soon enough come around, and for such a smash up to happen twice would wreck her peace forever. So he wouldn't do it, malice and injustice no part of him, fantasies only grain for the mill of his trade, having long since learned where imagination ended and actual life began.

Such speculation took him to where a chill wind rippled the water, two swans sliding towards the bushes, more as if thinking to find cover than have a quick fuck. Ruts being filled by yesterday's rain, he gave way to a passing woman, and took in what he could without seeming to stare, hoping his manoeuvre to leave her the drier part of the path was plain.

Her head was angled towards the ground, but not so much that he couldn't see a sign of tightness around the mouth, perhaps due to anxiety as much as age, for she couldn't have been much more than forty. She might have stepped from an Edwardian album, being handsome though not classically beautiful, mysterious because interesting and independent, coat blown by a renewing breeze to show a high necked pale brown blouse with a broad tie of narrow darker brown bands hanging between the folds of her small bosom, giving the neat aspect of a north American with dark Colette styled hair.

In the photoflash of a moment, he would have said something was missing in a life which ought to have been exciting but wasn't, though formerly an event he couldn't guess at had provided sufficient memories for her to be alone, while beginning to wonder on her solitary walk around the lake if it might be good to mix with anyone interesting again, her lips showing a subtle mark of enquiry and discontent.

Any intriguing woman passed on the street sent a wave of desire through him, always had, as if he'd only to see their face during an orgasm and discover the greatest love of his life. But the lady by the lake could have no part of him. Her passing merely enlivened the morning, for which he was grateful, and sorry he couldn't tell her so. Such faces filled his mind with possibilities, yet one of the first women met that way had been Jenny, on coming out of the factory arm in arm with a friend, smiling as if she could only be at ease with other women.

Perhaps all his clandestine scrutinies were an attempt to retrieve her image from the time they were in love, before she got pregnant by a man who wanted neither her nor the child, and before her marriage to George who later required almost more than anyone had to give.

Looking along the shore from the sluice gate at the top end of the water recalled scenery from *The Woman in White*, but the Hall beyond was a monument of civilization resplendent against slowly shifting clouds. You live in order to create memories, an incident from the past swamping in, whether pleasant or not, and you relish the free show with all its resonances, because when you're dead there'll be no more. If he had turned into smithereens on the motorway back to London every memory would have been fighting for space in the final second, before the exhibition hall of his mind was blacked out forever, the psychic pile up of all time, a reflection that only increased his feeling for life.

SIX

Arthur, driving as carefully as all get-out over Basford Crossing, thought that Brian had never come up for a gasp of real
air since leaving home, because working for television cut him
off from ordinary life. He spends his time scribbling, sticks to
his work but admits it's an easy life, having enough in his
loaf to earn money by writing scripts, which I never thought
anybody in our family would do. Derek (who's probably at
the pub already) slid out of hard sweat as well, only me to
carry the can, except I jacked work in when the firm went
bust and I was supposed to be too old to go on. Grandad
shoed ponies down the pit till he was seventy, but I was glad
to let others have a turn.

A lot of factories were closing at the time, the government
glad to see them go, everybody chucked on the scrapheap
and more like slaves than when they'd got places to work
in. Now there's a Labour government but they're no better
than the Tories because they don't care about ordinary
people either.

What I can't understand though is why I've got such a
bone idle bastard like Harold for a son. If I say anything
about him wearing a ponytail and an earring, when he calls
to cadge some money, he looks as if there's a bomb ticking
inside him ready to explode, though I'd give him more than
a run for his money if he made a move.

Now and again he spins a yarn that he's got a job, and likes it because it's such interesting work, says he's friendly with everybody and wants to stick it for the rest of his life, it's just what he's always wanted, and what a shame he didn't find it years ago. He sits there like a useless wanker, telling me how he works so hard the firm can't do without him, that he's so well in with the gaffer he's on the way to marrying his daughter and being made a foreman, and when he is he'll take out a mortgage on a bungalow and they'll have a few kids, and go for their holidays to Skegness or the New Forest.

A pack of fucking lies because I know he's only taking the piss, which makes me want to punch him in the chops and tell him to wrap it up or he'll get another, but for some reason I can't, want to see how far he'll go, and then it's as I expect because a week later the job, if he had one, is no longer a novelty, or he gets a black look from the foreman and tells him to stuff the job where a monkey shoves its nuts. Then he comes to us and asks to borrow twenty quid, like he did last month.

'I'm stony broke. I ain't even got the price of a pint.'

'You should have thought of that before you chucked your job.'

'I didn't chuck it. I was kicked out.'

'Everybody gets kicked out if they tell the foreman to fuck off.'

'How did you know I said that?'

How? It was just what he'd wanted to say a hundred times a day when he'd worked in the factory, but hadn't because he'd got to earn a living, and needed his fourteen pounds for ale and women at the weekend. 'It's what everybody wants to say who's at work, and you were daft enough to say it.'

'He asked for it.'

'They all do. But you don't say it.'

86

'The fuckface was picking on me. He had it in for me right from the start, but I stuck it as long as I could. Anyway, it's too late now. All I want is twenty quid for a packet o' fags and a pint. It's Saturday night, and I'm flat broke.'

'Where do you think I've got twenty quid? Well, I did print a batch this morning, but I'm waiting for the ink to dry, though I don't think you'll be able to pass 'em over the counter because like a prat I put the Queen's head on upside down.'

'Very funny.' The smile didn't do much for his face, as he stretched his legs to their fullest extent. 'What a fucking country. It must be the deadest place in the world. I wish I'd got a lot more than twenty quid, and if I had do you know what I'd do with it?'

Arthur was too fed up to guess, unless to suggest a one way ticket to a less boring country on the other side of the world, where he could stay for good. 'No, I don't.'

'I'd buy as much dynamite as I could get my hands on and blow up the Houses of Parliament. Blow all them government fuckpigs to bits. They just fuck everything up, the bone idle lot.'

Arthur wondered what he had done to deserve such a son, whom he'd taken fishing up the canal as a child on the crossbar of his bike, nothing Harold liked better when he had his own little rod and line. He would drive him to all the choice spots in the county, from Cresswell Crags to Hickling Pastures, proud that by eight he could read a map and navigate. At the first mention of hunger he stopped at the nearest café for cakes and a bottle of pop. He bought him an air rifle, books about cars and aeroplanes, even an electric guitar, but on splitting up with Doreen he had lost sight of him for ten years.

'Anyway, why the fuck should I work? What's in it for me?

You slog your bollocks off day after boring day, and get a miserable few quid at the end of the week. So what? It ain't worth it. In any case there's plenty of other mugs to do the work, so I can't feel guilty.'

Something had gone wrong with Harold in his twenties, but Arthur didn't blame himself: it would have happened whether he'd stayed with Doreen or not. True, he had spoiled him rotten, but it was heartbreaking to recall how they used to be so friendly. He had given him more than he'd ever had, which should have made him willing to work and settle down. So what had gone wrong?

Harold's tea was getting cold, and Arthur knew that as a young man he would have sent it down scalding and been waiting for another. He watched him break up the biscuits without eating, so he wasn't hungry, didn't deserve one never mind twenty pounds. He's idle like a lot of blokes these days, who rely on giros not to go looking for work, and aren't interested unless they're offered a job for five hundred pounds a week, or there's a vacancy for a pop star.

It wasn't easy to get work, he knew. When he left school you picked a job from scores of others, and if you didn't like it after a week could tell the gaffer where to stick it, then get another. Not that he had. He'd stayed at the bike factory more than ten years, though often enough thought of packing it in. 'And if you blew everybody up in Parliament things would be just the same when the dust settled.'

Harold laughed. 'I know, but I'd feel a lot better, wouldn't I?'

'For five minutes you would. You think it hasn't been hard for all of us?'

'On no!' He lay full length along the sofa. 'Please don't start telling me how much you suffered as a kid, when you only had a donkey's foreskin between the seven of you for

88

Sunday dinner, and one pair of shoes in the family so's you could only go out one at a time when it was snowing. I don't want to get tears all over your nice new sofa. I just couldn't bear hearing about when your dad was on the dole and knocked you about. I've had to listen to such fucking rubbish all my life, and I'm fed up to here with it.'

He stabbed two fingers viciously at his throat, and Arthur regretted they hadn't got steel points at the ends. He knew that if he didn't give him any money he would get it from somebody, being good looking and charming when he wanted. He also had a swaggering self-confidence, as if spoiling him as a kid had actually done him some good, but at the worst of times he looked like Grandfather Merton down on his luck, though Merton would have kicked him from arsehole to breakfast time as soon as look at him.

You didn't know what to think. Last year he and Avril had gone down town for her birthday, thinking to have a drink in the Royal Children. From the doorway they saw Harold with two attractive women, the three of them as close as if he was planning to have one one night and the other the next, or maybe both at the same time. Harold was startled at seeing his father, in no way wanting to be disturbed, so they left him to his love talk, and had their drink in the Trip to Jerusalem.

Harold usually had some woman to sponge off, who might be married or not, though Arthur couldn't fault him for that. He probably didn't need twenty quid any-way, and had only called to play his favourite game of winding the old man up. When Avril came in from the kitchen he sat up and smiled. 'Hello, duck, I wondered when you were going to come in again and sit by my side.'

'You've let your tea get cold,' she said. 'And look what

you've done with those biscuits. You've crumpled them all up. That wasn't very nice.'

'I'm sorry, love. I was so busy listening to dear old dad. He nearly had me sobbing my socks off again about the bad old days. I was hoping you'd come back in and save me. He's not very glad to see me. All I want though is to say how marvellous you look today. But then, you always do.'

'Listen to him! I never know how to take all those things he says.'

'I'll put my boot in your big mouth if you don't shut your rattle.' Arthur's fist was twitching to be given flight. 'Just see if I don't.'

The silence frightened Harold. 'I was only trying to be sociable.'

'Try somewhere else.'

Avril, as usual, diverted them from their antipathy. 'If you don't stop annoying Arthur I won't make you another cup of tea. But drink it while it's hot. And eat those biscuits, or you'll have me to answer to.'

Harold went to the window. 'I've been thinking things over.'

Arthur grunted. 'Not again.'

'I have, though. I'm going to get a haircut, and take this earring off. I'll even buy myself a proper shirt, and a suit.'

'You'll look even more handsome,' Avril said.

'I want to change my life.' He waved off her compliment. 'I'm fed up with being the way I am.' When biscuits were finished, and swilled down with tea, he stood tall in stretching himself, the same way as Arthur a few minutes earlier, showing them as so physically alike that Avril added: 'I'm sure you can change yourself if you want to.'

'I will. You'll see. It's the boredom that's killing me. And I'm tired of being like this. I'm just not myself, so things have got to alter. I want to stop relying on other people, as well. That's why I want twenty quid, just to start me off.'

She was too soft on him, and however much Arthur argued against it, it made little difference. Harold went whistling down the street. 'Poor chap,' she said. 'He told me on his way back from the bathroom that he didn't have a penny to his name, so I couldn't see him without the price of a glass of beer.'

Ten years ago she had been left a few thousand pounds by an aunt, and Arthur never asked how much. She kept it in a building society, and used the interest for a holiday now and again. What she gave Harold would come out of that. 'You give in to him every time.'

'Yes, but he is your son, you know.'

'I'm not so sure about that.'

'I am. I've never seen two people so alike, allowing for the difference of age. It amazes me every time I see the two of you together. He looks just like you when I first met you.'

Which seemed, if anything, to please him. 'It's the way he carries on, but he's a lot different to me on the inside. And the trouble with giving him money is he might spend it on drugs. That's what frightens me.'

'He won't get much on twenty pounds. Anyway, he doesn't need drugs to keep his spirits up. And you heard what he said about changing the way he looks. I think he means it.'

'We'll see about that.' He stood, bereft for a moment, as if missing hard work at the factory. 'I've always loved him, and he knows it. I just hope he don't get on drugs.'

'I can't think he's ever taken more than a puff or two of marijuana, if that.'

'I've never even swallowed an aspro,' he said.

'That's because you're hopped up all the time.'

91

He drew her close for a kiss. 'I must have been stoned out of my mind when I first made a grab at you.'

'You mean just after you backed into my front bumper at the supermarket?'

'It was the only thing I could do. I saw this smashing young woman in my mirror, and got a hard on, so it made me clumsy. You didn't half tell me off.'

'You dented my lovely new car, that's why.'

'I'd never heard such language. I thought you were going to rip my eyes out.'

'There was no other way to get through to you. You just stood there.'

'Then I bought you a cup of coffee.'

'And you kept trying to hold my hand.'

'It was only to steady my nerves.'

'I was glad you did. My hands were freezing, and yours were burning hot.'

He looked at the framed photograph of Isambard Kingdom Brunel, in its frame on the wall, the famous engineer crowned by a stovepipe hat and standing against a heap of enormous chainlinks. 'I got your bumper off next day, and took it to the factory. Hammered it as good as new. Good job I'd done some panel beating in my time. But I still like nudging into your front bumpers.'

'You aren't doing badly just now.'

'It's only because I love you.'

'If I didn't know that I wouldn't know anything, would I?'

'That's what I like to hear.'

'Oh, I'll always say that to you.'

'You mean you tell lies sometimes?'

'Not these days I don't, but I've never lied to you. I only lied to stop people getting hurt, though it didn't do me much good. Or them, either.'

Talk flowed with an ease he hadn't thought possible with someone so long lived with. After six months – and he supposed it had been as much his fault as hers – he and Doreen had fallen into a putrid trap of resentment and animosity, the first words on whatever matter fuelling them into days of unspoken dislike.

At first Avril hadn't appeared to be his sort at all, though she was no less attractive for that, but she had confidence in all she said, which made her so easygoing that they soon got to know each other as much as two people ever could. Nothing spoken was given too much importance, and there was no need to worry about what might be hidden between their words.

Her years as a catering manageress had taught her how to deal with people, but since being made redundant she did dressmaking, studied botany and bird recognition, and was learning to read music, which told him more about her than if she hadn't had such hobbies.

He used to joke that marrying him had brought her down in the world, to which she replied that since they loved each other what could it matter, providing of course that he came up a few steps to meet her now and again, though not right to her level, because then they would have nothing to argue about, and she would see no reason to laugh at his stories. 'On the other hand I don't think I ever have told a lie. At least I can't remember when I did.'

'You must have done, once.'

'I could never be bothered.' She lit a cigarette. 'Nobody's worth lying to. You have to hate somebody, to lie to them. Or be frightened by them.'

He'd always thought that everybody lied, that lying was a way of getting what you wanted, or of survival in a perilous situation, or even as a means of entertainment. Life would be dull if people didn't lie.

'Mind you,' she said mischievously, 'there are lies, and lies. You tell lies to make me laugh when you want to cheer me up, or when you've got nothing to say and can't bear to stay quiet. I sometimes think you ought to have been an actor. You'd have been good on the stage.'

He growled into her ear. 'I'd have played Frankenstein, or Dracula. When I tried it in Sunday School they threw me out because I frightened the other kids to death. I'll tell you about it sometime.'

'I couldn't act to save my life,' she laughed. 'That's why I've never been one for telling lies. I don't feel threatened enough, not by you anyway. And it's unnecessary to lie to somebody if you love them.'

'Now you tell me,' he said. You never knew what a woman was thinking, no more than she could tell what was in your mind, but to Avril it didn't matter, and there was no need for either to fish for each other's thoughts. They talked about whatever was in their minds and in his better moods he knew he had been waiting nearly half his life to meet her. 'The sun's come out, so let's have a look at the garden, before it goes back in again.'

SEVEN

When Derek mounted the steps of The Crossbow for a better view the sweet and playful air seemed to promise eternal life. Beyond the bungalows and council houses stood the grey tower blocks of the tobacco warehouse. Then, as far as the crest – where in the old days a mass of small dwellings with their smoking chimneys had lapped up the hillside like a hurriedly made rug – came the dragons' teeth of highrise hencoops nobody had ever wanted to live in. 'The street where I grew up has been bulldozed.'

To see him so assiduously reconnoitring the landscape made Eileen think of the verses in the Bible she had read aloud at the Sunday School her father had sent all his kids to. No one who went into the terrain Derek looked at would come back with a bunch of grapes hanging from a stick and say it was the Promised Land, though it was all they had and couldn't be liked any the less for that. 'The house I was brought up in's gone as well.'

He came down to join her, touched the back of her neck with affection. 'We got here early.'

'We always do, but it's better than being late, and I don't mind waiting on an evening like this.'

People were going up the wooden steps to the lower floor of the pub, but he and Eileen sauntered around the large car park bordered by bushes and trees of what had once been a

95

triangle of dense jungle between road railway and canal. In the days before the pub was built Arthur, after coming out of the army with a pair of heavy duty wirecutters, scorned warning notices and boundary fences. Infantry training had taught him to move across terrain without being seen (a childhood skill, in any case) lumbered with fishing tackle, a knapsack of food and drink, and often a bicycle. He ensconced himself where the fishes bit, in spite of juddering trains and the noise of motor traffic.

Derek smoothed his black militarily trimmed moustache. 'As a kid I often walked the two miles to get here.'

'Nobody does that now,' she said. 'They jump into cars or get on their motorbikes to go a hundred yards. They've lost the use of their legs by being stuck at video games or flopped in front of the television.'

On any spare day the two of them set off up the Trent valley, or left the car at a Derbyshire village and did a circuit of ten or so miles, each with Swift binoculars to spot what birds were flying. Rain didn't put them off, though better if a Pennine wind blew air at their ribs. 'I wonder how long they'll be?'

'Not too long,' she said. 'They're never late for a party in a pub. It's you who made us get here early.'

'I've always been like that. I can't think why, except that in my job you've got to be punctual. I'd be letting the others down if I wasn't, and I wouldn't like anybody to let me down.'

His work at the surveyor's office led Arthur to twit him about complicating the traffic system: 'I can just imagine you getting to work at half past nine. You don't have anything to do, and you're dead frightened of being laid off, so you light your fags or pipes, and make some tea. Then you put your heads together, till somebody says: "When I came in on my push-bike this morning the traffic was flowing like water, not a hitch anywhere, so what about another one-way system, to balls it all up?"'

'Did you see that magpie?'

He trawled fingers through short thick hair that would never fall out. 'A beauty, wasn't it?'

'They get fat from rummaging for leftovers in the pub dustbins.'

'It was so tame you could have touched it.'

'You nearly ran one over coming in,' she said. 'But you never do, they're so quick. Let's walk around a bit. We might see another. When Arthur and Avril and Brian get here they'll know our car.'

'Brian used to take me walking in this area. We'd have a bird recognition book, and one on flowers and trees, so we stopped every few minutes to look something up. I've never forgotten what I learned, though I was only ten at the time. When we were tired he took me to a cottage on a lane near Cossall where they sold lemonade and sweets out of a little side window.'

Such outings jumped to mind because the three brothers were getting together. 'If we heard a cuckoo we'd try to find the nest, but it was too far away, or hidden too cunningly in the bushes. The nest we did find always belonged to another bird. Brian would sometimes thump me if I named the wrong flower, or couldn't tell what sort of a bird was flitting over.'

'I know he's got a temper, but why did he do that?'

'Something was eating him up. I never knew what it was. He just got ratty and took it out on me. But I tried not to lose my temper like that with our two kids, even though they did drive me half barmy at times.'

In the sixties the family was supposed to be outdated and the cause of all mental troubles, everything the fault of your parents, or the claustrophobia of the home, but he hadn't believed it, because he and Eileen were too busy making sure the kids had all they'd lacked when young but without spoiling them. Those who spouted that the family was done for had grown up with more than he'd had as a kid, which made their attitudes hard to credit.

'But just think of Jenny,' she said, 'who had seven to bring up. It's not a family, it's a crowd. And look at all the people going into the pub. We'll be lucky to have that many friends and family at our party when we're seventy.'

'Well, the years'll whistle by, so it won't be long, now that the kids are off our hands.'

'The house is peaceful, though I'm glad they don't live too far away.'

'And we've got more money as well,' he said, 'with your job and mine. I'm looking forward to getting under the Channel to France next month. Maybe we'll try Spain this year.'

'I like Austria, or Switzerland.'

'I know, but we ought to go somewhere different.'

They talked about Avril because her prognosis didn't look good, and hoped the chemotherapy would work. She had knitted into the family like the warp and weft of cloth, and they all liked her, so how would Arthur manage if she died? Meeting her had been the best thing in his life, and they got on so well it would be awful for him to be on his own. Since all their parents had died ten years ago nothing bad had happened, but you would be daft if you expected the peace to go on forever, yet you do. So now Avril had cancer, but she was taking it well and didn't really look ill, so they could only hope everything would be all right.

Derek rolled the glasses till all details were clear. The past was built over, and good riddance to the slums, a word Arthur and Brian didn't like. Being older they'd lived through earlier days, though when the three of them sat reminiscing in a pub, talking politics and bringing up the old times, they seemed much the same age. Arthur and Brian often turned their experiences into a comic show, laughter proving them brothers to the bone.

To lack a meal in those times wasn't rare for Brian and Arthur, but it hadn't been good in the forties, either, even after the war when everybody had work and life was supposed to be easier. One winter he had walked miles trying to buy coal or coke for the fire, and often he was lucky if he carried a half hundredweight home in a sack on his eight-year shoulders, though at the time there seemed no reason for whining, because everybody was doing it.

From their different perambulations they met again among the cars, Derek coming from behind to say: 'Love you, duck!'

'Oh, that's a relief,' she said. 'I was just thinking we're the only ones in the family who didn't get divorced.'

'I hope you're not disappointed.' His brothers and sisters had all split up, but with a bit of effort they might have stayed together, though Derek laughed at his self-assurance on saying so, since he hadn't been through what Arthur had. As for Brian, he only hitched up with difficult women, though you couldn't blame them for his divorces because he was probably just as tormenting to live with. Only Jenny would have had the saintliness to keep him in his place, but he'd done a runner. If he hadn't, it wouldn't have been as bad for her as caring for a paraplegic all those years. 'We were too busy earning a living and looking after the kids.'

'We loved each other, I suppose.'

'Still do, don't we?' he smiled.

She took his arm as they strolled towards the pub steps.

'I'm longing to see Brian's face when he sets eyes on Jenny. How long is it since they met?'

He put the binoculars into his pocket. 'A good few years. She's seventy, so I can't see him going daft over her.'

'He's seventy as well. I don't expect she'll see much in him, either.'

He took out his pipe. 'None of us are toy boys anymore. Brian once told me that according to the French the ideal age for a man's girlfriend is half his age plus seven.'

'Men would say that, wouldn't they?'

'So any woman much older than forty wouldn't do for him.'

'He'd be a fool if he believed it,' she said. 'Anyway, I'd say the best age for a woman's boyfriend is half her age minus seven. That would make mine twenty-three, when I ran away with him.'

'I'd kick your arse if you did.'

'I'd put ground glass in your tea before you could think of it.' She laughed at him laughing. 'Brian's only ever lived by his own rules, and he doesn't know what they are most of the time. He'd have been cleverer keeping to a quiet life, I sometimes think. But he lives off other people's experiences most of the time. Have you noticed how his ears start to wiggle when we talk about what goes on in our street? He's got the best of both worlds.'

'He can still seem pretty miserable.'

'No, he just puts it on.'

'Mind you, he's happy when the three of us go out together with our caps on, and sees there's not much difference between us and everybody else in the pub.'

'That's what he comes up for,' she said. 'He likes having two lives.'

'Who wouldn't? Two's bound to be better than one.' He

scooped the dottle from his pipe and slopped it onto the gravel. 'But having only one is all I've got time for.'

'Same with most people. He can't live with only one, though. I wonder how much he thinks about London when he's up here with us? And do we cross his mind when he's down there?'

'He phones us now and again,' Derek said, 'and writes letters, so he must. He keeps in touch, and we like him to. He always phones to let us know when something of his is coming up on the telly.' He puffed his curved briar into life. 'I'm ready for a drink.'

'I wonder if there'll be any food?'

'Tons, I expect. She's got seven kids and all the in-laws to lay things on for her.'

'I told you we shouldn't have eaten before we came.'

'You said you were hungry.'

'I couldn't let you eat on your own, could I?'

'I wouldn't have minded,' he said.

'You always say that.' She turned at the noise of an engine. 'Anyway, here they are.'

EIGHT

'We don't need navigation,' Avril said. 'The car must be smelling the beer.'

'That's because I've trained it.' Arthur drove along the wide tree lined road. 'See that froth on the windscreen when I press the button? It's Shipstone's finest ale.'

The sunlight nevertheless dimmed in his mind to a darkening afternoon before the alligator of cancer had dragged Avril down, when he carried two large plastic bags of fallen Bramleys into the kitchen, for them to sit at the table and peel, a common autumn duty to cut out the cores and bad bits, and slice them up to make stewed apple and purée.

'You'd do better to put the light on,' she said, 'or you'll nick your finger like you did last time. I don't like to see blood in the saucepan.'

The striplight across the ceiling illuminated the dining-kitchen: sink, fridge, washing machine, stove, microwave, working tops, and the formica table they sat at. Cupboards and walls were painted white, Avril wanting life clean and convenient after her catering days.

He took up a butcher's steel to sharpen a short wooden handled knife bought from a market stall in Spain. 'You'll tear the apples with that chrome one, and use twice the energy than if it was like a razor.'

'You've got your way,' – she placed a large pyrex bowl in the middle of the table – 'and I've got mine.'

'Mine's better.'

'We shall have to see about that. You always end by cutting your finger.'

'This time I won't.'

She emptied a plastic bag of apples into a larger bowl, and took one out to start work. Arthur sorted one of the biggest. 'Don't leave all the little ones to me,' she said.

'I like to do the big 'uns first, and see the heap go down.'

'We've got a long way to go before you'll notice.'

'Ah,' he said, 'so I can see.'

'So take some of the small ones as well.'

'It's just that I like the big 'uns, and I shan't mind if you pick 'em as well. Anyway, I'm doing you a favour, because they're too big for your little hands.'

'My hands aren't little. And if they were I wouldn't moan about it. I never moan.'

'It sounds like it to me.'

They bickered, yet without irritation. 'If you call that moaning I don't know what you'd say if I did moan.'

'I don't think I've ever heard you moan,' he admitted.

'I hope you never will. If I did, you'd know it.'

He scooped peelings into the compost bucket by his feet. 'You never do, though. Maybe that's why I love you.'

'Is that the only reason?'

'There's lots, but isn't that enough?'

'It could be, but I won't want you to disappoint me.'

'I try not to.'

'Just be yourself,' she said, 'and you'll be all right.'

He placed a large apple before him, levelled the knife so as to centre it by the core, laid his palm on the dull side of the blade, and pressed, hoping to see two unblemished hemispheres of white fruit as the apple fell apart. But the zig-zagging thread of a black tunnel marred it, a miniature coalmining beetle eating its way along a gallery towards the heart, more than halfway there, as if going full pelt to get a big Christmas bonus. Excavations were necessary, even before cutting off the peel. 'I can't imagine our Brian sitting at a table, and slicing apples hour after hour.'

Her smaller and more perfect apple was soon finished. 'I expect he'd do it if he had to.'

'If somebody tried to make him he'd get out of it. Can you see him sitting all nice and quiet like me as he worked? He's far too canny to get sergeant-majored into this.'

She reached for another. 'You mean you don't like to do it? I can read you like a book.'

'And what page are you on now, sharpshit?'

'I can see you aren't doing very well.'

'That's because you pick all the little 'uns, and leave the monsters to me.' He sliced the completed apple into the bowl. 'I love doing this, you know I do.'

'Tell me another.'

'Have I ever complained?'

'No, but I can tell by the look on your face that you don't exactly enjoy it.'

'Do you expect me to look as if I've just opened the newspaper to page three? I'm concentrating. I love cutting up apples. The first thing I said when I learned to talk was to ask mam if she'd got any apples that wanted cutting up. When she said no I cried so loud people in Derby thought there was another riot in Nottingham. I used to go scrumping, and no orchard was safe. Every day I'd come back with my jumper full of apples so's I could sit at the table cutting 'em up. Mam had to drag me away when she wanted to put newspaper and jam jars on the table so that we could have some tea with our bread and lard.'

He kissed her on the mouth. 'I was dreaming about 'em all last night, and thought I was in paradise. Apples was falling from a tree. You was there as well, and gave me one to eat. You looked at me in a very funny way, but before I could take one I woke up.' His aspect turned to dark brooding. 'On the other hand, when I get my claws on Oliver, who out of the goodness of his heart – so don't tell me – gave us these two bags of scabby drops I'll tell him where to shove 'em.'

'A man at his age can't climb the trees to pick them fresh,' she said. 'Nor can he send his wife up. You know she's got arthritis.'

'That's what he says. She's so fat it takes all his strength to get her upstairs at night. Anyway, when I see him I'll take this knife' – he spun it a half circle before spearing the next apple – 'cut his heart out, and throw it on the compost heap he's always bragging about.'

'It's very generous of him.' She expertly sliced half an apple into the bowl, each piece exactly the same size. 'Every year he gives us these Bramleys. The delicious stewed apple lasts us all winter, and I've never known anyone gobble it like you, especially when I put it in a tart with a nice thin crust. So get on with it. You've only done two, and I'm on my fifth. You're too busy talking.'

'I can cut apples up and talk at the same time.'

'I know you can, but you aren't.'

He sliced another half into the bowl. 'Oliver doesn't only give us apples. He brings you a bunch of chrysanthemums as well.'

'Yes, beautiful big white ones.'

'I think he fancies you.'

She laughed. 'A man who's had six kids?'

'They're grown up. He's got plenty of time on his hands.'

'He spends every spare minute in his garden. Even his wife says she doesn't see anything of him.'

'Yeh, he potters there every day, even in December when it looks like something left over from the First World War. He's on his hands and knees by the apple trees praying for a good harvest so's he can give more to us. He hates apples himself, he told me. He gives 'em out to everybody else, to make their lives a misery when they have to cut 'em up like this. He knows what he's doing. It don't bear thinking about. One day the whole district's going to rise up against him. You'll know who they are as they go by the window because they'll all have cut fingers, and be swivel-eyed from staring at too much apple skin.'

'He's generous, that's all I know. I thought he was supposed to be your friend?'

'What difference does that make?'

'He helped you when you had that allotment. Hey,' she cried, 'that was a whole apple you threw in the compost bucket.'

He picked it out: it was rotten all the way through. 'He had to. We had the plot in common. Still, you're right, he's a good sort. I've never known anybody so good hearted. We used to have some right old times at that allotment on long summer nights.'

'Yes, the state you were in when you got home.'

He held up his knife. 'I've done three. It must make a difference to if you was on your own.'

'I wouldn't be doing it on my own, would I?'

'You would if I wasn't good enough to give you a hand.'

'I don't know how you could have had so much that night you got back. You came in and dropped the onions all over the floor.'

'That was an accident. I tripped over the carpet.'

'You should have seen yourself, trying to pick everything up. All I could do was laugh.'

'I wasn't drunk. I never get drunk, you know that. It was just that Oliver had brought these six packs of lager out of his car, and we sat on the seat talking. We started at seven, and it didn't get dark till ten. He was telling me what a tartar his mother had been to him and his five brothers. All of them worked down the pit, and when they came in with their wage packets they had to put them on the table unopened. She sat there in a chair like Queen Elizabeth, and slit each one open with a pearl-handled paperknife. She gave each of the lads five bob back for spending money.'

'That wasn't much.'

'That's what Oliver said. But none of them dared say anything. She kept the rest of the money, for housekeeping. Even when they were grown up men of twenty-one they still had to hand in their wage packets every payday. "Why didn't you just tell her to piss off?" I said to Oliver. "You don't know what she was like," he said. "We were terrified of her. We daren't say a word. We'd been brought up to it from babies, so none of us knew any different. She fed us all right, or just about. She had to if she wanted us to go on working hard and bringing in our money. When we wanted to piss in the toilet she told us we had to sit down to do it, not like in other places where you could stand up, in case we splashed her precious bit of pink carpet. She was dead hot on that. When I was twenty-two I met a nice girl and wanted to bring her home to tea, and when I told my mother, you can't guess what she said." I told him I didn't suppose anybody could: "What did the old cow say?" "Well," he said, "she told me I could bring her home to tea if I liked, but I'd have to pay the expense of it out of my own money."

'I was shocked to the backbone: "And did you?" "What could I do?" "And what did your mother think of her?" "Oh, she was polite," Oliver said, "I will say that, but that's about all. Six months later I got married." "What," I said, "to your mother?" "No, the girl, you daft prat." "And did your mother get into bed with you and your girl when you went on your honeymoon?" "Don't be so fucking soft." "Well, I've got to wonder," I said. "But what did your mother do with all the money you and your brothers earned at the pit?" I was dying to know. "Oh," he said, "she and me dad used to go travelling. They went all over the place. One time they went to the Bahamas, another year they went to Australia, to see one of her brothers, who'd got as far away from her as he could, but she still found him. Over the years they went everywhere. I don't think she liked it much, because she used to complain at the scruffy hotels and rotten food. But that didn't stop her. I don't know why she did it, except maybe she was punishing herself for what she was doing to us."

'You can imagine how easy it was to get through so many cans of beer while he told me all that,' Arthur said. 'And he wasn't bitter about it, only a bit puzzled as to why him and his brothers had put up with it for so long.'

'Is that a true story? But cut up another apple while you tell me.'

He reached for the smallest. 'It was just as he told it.'

'And what happened to her in the end?'

'She died, only last year. The old man pegged out ten years before. I suppose he couldn't take anymore. She was ninety-seven, and the lads were frightened of her right to the end. They were all married, but had to visit her every week so's she could tell them what work to do about the house. Only a month before she died she told them to paint her kitchen, and they set to and did it. It never occurred to them to argue. She was bright and bossy to the end. Oliver's older than me, and I could see his hands shaking while he lifted can after can to his lips. That's why I drank so much: I had to keep up. He said he'd never talked to anybody about it, and that I was a real pal for listening. It all goes to show how you can have a rotten mother like that, and the kids still turn out to be good sorts.'

'I thought your mother was a very nice woman,' Avril said in her silkiest voice.

'Oh, did you?' The knife, due to clumsiness, or from having changed to smaller apples, nicked the ball of his thumb, the skin turning a deep red.

'You're bleeding.'

'Am I? Where?'

'Look at it!' She crossed the kitchen for a sheet of paper towel. 'Put this around while I get a plaster.'

He did as he was told. 'Don't worry, it's only blood. Pass me a basin, and I'll save it for breakfast. I can carry on like this.'

'Wait till it dries.'

'Anyway,' he said, 'what were you saying about my mother?'

'I said even though Vera was a good woman *you* didn't turn out too bad.' After her second husband died and she was on her own again, happy in her ground-floor flat whose rent was paid by the council, they took her once a week to the supermarket, and made sure she wanted for nothing. Derek and Eileen also kept a watch over her, and though Brian couldn't get up often from London he had a telephone installed and took care of the bills. In her old age cataracts were removed from both eyes at the hospital and she was able to see again, so that when she died at eighty-five she had a fag in one hand and a mug of tea in the other, while watching television.

'Come on,' Avril said, 'take that bit of paper towel away and I'll put this plaster on. The blood will come through if you don't.'

'No, don't bother. It's dry now.'

'Oh, you shirker. Look at all those apples still to be done.'

'There ain't so many. It won't take long, after I've made a cup of tea.'

'So that's how you mean to get out of it?'

'You want one as well, don't you?'

'All right, but I want more help with all these. There's still the other bag, don't forget.'

'Wait till I get my hands on Oliver.'

'It's not his fault. And I don't think you can blame his mother, either. The poor woman must have had a hell of a time bringing up six coalminers. No wonder she was so strict.'

'Yeh, she had to go to Australia to unwind.' He dashed three spoons of tea in the pot and set cups on the table. 'I haven't told you I'm investing in a chainsaw, have I?'

'A what?'

'There's a model you can charge up from the mains and take outside without having to plug in a lead.'

She spilled some tea over the apple leavings. 'Oh what a wicked thought! Just because you're too idle to cut up a few apples.'

'I love you being so quick on the uptake. But the nights are pulling in, so I'll sneak out in my camouflage suit, my face black with boot polish, while Oliver and his missus are upstairs sleeping off their cider. With the chainsaw slung over my back like an anti-tank weapon, I'll get over the wall, and zig-zag across his garden – like we did in the army. Then I'll switch on the chainsaw and shout: "Timber!" every time an apple tree goes down.'

'I'll bet you would, you rotter.'

'I've got to. Even if he lives to be ninety he'll still come wheeling his bags of Bramleys from door to door in a pram, just to make people's lives miserable. Anyway, have another cup of tea. You lost half of that one laughing. Oliver and me had some good times together. I just hope his trees get blight and stop breeding.'

'I will have more tea,' she said. 'But when you've poured it you can help me cut up the rest of these apples. With two bags done we'll have enough for the winter.'

He tapped her wrist. 'You missed a bad bit on that one.'

'No, I didn't. Some peel fell on it.' She flicked it away. Rain came at the window like the rattle of unstrung beads. 'I thought that was going to happen.'

He scooped heaps of chippings into a plastic bucket, then cut the rot from the biggest apple remaining. 'I saw that forecast as well, but I shopped around till I got a better one. I started on Radio Four, and on Radio One the prospects still didn't seem good so I switched channels around the telly till I found one which said it was going to be fine all day. Searching for a good forecast gives me something to do when I'm not cutting up apples.'

'You can always work in the garden if you're bored.'

'Not when it's pissing down. It's a sea of mud out there. No wonder Brian lives in London. It rains less, and it ain't as cold.'

'If everybody lived in the south nobody would be up here, would they?'

'I wouldn't want to live there, though I don't mind having a look at it now and again. I expect you miss it more than I do.'

'You live where you live.' Her fingers were speedy, each piece neatly cut. 'I've always been happy enough up here.'

'Brian loves it here, but he's got to be where the work is.'

'Look, we're getting through them now. See how quickly they go when both of us are at it?'

Half a dozen left, and he couldn't wait. 'I think we'll deserve a treat when it's done.'

'What do you have in mind?'

'I don't know. Have you got any ideas?'

'Why should I have?'

He recalled the Medieval Night Out they'd gone to five years ago in Warwickshire. He'd had a beard and weighed a couple of stone more, till Avril put him on a diet and he lost them. A hundred people in two coaches from Nottingham were sat at long tables in a great wainscotted hall, fires erupting at either end, placecards indicating your seat bent double on the halfway mark and looking like miniature soldiers' bivouacs between the knives and spoons. Written on the side of his was: Thane Arthur Seaton.

A couple of Great Danes bigger than Shetland Ponies and twice as rugged plodded up and down as if hoping to get jobs as mobile ornaments in the back of ex-colliers' Rovers, though Arthur assumed they were more for flinging bits of dinner to like Charles Laughton in *Henry the Eighth*. Pots of mulled wine with cloves were put into your hands as soon as you went in, with chicken legs and venison sticks, and sausages like pricks worn to a frazzle after an orgy, to while away the time till the barons of beef roasting on spits were done, Arthur thinking it a pity they weren't real barons.

Scullions ran up and down with earthenware platters laying slabs of burnt offering on everybody's plate, and serving wenches with their tits about to jump for freedom walked around making sure your flagon of mead never got below

113

the halfway mark. Mine Host had done his best to put wives and husbands as far apart as possible.

After apples and frumenty for dessert one of the wenches came to see if Arthur wanted anything else, a question which nearly choked him. 'What's your name, love?'

'Sarah.'

'I had a sister called Sarah, and I thought she was the loveliest girl in the world – till I met you.'

'Oh, you liar.'

'I never say anything I don't mean.' After more such talk she was on his knee, and he was gratified to feel the pure heat from her arse scorching through his trousers as she put her face forward for another kiss, such warmth not known since Brenda used to plonk herself in the same place to lighten the mood before going up the wooden hill when Jack was on nights.

Short of dragging this lovely girl (from Sutton Coldfield) under the table and sliding the mutton dagger home – burbles of enjoyment hidden by the jollity above – there was little he could do but see to her breasts now and again, which she didn't mind, perhaps liking to be on daddy's knee while he whispered into each delicate oyster ear as she wrote her phone number on the back of his placecard, and slid it unseen into his jacket pocket.

'I thought it would end in an orgy,' he said on the steps of the coach.

'You look a bit cheated that it didn't,' Avril said. 'I suppose it would have been amusing, except the man at our table was overweight, and he had a beard with bits of grey in it, so I didn't fancy him. You should have heard the language when the woman across from me told her swain to get lost as well. Then we sat talking, which was a lot more interesting.'

The apples done, he drew her into his arms for a kiss,

but her lips were there first. 'So this is what you had in mind?'

'It must be the apples. They act on me like Spanish fly.'

'It feels as if you've been to the chemist's and bought a box of those Viagra pills.'

'When I'm ninety I'll get the doctor to put me on 'em. Apples'll do till then.'

'You've got something to thank Oliver for, after all.'

'Don't be cheeky, and come to bed.'

'I wondered when you were going to ask me.'

'Well, now I have.'

NINE

Eileen pointed: 'Here they come.'

A pigeon got lift-off at the screech of Arthur's horn, and he backed into a free space in case a hurried departure should be necessary. Old habits died hard.

Brian, glad to flex knees and stretch his aching thighs, opened the door to get Avril safely out and standing. Then he embraced Derek, and kissed Eileen. 'All right, then?'

Derek showed the same broad smile as when he was a kid. 'Have a good run from London?'

'You know me. I got on the outer lane and steamed up at ninety. I hope the police cars I passed didn't get my number. If those camera signs are working they've got my mug in a thousand copshops.'

Derek was taller than his father had been, a sober pipe-smoking man Brian sometimes envied for going through every crisis with a show of optimism, though he didn't cop out of violence if he or anyone in the family was threatened. Brian was once alarmed to hear his invective against other drivers as he launched his BMW beyond the lights, a dangerous temper under his uncle-like exterior that needed much control to keep in check. 'I suppose we can go in now. She'll be due in ten minutes.'

'He can't wait to see his old flame,' Avril smiled. 'She won't run away, so don't get impatient.'

Derek, halfway up the steps, knocked his briar out on the rail, sparks flying by his shoes, Brian and Arthur a rearguard behind Avril and Eileen, the five advancing into a spacious curving saloon parted by a wide stairway. A notice between the banisters saying PRIVATE meant that the upper floor was for family and friends only, and that interlopers, or those who couldn't read, would be seen off by Jenny's sons and daughters.

They were welcomed by a round-faced fifty-ish woman whom Brian surmised hadn't had a happy life – though with no hopes for pumping he would have to imagine why, and hope to get it right. 'I'd know you anywhere,' she said to Arthur. 'And these are your brothers and their wives?'

He did the introductions.

'I'm glad you could all come,' she said. 'I'm Jenny's daughter, Eunice. She'll be here soon, and won't she get the surprise of her life!' She smiled at Brian. 'We've heard all about you, though.'

A score or so were already in the room, talking in groups or standing at the bar. 'I hope not too much.'

'She always said you were her first love. But I'll see you later. I've got to go now, and talk to my brothers, to make sure everything's all right for when she comes.'

He went to the bar, a rum and coke for Avril, and a shandy for Eileen who would be driving Derek home, then three pints. Old people far outnumbered the young, and they talked mostly to each other, so that if he pushed a way in they would only wonder what this funny old bogger wanted.

'We'll sit at that table near the window,' Arthur said, knowing Avril couldn't stand for too long. He called the barman to clear the vandalized graveyard of empties.

Curtains were ruched aside, the landscape more impressive from higher up, though Brian sat with his back to the window, looking at people rather than the same old view. A slim fortyish man with fair wavy hair and wearing a cardigan was laying out a speaker system.

'Are you Brian Seaton?'

He noted the woman's plain grey dress buttoned up the front, and one leg thicker than the other from a reinforcing bandage. About sixty, she must have been handsome when young, her wreck of a face still suggesting mischief. 'How's your sister, Jane? We used to go out together, and I haven't seen her for years.'

'She died about eight years ago.' He had forgotten the exact date, and didn't want to mention cancer, with Avril so close, but he had to, and did, Avril knowing well enough what had killed Jane. The woman's face went small with pain. He was sorry to spoil her evening. 'I didn't like to tell you.'

'She was such a happy person. We used to dress up to the nines and go out to Yates's on Saturday night. I haven't seen her since she got married, but we did have some good times together.'

He smiled at her memories. Nor were his own dead for him, though he rarely thought of Jane. Like their elder sister Margaret she was out of his mind for months at a time, till a remark brought her so clearly back she might still have been alive. Realizing she was not, he felt like weeping, while surmising that all families had casualties in equal proportion.

'We went to the same school,' she said. 'But after she got married we lost touch. Then I got married as well, and had to bring up five kids. How many did Jane have?'

'Two.' Arthur was listening. 'One with each husband.' He wanted to get rid of her: 'Would you like to sit down and have a drink?'

'There isn't a seat.'

'You can sit on Brian's knee. His wife won't mind. She's in London.'

'What a bleddy cheek!'

'You're blushing,' he said, 'and none of us are.'

'You mean I can still blush?' She laughed. 'I thought them days was over. But my husband's over there, so I must be getting back.'

'Which one's that?' Arthur wanted to know.

'Him against the bar looking as if he's lost something.' A tall elderly man in a grey suit, black sleeked hair, and a thin sour face, turned with a glare in their direction. The white head of a chrysanthemum glistened in his buttonhole like a miniaturized deathray.

'You'd better go back, by the look of him,' Arthur said, 'or he'll come over and give you a pasting for talking to strange men. I shan't tell him you can still blush.'

'I'd scratch his bleddy eyes out if he even thought of laying a hand on me. I can tell you're Jane's brother, though. Now I can see why we used to have so much fun. If I told you one half of the things we used to get up to you wouldn't believe me.'

Arthur put the remains of a pint into his throat. 'I thought she'd never go. I don't think she knew our Jane at all. Somebody mentioned we had a sister of that name and she came over to get off with you,' he said to Brian. 'Jane wouldn't have been seen dead with a person like that.'

'Jane used to go out with Betty Smith,' Derek said. 'They worked at a little factory in the next street, where they made pot dogs. They sat at a bench painting them after they came out of the kiln. I walked in when I was a kid, and saw them doing it.'

'I remember them pot dogs.' Arthur flexed himself for a laugh. 'When she brought her rejects home I'd set 'em up on the shelf in our bedroom, and shoot 'em to bits with my air rifle.'

'You once used old Ma Bull for target practice as well,' Derek said.

Arthur reached for the empty glasses and took out a tenner. 'John Smith's bitter, in't it?'

'I can just imagine you lot when you were young.' Avril's smile came easily, though she was fragile, Brian saw, and vulnerable, pain somewhere in her body, only sipping at her drink.

'Arthur's told me a few things, but I'm sure he left a lot out.'

'We were as good as gold,' Brian said. 'We always got top marks at Sunday School. You couldn't get in our parlour for Bibles.'

'When they were knocking those old houses down in Radford,' Eileen held Avril's hand, 'Derek and Arthur took a bag of tools like thieves in the night. Arthur steadied the ladder while Derek shinned up and unscrewed the street signs. How they got them down I'll never know. They were real iron, and weighed a ton, but they'd only have been smashed into rubble. Now they're fixed on a wall in our back garden, and look as good as new. When Brian stays with us and uses the outside toilet he says: "Shan't be a minute. Just going down Salisbury Street."'

'That's right.' Whenever he looked at it he saw the houses still attached, short terraces angling off to stop at the Berlin wall of the bike factory, the district alive with the smell of machinery, petrol, horse shit, and a whiff of fag smoke and stale beer when a pub door opened and slammed to.

'Sup this.' Arthur set their pints on the little square mats. 'Nottingham ale would be on the National Health, if I had my say. "Not feeling on top form, lad? Wait while I write a

121

prescription. It's four pints a day before your tea, and four pints after. A month ought to see you right, but if you still feel peaky, come and see me again. Oh, and just a minute. They won't run out of ale. You look a bit off colour. I want you to swallow a handful of Viagra pills with your beer, before going to bed with your wife."'

'Brian can get Viagras on private medicine,' Derek said.

'I know. He was popping 'em all the way here, in case Jenny pulls him on for old time's sake.'

Brian slewed much of his pint, to keep up with his brothers. He wiped his mouth, then speculated on whether the amount of spunk he had shot in his life would have been enough to drown in.

'It would have poisoned you first,' Arthur said.

Maybe the ink he had used was a safer bet for suicide. Gallons of both, but neither death was tempting. The collective bulk of matches struck for fires and cigars could have made a tree from which to hang himself, though he'd only ever thought of such an end to scorn himself out of doing it. Every morning he mainlined ink from a fat Mont Blanc into his upper arm, one side one day and the other the next, at which notion they laughed, as did he.

'I wouldn't mind a shot in the arse from that magic pen if I could live the way you do,' Arthur said. 'But I don't think what I wrote would get put on' – though his letters, Brian recalled, had never been dull, and during the days of his being poor in London, there'd often be a pound note attached for him to buy food. 'This fat pen cost a couple of hundred quid or so.'

'It'd buy a lot of beer.' Arthur handed it back. 'A workman's got to have good tools, so's he can't blame 'em if anything goes wrong.'

Those near the bar were facing the entrance, as if a pigeon

had flown in, no noise but the rattle of jars. 'I think she's on her way up,' a man said, but as if not wanting to be heard.

Brian's blood pressure had always been of the lowest, but wouldn't it be perfect, he thought, if a massive heart attack sent me into oblivion (I should be so lucky), clogs popped at the sight of her? He found a good position for the view, and the excitement of being among people with whom he felt little connection made him wonder whether his sundering from Jenny (and perhaps others like her) was yet final.

She came up the stairs between two of her daughters, though free of their arms, an erect figure taking one step at a time, not like the Queen of Sheba to music by Handel, or Good Queen Bess to the strains of Tallis, but a bemused and ordinary woman surprised by a gathering she hadn't expected.

The neat dark curls around her pale forehead were dyed, because formerly they had been turning white. An open grey cardigan showed a white blouse buttoned to the neck with a purple brooch, a grey skirt below. He focussed on her face, uncertain why such coercion was necessary, noting the serene aspect of someone who had come through the test of a lifetime, a glow of innocence yet authority from a person few in the room could finally know.

After the first surprise she liked what she saw, as if part of getting back into a world which little resembled what she had known before, which she had inhabited for as long as many people in the room had lived, to go by the stones near George's grave, of those who had been born and had died in the time spent caring for him. George had clawed at her skirt near the end, asking for poison. When she sat by him in the hospital the nurse told her that he had used a knife from the breakfast tray to jag at his sticklike wrists.

Jenny would have given him all she had, but life was

precious, and death a cliff with a long drop, to be gone over only when the time came, so he had to be tended as long as a crumb of life remained. After such years knowing that she had little to give, her spirit broke over and over again, as if she too might be nearing the end, weariness forcing her to sit down, almost as helpless as he, until the dying voice called that he wanted this or that, or just to say he was alive and needed to know that she was also. Sometimes too weak to lift him, she'd get one of her sons to help, wondering how far off the day was when she could do no more.

In the hospital she heard sounds telling her he wanted to die, and she stroked the white brow, his almost weightless body hidden by the sheet. 'I can't help you to do a thing like that. I just can't. What shall I do if you pass away?' Guilt at thinking it was best for him to die kept them closer. 'What will I have to live for after you've gone?'

'I shall have to live for myself,' was in her mind as she took the final step into the large room crowded with people to celebrate her birthday.

Her head turned left and right. She took her time assessing those she knew, or hadn't seen for a while, or those of her own family, an expression altering from shock to suspicious delight while letting out a little cry.

The small teeth, as she smiled, were too even not to be false, the subtly fluctuating features showing not so much astonishment as that a trick had been played (which it had) whose purpose she needed time to think about. Such solicitousness for her well being seemed less deserved because so unexpected. Drawn into a trap, she didn't know what to say. Those in the room wanted to hear words that she couldn't yet get from her lips, like what a wonderful family they were to have set up such fairy-tale splendour, arranged to celebrate the end of her ordeal.

124

Age had drawn lines on her forehead which he remembered emphasized as well on the young girl, after his telling an obvious lie, or weaving a clumsy fantasy to divert her from going somewhere he did not want to follow, or even only to astound her out of silence. A smile transformed the skin on her sometimes melancholy face, the same now as she looked over the culinary abundance brought by the women and spread over the table: sausages, slices of ham, sandwiches, various salads, and a large iced cake with a single candle in the middle as if to make it easy for her when so much had formerly been hard, or as if all the years looking after George were to be extinguished in a single breath. Or maybe it was to mark Year One of her new life.

She took in what had been done, lips half opened as if to speak, but once more changing her mind, not wanting them to think she was too astounded by their secret efforts. The scene would make a precious memory, and he thought that whoever awarded campaign medals for the Battle of Life weren't knowing or willing enough to give one to such as her. Maybe those calling happy birthday thought the same, taking her hand before letting others have their turn. She had registered him in that long preliminary gaze.

'You'd better go and claim your kiss,' Arthur said.

The small box in his pocket, with its silver Celtic cross in a bed of cotton wool, had seemed the right present. Anything more elaborate would be showy, or facetious, or lack significance – not be worthy of her. No way of telling, it would have to do, too late to drive back and get something else. He had traipsed around Covent Garden, browsing at every stall till the glittering merchandise half blinded him. After a cup of watery coffee between forays he thought he might not go to the party, feeling so little enthusiasm in searching assiduously for token or trinket.

Now, he was in the same room with her, and knew they had to talk.

'Let the mob go first,' he said to Arthur. He foresaw a sad smile at the memory of their early days when he gave her the present: a press of the hand, even a quick kiss, though he had no right to one, nor even much desire. After saying hello he was only here to watch, an outsider if ever there was one, foolishly conspicuous, yet as welcome as anybody else. At the same time he felt as shy as a youth, and she the first girl he must try to get off with.

Jenny left whoever she was talking to, and stood before him. 'I'm ever so glad you're here. You're the biggest surprise of all.'

'I jumped at the opportunity to see you.'

'I didn't expect to see you tonight, but I was hoping to meet you again some time.'

They'd played a game in her parlour after making love, or when sitting a few feet apart on a fallen tree at the edge of a field smelling of cornstalks at the end of summer, of looking deep and long into each other's eyes, and whoever blinked first didn't love the other. He looked away, wondering how it was that lost loves endured the longest.

'And you drove all the way up from London especially?'

'I couldn't not. As soon as I heard about the party.' He smiled, for it was true enough, but how genuine did it sound to her? She must know he'd come to see his family at the same time. 'I got a letter from your daughter, and put the date in my diary, in big red letters.'

She held one of his hands in hers. 'I'm glad you did. I can't tell you how much.'

If he gave her the small container in his pocket she would need to take her hands from his to see what it was. Yet he had to. 'I brought you this. Happy birthday!'

She held the box, as if to make sure it was hers and would not be taken back, but didn't open it to see what was inside, which disappointed him, as if she thought it too insignificant. Or maybe she wanted to make the most of their meeting, and didn't want to lose the warmth of his hands either. 'I'm still dazed about what I've found here tonight – and not only this' – she waved towards the tables. 'I feel like a young girl again. But if only we could look as young as we feel! I'm seventy, I know, but I don't feel it at the moment.'

'I suppose if anybody does feel their age they're dead from the neck up. But I thought you must be about forty when you came up the stairs. You were a real picture. I'll never forget it. Forty's all you looked.'

Such teasing could do no harm, since she knew the score, though her smile showed a multitude of emotions. 'Ah, well, there are times when I feel a hundred.'

'The same for all of us. But I've heard about your life. I can imagine what it was like.'

'Can you?'

Well, he'd asked for that. Of course he couldn't. Idle talk was out of place. Her tone said that he didn't and never could, and he knew she was on the point of saying he didn't know one half, when she said it. Nothing more, either, that he could respond with, too great a gap, always had been, so much water under the bridge, such cruel differences separating them. It needed all the time of the years not spent together for them to say any more.

She put the present into her black handbag. 'My eldest son's over there. Come with me and meet him.' Her warm hand drew him between two women, who smiled as if wondering whether the birthday would turn into a wedding.

'Ronald,' Jenny said, 'I want you to meet Brian. He's a very old friend of mine.'

Tall and tending to corpulence, he wore a navy-blue waistcoated suit, white shirt and a colourful reddish tie, stood with amiable dignity, his back to the bar, an aspect of being pleased with life, as if he scorned to question that there could be anything more to know about himself than had been obvious from birth, confident that such an attitude had done nothing but good – a prosperous hardworking man who took no nonsense from anybody but could be kindly as well.

The handshake was firm, his smile as if offering to be a friend for life, and that if he wasn't taken up it could be no fault of his. 'She's often told us about you.'

'I hope I didn't sound too much of a villain.'

He laughed. 'No, it was the other way, mostly.'

If proof of belonging was that you had no secrets among the people you mixed with, then he was surely one of them. 'Thank God for that!'

'Ronald has his own business,' Jenny said, with some pride.

'It sounds very grand.' He let his cigarette ash fall to the floor. 'It's just a family thing, though we do well enough, a place called Leen Technology. I deal in software and superpower, you might say. I suppose you're all plugged into computers, with your job?'

'Not yet.' Brian held up his pen. 'This is the smallest word processor in the world! But when I do get wired up, and I'll have to, sooner or later, I'll call you.'

Ronald gave him his card. 'Anytime. I'll sort out the best deal for you, as a friend of the family, plus all the advice to get yourself on line.'

Jenny introduced him to Ronald's wife Sylvia, a tall woman wearing a black and white dotted dress, with blonde hair pulled close to her head and ending in a short ponytail over the back of her neck. She had the full figure of a woman in her forties, worth getting to know, he thought, with those interesting lips and opaque cornflower blue eyes, his usual quick look confirming her as the most attractive woman in the room, though he didn't suppose, to go by her cool handshake, that he would get very far in trying to become more acquainted, especially at a 70th birthday party when he was known to be the same age.

'Brian's come up specially from London,' Jenny said, which fact brought a smile from Sylvia: 'That was good of you.'

He hoped to hear more, but she looked with a proud kind of vacancy into the crowd, sure she missed nothing by standing aloof. 'I wanted to see her,' he said, though he hadn't thought of her for months or even years at a time. 'She's always meant a lot to me.'

'It's the same for the rest of us,' Sylvia said.

When Ronald offered him a drink he wanted to say yes, talk to him more, soak down a few jars in his and Sylvia's company, but was tugged away by some perverse instinct which nine times out of ten led him to refuse whatever might turn out to be enjoyable: 'Thanks, but I've got one at our table over there.'

'Any time you like, and it'll be my pleasure.'

They shook hands on it, and Jenny walked with her daughter-in-law to another part of the room.

The man with the microphone bellowed out words with the sincerity of an old-fashioned tuppenny hop. 'You can't hear yourself think over that racket,' Arthur said, 'never mind talk.'

The lyrics knocked at the back of his head, telling about love not being all it was said to be when a sweetheart walked off with your best friend. His performance enlivened the party, such a noise level that no one could hear unless they were shouted at, the pitch only normal to people whose ears had been battered by it all their lives, but the coarse-grained emery paper scraping back and forth across Brian's skull honed away what brains were inside.

Double-glazed windows in London cut down noise, but if he opened a window for a lungful of petrol-soaked air, the grinding of cars and thump of pneumatic drills, the screaming bandsaws from renovations in the next house, forced him to turn up Radio Three more than he cared to. Stereo systems in open-topped cars belted out jungle music that shook the backbone, and he craved a three-o-three Short Lee Enfield service rifle to pot one of the tyres, and kill the driver when he got out to look. People preferred overwhelming noise to quiet thoughts that would drive them insane, not knowing that only silence enabled you to be yourself.

'If I open a pub door and hear this,' Arthur shouted, 'I slam the bogger shut, and find another where it's quiet. The factory was bad, but this'll send me deaf if I stay much longer.' Avril was pale from the effort of leaving the house, and Arthur knew he must get her back to rest, whatever she said about not wanting to spoil their evening. 'I don't think I can stand it much longer,' Eileen said.

The decibel count wiped away all functions of the brain or mind, eyes swivelling and hands twitching to close on the singer's throat. Brian wondered how much more he could take, and whether it could be used as a reason to leave. 'I'm glad I'm not the only one who thinks so.'

'It's not a bad performance,' Derek bawled. 'At least it's got some melody' – though agreeing it was too loud. 'I thought he was miming, but it's him right enough. They must have headhunted him from a miners' welfare.'

Arthur said he would have one more pint. 'The noise makes it taste soapy.' Derek went for them, but Brian looked into the mass, hoping yet not hoping to see Jenny, though enough had been said, the experience tasted, time to cut, thinking he wouldn't find her yet impelled to try.

A bridgehead into the crush, careful not to knock drinks or tread on toes, he parted a man and a woman shouting to each other through their smiles. The noise seemed to blind as well as deafen. He waved to Ronald at the bar, and went to him, putting his ear close to get the response 'I'm looking for Jenny.'

'She must be somewhere. I'm sure we haven't lost her. Try another recce: you'll find her.'

She was talking to a man and his wife. 'I have to go now,' he said.

'You needn't shout. I can hear you.' Maybe everybody had ears that noise couldn't chasten. 'I'm sorry you're going,' she said. 'I really am.'

'We'll leave you to your old flame,' the woman gave a dirty laugh, and pulled her husband away.

'I'd like to stay, but I can see you've got lots to keep you busy. And Arthur's wife isn't feeling well. She's on chemotherapy.' To mention the noise would grate against the perfection of her party, and she might remind him of the indescribable sounds of the Goose Fair, or the dances at the youth club, or the bedlam in some of the pubs when singing began on a Saturday night.

'Oh, I'm ever so sorry to hear that. I hope she'll be all right. But you haven't had anything to eat.' She pointed to food heaped on the large trestle table, where people were loading their paper plates. 'You must be starving.'

'No, I'm not, love.'

She held his hands. 'Of all the people! If I'd known about the party I still wouldn't have expected you. They're such devils, springing it on me like this. When I came up the

131

stairs I thought I was just going to have a meal with Ronald and Sylvia.'

'They're fond of you, that's why they did it.'

'I know. They've always been good to me.'

'And you've been good to them.'

'I don't know about that, though I did bring seven of 'em up. And I do love them all.'

He wondered if she would have stayed with George for so long if they'd had no children, then he knew that she would, on feeling the intense warmth from her hands. 'I'll call for you at home next time, but I'll phone first so that you won't get such a shock.'

'Oh yes, come and see me whenever you like. We can talk when you do. I'd like that. We can't do it here, I realize.' She looked into his eyes. 'We did have some good times when we were young, didn't we? I used to wish they could go on forever.'

'So did I.'

'Do you remember when we sat in the living room at home afterwards, and listened to Joe Loss on the wireless?'

'I do.'

'It's a shame such times can't come back.'

'We had them, that's the main thing. Nobody can take 'em away.'

'That's true.' The same old youthful glow was in her eyes, till she added that they'd had their ups and downs as well. He couldn't deny it: 'But you only remember the good times,' he said.

'You've got to, haven't you? It really has been a tonic seeing you.'

'For me too.' Derek and Eileen were standing, Arthur and Avril already by the door. 'I must be off, though. I don't want to keep the others waiting.'

'If you've got to,' she said, in the same cool tone as when he had proposed leaving her in Ripley market and cycling alone to Matlock. 'I suppose we should have met somewhere else, but we can next time, can't we?'

Lip-reading as much as hearing gave her words added importance. 'I'll be sure to arrange it.'

'I know you will.' She leaned, and he took her by the shoulders, as so often before, and drew her into a kiss, thinking one for each cheek, as she perhaps expected, but their lips pressed hard, neither wanting to let go, as if the gate latch had already clicked and her parents were on their way up the garden path, Jenny and he locked in a final passionate kiss before his long traipse home through the misty darkness.

Eyes closed as if to make the moment last, their ancient past putting sugar into the kiss, a mellowed regret at not having kept their love alight, a kiss in mourning for the chance they'd let vanish – neither caring about whoever looked on from the crowd.

'I'll see you again, duck,' he said in the homely lingo of so long back, not knowing who had drawn off first.

Many wanted her to themselves: children, grandchildren, great-grandchildren, cousins and inlaws and nephews and nieces and friends, and to give some of herself to everyone would take whatever was left of the evening. She let go of his hand. 'I'll look forward to it. But now I must talk some more to the others.'

TEN

'I'd never have believed it, you kissing a seventy-year-old woman like that.' They walked into more silence the closer they got to the cars. Avril felt it necessary to tell Arthur that Brian was seventy as well.

'That's true, but he don't look anywhere near it.'

'It was romantic,' Eileen said. 'I hope somebody kisses me like that when I'm seventy.'

'I will.' Derek filled his pipe. 'I promise.'

'Oh, you!' she laughed.

'Anyway, you've seen her.' He put the pipe back in his pocket because Eileen wouldn't let him smoke in the car. 'It's all over now.'

Brian couldn't think it was. 'So it seems.'

'I wondered what he was up to,' Arthur said. 'Everybody was staring, but you was too far gone to notice. They wanted to hear you pop the question, though I'll bet they're laughing their heads off now you've scarpered. I've never seen such a mad, passionate kiss.'

Banter eased his emptiness, brought from it by seeing a tip of the last sunlight on a leaf as if it had been rinsed. They were in love with the past rather than each other, and if he called on her they might talk the nostalgia away, though maybe he needed to get rid of it more than she wanted it clear of herself. He couldn't say why he felt the urge to kick something so precious, because nothing was finished till the blackout came down and you were dropped into the same common hole never to see daylight again.

'I'll see you in the morning,' he said to Derek and Eileen. 'We'll talk for an hour, then I'll make for Trent Bridge and head south.'

Eileen sorted car keys from her pocket. 'We'll have the coffee ready.'

'I enjoyed the party,' Arthur turned on the ignition, 'but that bloody noise was the limit.'

'I heard a couple say they thought it was too loud,' Avril said. 'I can still hear it.'

She was exhausted, and every second, when not talking, Arthur was filled with misery thinking about her illness. 'I'll get you home as quick as I can. I shouldn't have kept you out so long.'

'I can't stay in all the time,' she said. 'And I wouldn't have come away earlier, even if you'd said I should.'

Mellow light gave the redbricked houses a glint of newness. It was uncanny for the district to be so quiet on a Saturday night. A westerly wind pushed clouds which would certainly throw down rain by tomorrow morning.

'You never see anybody walking,' Brian said. 'Maybe they're already in the pubs.'

'People are watching the telly,' Arthur said. 'The old 'uns, anyway. The young 'uns are downtown boozing and getting into fights. They come back with black eyes and blood all over their clothes. Shows they had a good time. Or they go to clubs and get drugged up to the eyeballs. Then some of 'em go mugging to get money to pay for a bit more. Nottingham's dangerous these days.'

'It always was,' Brian said.

136

'I don't know about that. We had fun when we were young. We got drunk now and again, but we didn't go mugging. We didn't take drugs. Whatever you do, never walk around Slab Square on Saturday night. Some blokes'd knife you as soon as look at you.'

'I've always gone where angels fear to tread,' Brian told him.

'You've been lucky.'

'My father used to say,' Avril said, 'that if you go where angels fear to tread only the Devil can lead you back.'

Basford Crossing was passed without comment. His life between leaving as a young man and meeting Jenny at her seventieth birthday party would hardly make the sitcom of the century. In the theatre it would come off after a week, to universal execration, while a painted triptych would send people away screaming. As the sound of music it would be more deafening than those forlorn lyrics at the party. Or so he imagined, though self-flattery was the first sign of the demented.

His second divorce had been of nobody's making but his own, because his previous experience of matrimonial hugger-mugger, and being ten years older than Jane, could have saved the marriage, especially when he knew that if you wanted to end an argument with your wife you only had to let her have the last word. Having the self-control to do it, and feel no injury to his self-esteem, he had made the attempt, but after a while she had spotted his manoeuvre, and with her taunts sent him into rages which she liked better than the peace and quiet he needed for his work. Living with someone and being in love, you imagined any problem could be worked out. It couldn't but, all the same, he had made it to three score and ten, sound in wind and limb, the same as Jenny, showing the common tenacity of both, and that being alive was victory enough.

Beyond the traffic lights at Sunrise Hill Arthur knew that Brian was chewing at the bits and bobs of his past, which could be unhealthy, though he knew it to be so because two brothers in the same car are like back to back houses in the closeness of their thoughts. As different as they can be, Arthur had his own and recalled how he had once seen a woman on a street corner up the road from the White Horse, looking as if she didn't know which direction to take, whom he then recognized as his old flame Brenda, talking to an aloof adolescent girl.

She was a bit more than forty, but hadn't aged as much as she might have done. He put on his best smile, knowing that after so long he couldn't look youthful either, but luckily he was togged up in a suit, wore the usual good overcoat, and had given his shoes their weekly gloss that morning.

In spite of her brown coat and sweater he knew she could still doll up to the nines for a Saturday night out. Jack would be a manager at the factory by now, so she must have a wardrobe full of smart dresses.

In spite of the trouble when Jack found out about their affair, she seemed glad to see him, as if she wouldn't object to a few more of those torrid days. Nor would he mind getting in to bed with her again. 'This is my daughter, Joan,' she said, 'who'll be fifteen next birthday.'

The girl was tall and thin, had short fair hair and grey eyes, and wore a blue and white anorak, pale trousers sharply creased, and trainer shoes. She stared as if hating all men, but especially him, and would have hated him even more if she knew him better, which didn't surprise him, having Jack for a father.

'I suppose you're proud?' Brenda said.

The change of tone suggested she'd like to bury a knife in his back. 'What about?'

'Haven't you got eyes to see?'

He soon enough had, as if thumped in the chest, not a serious blow, but the reverberation yanked him sufficiently clear of himself to look at the girl again, at which stare she turned to see whether the shop display of jeans and sports clothes had anything on offer. 'She looks well.'

'A bloody handful, I can tell you, but she'll be away in a year or two, if I know her.'

He took a twenty out of his wallet, but didn't give it directly to his daughter in case she smelled a rat – and a big slimy one at that. Brenda read him like a book, amused at his daft pride. 'Don't think you've got any rights over her. Understand?' She took the money, knowing him capable of causing a fuss. 'I'll give it her. She'll think I've decided to be nice for a change. I'm always telling her she can't have everything, because she's already spoiled rotten. Jack thinks the world of her, at least when he forgets she might not be his.'

'How is he, then?' – the arse-crawling bastard.

'He's a pain most of the time. Luckily I don't see much of him. He still works every hour God sends.'

Joan's settled features showed in the shop window, and it was obvious from the way she stood, and her intent look at the goods laid out – as if she wanted them all, and by God she would have them – that she couldn't be anybody's daughter but his.

'Take a good goz,' Brenda said. 'I've taken a lot of stick over it from Jack. Being so blind's turned him bitter, whenever he thinks about us.'

'Mam!' Joan called, 'I want a pair of jeans.'

'Oh all right. Which ones this time?'

Arthur turned to go. 'See you, then, Joan.'

'No, you won't,' Brenda said. 'She's mine, not yours.'

'She's a nice girl, though.'

'You think so? That's because I brought her up.'

Some kids turn out to be good no matter what their parents are like, he wanted to say. 'I expect that's true.'

'You bet it is.'

'Come on, mam, I want to talk about which ones you like. Then you won't complain if I pick the ones I want.'

'She's a real sharpshit.' He was delighted, and heard her say when her mother paused at the shop entrance: 'Who's that bloke, then?'

Brenda laughed. 'Never you mind.'

'One of your toy boys, I suppose. Looks like he still fancies you.'

He'd seen neither since, no point looking, in spite of Joan's face now and again vividly before him. Sometimes he wondered whether she really was his daughter, yet knew she was because she didn't have the tight miserable face of Jack. Maybe he had one or two more kids scattered around, and would turn into a doddery old man buttonholing people in the street wanting to find out, and getting kicked in every time for putting such a question.

Nowadays you can get a DNA test if you aren't sure (though it hadn't occurred to Jack) so maybe those happy fuck-a-day times are over. Soon there'll be do-it-yourself DNA booths at every service station, big signs flashing twenty-four hours a day saying: TRY DNA WITH YOUR KIDS. A POUND A GO. REDUCTIONS FOR FAMILIES! Blood all up and down the motorway. He couldn't help feeling sorry for any bloke whose wife had a kid he thought was his but wasn't. In the old days you didn't even care about catching AIDS.

He clipped another set of lights, a touch on the brake pedal passing the constabulary headquarters. 'The cops must have your number by now,' Brian said.

'They have. Didn't you see them give me the nod as we went by? They know me, always Arthuring me and my old ducking me when I see one in a pub. "Have a pint on us, Mr Seaton." He's even younger than Harold. Coppers look like kids who've just had a uniform and cosh in their Christmas stockings. "I saw you pass our headquarters in your old tin lizzie, and you were doing a tad over fifty in a thirty mile zone. We have a very wide view from the second storey." "I was only doing twenty-six and three quarters," I say. "We clocked you, Arthur, just for the fun of it. When you're ninety and got Alzheimer's as well you'll have to slow down a bit." They've known me so long they talk about me all the time.'

'In the old days you wanted to hang all the coppers from lamp posts,' Brian reminded him.

'That's when I thought they'd like to hang me, or bang me up for ten years. But we all belong to the same outfit in the end.'

Avril went down the garden path to deactivate the burglar alarm. 'She always does it,' Arthur said, 'because I once plugged in the wrong number. Before I knew what was happening the bells of hell sounded all up and down the street. There was a policeman at the front door, one at the back, and one coming down the chimney. I've never seen them move so fast. While they was at it a couple of fire engines covered the house in foam. Smart lads, them firemen. The only way you could tell the coppers from Eskimos was when they ran out of the house shouting into their radios. They gave me a right bollocking, so now I let Avril do it.'

He filled the empty kettle for the next mashing of tea so that Avril would only have to flick the switch with her good arm. 'Just sit down,' he told her. He brought out bread, butter, cheese, a jar of homegrown onions, their garden tomatoes, radishes, hearts of lettuce, and a large pork pie.

'We should have filled up at the party,' Brian said, 'except none of us were hungry.'

'In the old days,' Arthur said, 'we'd eat everything we could get our hands on, because we were never sure where our next meal was coming from.'

Brian relished the crust, jelly and rich spiced meat of the pork pie, never trusting any in London that might come from Sweeney Todd Limited. 'You might cut one open, and find a shirt button inside.'

'Avril gets the best Melton Mowbray.' Arthur uncorked a bottle of Valdepenas. 'It's corn in Egypt in this house. I'm glad we had it rough when we was young. Kids today don't know they're born.'

'Here we go again,' Avril laughed, as he filled her glass.

'But I want everybody to have enough to eat. And there was people worse off than us, like all them starving to death in Poland. The Germans did it on purpose. It don't bear thinking about. If them kids could have had half what we had they'd have thought they was in paradise.

'A few years ago at work an apprentice was sent to me so that I could teach him how to saw metal. At lunch break he opens his box and takes out some sandwiches his mother must have packed for him. "Bloody hell," he said, "not cheese again. I had that yesterday," and he flung the whole packet straight into the rubbish bin. I shot up, and put my fist under his nose. "You young bastard," I shouted, "you ought to fucking die for doing that. If I see you do it again I'll kill you. You should be ashamed of yourself."

'I just about went mad. I must have terrified the poor bogger, but it served him right. The other blokes agreed with me. "I'd have given my right arm for them sandwiches

142

once upon a time," I told him. After the break I said to the foreman: "Get that kid out of my sight. I don't want him working with me." And in a couple of days he was put somewhere else.'

Brian asked how he got the job, knowing that a metal sawyer was only qualified after a long apprenticeship. 'I was made redundant at the bike factory,' Arthur said, 'but while I was there I worked every machine they had. I could only get a job as a van driver when I left, fetching and carrying the firm's metal products all over the Midlands. I was standing in the main assembly shop one day, where the metal was cut for making the arms of robots that we supplied to car firms and automated factories, and I said to the foreman: "I can do that job." "Well," he said, "we'll be shorthanded after Joe leaves next week, and we haven't trained anybody to take over yet. Give it a go, and we'll see how you get on. We can easily get another van driver, but we can't get metal-cutters. Joe will tell you what you don't know."

'I was bluffing a lot, and after Joe left I couldn't work out a blueprint thrown on the bench showing the shape and size of some metal to be sawn. But I asked around, and one of the other blokes would put me right. It took me nearly a year to get the hang of it properly, but the man I took over from left because the work was too heavy, even though he was younger than me. Big pieces of steel and brass had to be lifted onto the machines for shaping, and you had to make exact calculations. The change to metric complicated things, but not for long. I even invented a special stop to the machine, which saved on the brass and steel. The firm was pleased, but I just thought it through, and did it.

'The noise wasn't as bad as in the bike factory. There'd be screeching for a few minutes, then it got quieter till next time. You had earmuffs, but hardly anybody wore them. If they went deaf they couldn't claim compensation. Goggles were provided against bits of metal flying about, but you only wore them now and again, and if something did get in your eye you put 'em on straightaway and said it had jumped in from underneath. When a bloke came in with a bad back from grafting all weekend in his garden he tripped over a box, and said he'd done it at work. He got a week off fully paid. I never had a day off because it was highly skilled and interesting. Some jobs took three days, another only three hours. I worked as a sawyer for eighteen years, and some of the young lads started calling me dad when they came to me for advice. I was nearly sixty, so couldn't get mad. But I got good money, and was never short of a crust. But I'll tell you one thing, no grub was ever left on my plate.'

'We even have to buy peanuts for the birdtable in the garden,' Avril said, 'because there are never any leftovers. We used to have lots of sparrows and greenfinches, bluetits as well, but there are hardly any now. I can't think where they've gone. We get more insects.'

Arthur topped up the glasses, though only a little for Avril. 'I used to think they'd died because of poison on the fields, but I've never seen any corpses. I've often wondered where birds go when they die.'

'Do you remember the sparrowhawk that came down?' Avril said. 'All the birds flew into the honeysuckle, so it didn't get any. Arthur would have had it for breakfast if he'd set a trap, but he didn't like what they fed on.'

Brian peeled the cellophane from a cigar and, on his way back to the table with an ashtray, glanced out of the window, seeing the colours of yellow marigolds, fuchsias, petunias, michaelmas daisies and geraniums planted by Avril while Arthur toiled at the vegetables. 'I've never seen a garden so neat.'

Arthur turned to her. 'We'll give you a tour in the morning.'

She blew smoke from her food, most of which had been left. 'When there's a cold east wind in winter and plenty of drizzle it doesn't look so good.'

'It's a wonder nobody comes over the fence and helps themselves,' Brian said.

'They'd be taking their life in their hands.' Arthur's lips went down. 'They'd have to climb over the garage, for a start, and if I caught them I've got a cavalry sabre under the bed that we found in a junk shop. I sharpened it like a razor at work. If anybody broke in I'd cut a piece off them. I wouldn't hesitate. You get let off if you kill somebody in your own house.'

Brian didn't doubt Arthur would wield it. 'Just show it to them, and they'd run a mile.'

'Everybody keeps their eyes open for everybody else in this street,' Avril said. 'We're on Neighbourhood Watch.'

'Alice next door lost her husband last year,' Arthur laughed, 'so her son paid for a phone to be installed by her bed, and I nearly pissed myself when I looked out of the window and saw three big chaps from the phone company coming down the path to install it. One man could have fixed it in ten minutes. You shove a cable through the wall, tie the connections, do a bit of making good, and it's finished. The three of them stayed half a day drinking Alice's tea. I'd have done it for her, but she didn't think to ask.'

'It's better than them being out of work, or walking the streets looking for a house to break into.' Avril stood to clear the table, till Arthur told her to sit down: 'It's my job, for a while.' He filled the kettle for a last cup before going to bed, as if they should have something in their stomachs as

145

ballast for settling bad dreams, or liquid to smooth the final moments of the day before saying goodnight.

Brian went up for a shower, then lay in the dark lulled by muted talk from the kitchen as Arthur finished the washing up and put it in the cupboards.

The next thing he heard was a thump at the door, and a mug of coffee set on his bedside table. 'Gerrup, you idle bastard, it's quarter to eight. You should have been in the factory an hour ago. How will you pay the rent if you get the sack?'

Part Two

ELEVEN

Motoring to visit his brothers he would either travel along the M1, or go up the Great North Road, depending on whether he intended calling at Derek's first, or at Arthur's. He would sometimes avoid the latter route due to a forecast of mist, and take his chance among coagulating lorry traffic on the motorway.

Whichever he chose, he could home in on either of his brothers' places as if a Decca navigator had been planted in his brain from birth, much as a bird might have its own inertial system. When his sister Margaret lay dying in the City Hospital he got there in two hours due to far less traffic, but nowadays, even steaming along the outside lane, he couldn't often reach the legal limit.

A car in front, which would not get into the middle lane and let him go by, ought to have been scorched by the dexterity of his curses but, without the guts or know-how to increase speed, or lacking the sense to shift back to where he belonged, annoyingly was not. Brian never supposed himself to be in a hurry, but the motorway existed, so it seemed sensible to make the best headway possible. His fine-tuned reactions had taught that the faster he went (within limits) the less energy was used, a throwback from his factory days.

Even so, somebody faster than you, with whatever philosophical justification, or most likely with none at all, would be coming up behind, a blood-red underslung gobbet of speed flashing white lights into the back of your skull, in which case you either became in his mind what the slowcoach was in front of you, or you got in and let him by, then came out again and fell in behind the same car still trying to thrust ahead but getting only as far as you had been a few moments before.

On the Great North Road (otherwise the A1 (M)) though mostly dual carriageway, the urge to go fast was less acute, since occasional traffic islands slowed you down. The more relaxing route could take up to an hour longer, because you were now and again slowed by a gaggle of juggernauts jockeying for position to overtake, the drivers no doubt fed up with seeing the same fat-arsed pantechnicon and boring logo for mile after mile, though for all their effort the only alteration in the scenery when they had finished their nerve cracking manoeuvre was a different number plate.

On the A1 (M), close to the A606 turn-off, he was reluctant to risk a stomach upset at a service station, so stopped to eat his sandwiches by peaceful Rutland Water. Having much of the parking area to himself, he wandered to the shore, the surface cut by the plumage of gliding swans, fields beyond subtly indicating that he was in a country with no name in the motoring atlas, a landscape from one of his dreams in which the seemingly unpeopled terrain belonged to him alone.

He recalled quizzing Arthur on the meaning of life, who had replied: 'What's the point thinking about what you can never know? I came out of my mother, and when I kick the bucket I'll go into the soil. No more daylight. Nothing at all. What more can you say?'

Looking across at the coastal indentations of the artificial lake created by engineers and surveyors, he felt no need either to wonder about where he would surely be going, yet could

150

imagine a Grand Deity responsible for every change of the universe, controlling the labyrinthine progress of all human and animal beings.

The chill wind of the winter's afternoon sent him to his car and on to Nottingham. Avril's chemotherapy was finished, nothing more to be done, corpuscle wreckers undermining her body with ravages invisible except to X-rays. She had been sent home, and Arthur was looking after her, with only optimism to deploy against the unstoppable course of her illness.

Driving over Trent Bridge he got in lane for his customary glance at the sluggish band of water wide enough to keep the two halves of the country from each other's throats. He had swam in it, rowed boats in it, played by its banks as a kid, walked and cycled along it, fished in it once with Arthur, and many a time fucked in the shrubbery along the Clifton bank. There was no other river for which he felt so much affection, sliding sinuously with never the same face, for which familiarity had bred love and never contempt.

He threaded the traffic, eyeing each signpost in case instinct let him down in the morass of roads and one-way turnings that, according to Arthur, Derek had taken such pleasure in creating. His latest script had been handed in and would go into production soon. Another lump sum was on its way but, he told Arthur, he would feel like vomiting when his name came up on the credits. Though the idea was more banal than usual, he had regretted not being able to laugh as loud as those in the studio on hearing it was to be called: 'Anyone for Dennis?'

Derek reminded him that the money he got for it would buy a lot of Alka Seltzers, and that nothing mattered as long as you made people laugh for half an hour and forget their

151

troubles. Let television live for them, and hope they stayed tuned in.

At the city centre cars spun in from every angle as he turned into Slab Square and cruised around to observe the people, well fed now and comfortably dressed in anoraks and bomber jackets and trainer shoes, no overalls or sports coats, or drab footwear. He saw black faces here and there, or someone wearing a Moslem pillbox hat, or turban, though he'd noticed that when such people opened their mouths the accent was often as Nottingham as the rest, language a perfect mixer.

Arthur helped him in with his camera bag, a holdall, a cardboard box of books and magazines, a couple of bottles of wine, and a carton of the best orange juice from the supermarket for Avril. 'How is she?'

'Not too well. But she always says she's all right. She'll never say how badly she feels. But she can't keep her food down anymore.'

'Does she rest a lot?'

'All she can. I'm glad you've come, though. She'll be glad to see you.'

She sat at the kitchen table in her usual place, as if dressed for going out, wearing a beige sweater, and a skirt as neat as if just back from the cleaners, her wig smoothly combed and so exactly placed one would never guess her affliction.

He kissed her on the lips. 'How are you, then?'

She smiled, 'Oh, so-so.'

'You look all right.'

She had drawn more into herself, gathering her resources to fight off what was attacking her; but the more she did so the weaker she became, which made her even less able to preserve her wellbeing. Science had failed, and it was up to her, she was on her own, she would get weaker, when the lack of resistance would leave only hope, as effective as a stick in a typhoon.

'Well, I've got to feel all right, haven't I?' She put a spoon into the bowl of half finished soup. 'It's just that I can't keep much down, though I'm trying.'

A stranger might assume the frail aspect to be her normal physique, but he recalled her former stateliness and wit on her countering Arthur's outlandish humour. She smiled, and lifted the spoon to her lips. 'Did you have a good run up?'

'Yes.' He sat by her. 'Not too much traffic on the A1. Hereward the Wake must have been asleep. But I did have a run-in with a camper van near Norman Cross.'

She gave her usual dry laugh of disbelief. 'You're a bit of a devil, if you ask me.'

'The bloody madhead drives too fast,' Arthur said.

'It wasn't my fault. I was on the outer lane, and this day-glo coloured vehicle with rusty bumpers swung out and nearly knocked me across the barrier, so for the next mile or two I worried him. I could see rats leaping out of the rusty holes thinking this was it. Then he lost his nerve and stopped on the verge, half tilted over. When I looked in my rear mirror he was shaking his fist because his engine had dropped out. At least I woke him up.'

'I used to think I was a good liar,' Arthur said, 'but I can't spin yarns like him.' His concern focussed on Avril, who let her half spoonful of soup fall into the bowl. She hurried out of the room, waving aside offers of help.

'She's gone to be sick again,' Arthur said after a silence. 'She can't even keep soup down. She takes tablets for that sort of thing, but they don't work anymore.'

The day would come when she'd no longer be in her usual chair, no help to give against what was killing her. 'Maybe there's something else she can take.'

Arthur shook his head. 'It gets harder to hope. I'll go and see how she is.'

153

He stood up to look at the framed photograph of Isambard Kingdom Brunel in his stove pipe hat standing against a background of outsized chainlinks, a smallish man with sensual lips, fine hands, and narrowed eyes, a slim cigar between his lips as if its smoke helped with thoughts of some mechanical contrivance not yet in anybody's imagination.

A white shirt showed under his waistcoat, and a thin chain coming from around his neck would be connected to a small circular slide rule in the left pocket, while another instrument, possibly a compass, swung an inch below the waistcoat. Untidy hair sprouted from under the rim of his hat, and his wrinkled trousers had shines at the folds, as if made of thin leather.

Hands in pockets, but with a youthful vigour in his attitude, he was relaxing after the inspection of some job in hand. Mud on his none too protective boots proved the day inclement, chainlinks behind stained with swathes of rain. He had looked forward to a sweet refreshing smoke while clambering over girders and stanchions, and his momentarily weary gaze may have been because he was impatient with the photographer and wanted to be back at work.

Brian had read that certain people would like to see the cigar eradicated from Brunel's lips, so that the young wouldn't be influenced by his seeming pleasure in tobacco, but he thought it better to airbrush out the chains behind him, which were symbolic of a greater evil than that of a well deserved smoke.

In Brunel's day people smoked and drank, fuelled them- selves with rich food (not to mention opium or lauda- num) and no doubt fucked all they could, and probably died younger than they might have done, but the civilizing benefits of their works had made life less brutal for those non-smoking teetotal vegetarian politically correct bigots of the present who cast an aura of sin over the simplest of pleasures.

Arthur, who hadn't smoked for a few months because of a chest infection, asked for a cigar when he came down. Brian passed one from his case. 'How is she?'

'Trying to sleep. She's better off in bed, but she wanted to put on a show, and greet you at the table.' He blew a smoke ring at the ceiling, which relaxed his features. 'Maybe she'll feel better in the morning. It's hard to know what to do, but after the nurse has been I'll get the doctor in as well.' He stood by the stove, and put some peeled potatoes into a saucepan. 'There's pork chops to slam under the grill, and mixed vegetables from the freezer.' He turned on the gas. 'We shan't go hungry. And I feel better when I'm doing something.'

'We could have eaten in town.'

He fitted the corkscrew to a bottle. 'There's no need to splash fifty quid on a meal. Last time you did I thought them turds was a bit off.'

'I'll pay the next food bill at the supermarket, then. But maybe the three of us'll have lunch at the White Hart sometime.'

Arthur doubted it, but liked the offer as he filled two glasses of red. 'They've ripped out all the small rooms since we last went, and made one big one, just to make more money.' He slid the glass across. 'They can pack more people in, though it looks the same on the outside.'

From staring into his wine he turned and grinned. 'With little rooms you can have a drink in each and think you've done a pub crawl. If it's raining you don't get wet, and you can talk to people. I don't drink much these days in case I have to drive Avril to the hospital, though I'd have to drink more than a drop before I couldn't drive.' He scissored a packet of

155

minestrone to heat while setting the table. 'I've got to look after both of us. I never did much around the house except washing up, but I'm getting a dab hand at it now.'

Arthur would always be able to care for himself, but the picture of him in the house alone, bereft, standing in the kitchen not knowing north from south, whether to go out or brew tea, if he should sit down or crawl into bed, laugh or cry, go and sit on a bench in the garden, or stay in and cut his throat, didn't bear thinking about. He had never lived on his own, and though Brian had heard it was good for self-knowledge it didn't stop you making mistakes, or lessen the suffering. Whoever said: 'know thyself' (and he was well aware of who it had been, but look where it had got Him) should have realized it would make little difference.

'Maybe we'll have a drink in town tomorrow,' Arthur said, 'I know I should stay in, but Avril gets upset if she thinks I don't go out because of her. I drive around now and again just to make her think she can look after herself.'

'We could call on Jenny. She'd like it if we nipped in to say hello.'

'You'd better phone and let her know.'

Brian found the number in his address book, did a quick tap-dance with his finger ends on the plastic base. 'I can tell your voice anywhere,' she said. 'You are a stranger, though.'

'How are you?'

'I'm all right. I always am, you know that.'

No use expecting her to tell him she wasn't. 'I'm staying a few days with Arthur and Avril.'

'How is she?'

'Not too good. She's sleeping at the moment.'

'Give her my love. I hope she gets better soon.'

'Me and Arthur wondered if we might call in the morning.'

'Of course you can. I'm always in.'

'About half past ten.'

He put the phone back. 'That's settled.'

'It'll give us somewhere to aim for,' Arthur said. 'But it'll depend on how Avril's feeling.' He cut into his chop. 'She might be all right. But she goes up and down. What the end will be don't bear thinking about.'

'She'll win through,' was all he could say, which neither of them could believe. Arthur had videoed a programme about an aircraft carrier sunk in the Norwegian Campaign. The English captain had locked his aeroplanes in their hangars instead of having them in the air looking for the German warships.

'It's a good job the bastard went down with his ship,' Arthur said, 'because nearly all the sailors drowned as well.' Not much talk left, as he stood to wash the pots. 'I'll be off to bed in a bit,' his worry and grief beyond measuring. 'We'll get an early start in the morning.'

Avril had been sick every half hour, so Arthur had been awake all night. 'We've got the nurse coming today, and Avril swears she can handle it on her own, but I'll stay behind to see that it goes all right. She always says she feels fine, and there's no cause to worry, so maybe they don't do as much for her as they could.'

Brian propped himself up so as not to spill coffee on the sheets. Rain swathed the house roofs, a depressing day, but after a soak in the bath he felt more lively, as he sat down to toast and coffee. 'Here's the key to the door,' Arthur said, 'in case you're back before me. She might have to go into the hospital, and if she does I'll go with her to see that she's all right.'

He put it into his waistcoat pocket. 'Are you sure there's

nothing I can do? I can fetch and carry, do anything you want.'

'No, I'm better off on my own. But give Jenny my love.' He allowed himself a smile. 'And if she pulls you into bed don't come crying to me afterwards and saying you've got her in the family way. I saw how when you kissed her at the party you couldn't tear yourself away.'

He wove between cars parked on both sides, and stopped at the Pakistani newsagent's for his *Guardian*, and Arthur's *Daily Mail*. The owner looked as if he would like him to buy something else, so he asked for a packet of cigars which Arthur could smoke later.

Rain cleared grit and insect smears from the windscreen, and streaks of London pigeon slime from the roof. Years ago he would wash and polish the car every week, a real bullshit job, or he got a couple of bob-a-job kids to do it for a quid.

So as not to arrive at Jenny's too early he drove like an old age pensioner, or a happy saver economizing on petrol, keeping to inner lanes and not overtaking on dual carriageways. Beyond Basford Crossing, uncertain of the way, instinct guided him by The Crossbow of the birthday party eleven weeks ago.

A Nottingham town plan was always in his side pocket (even when driving through France) so he pulled in, to find himself only a few hundred yards from where she lived, thinking he would have driven away if he hadn't phoned already. The two-storeyed modern house was at the end of a quiet and peaceful drive, where those who didn't live in the area were easily observed, neighbourhood watch never a new concept in Nottingham.

During the time it took to get to the door he noted the lawn well kept to the kerb, and wondered what sort of car was in her garage. He followed her into the living room, her bruised legs looking as if they caused some pain.

She sat with hands on lap, calm and smiling, waiting for him to talk, like royalty on whom such onus could never be put. It was impossible to know what lay behind her untroubled gaze. Only speech might show how happy or otherwise she was, but she gave no sign either way.

Entertaining his girlfriends had never been a problem. They would think him empty and dull if he didn't keep the patter going, though not so much that she would think him a motormouth. You paused now and again, to let her talk, but such calculations would make no sense to Jenny.

'I'm really glad to see you,' she said, 'I can't forget how you made the effort to come up specially for my birthday party.'

There was little to say, as if she was too important for facile chat. Being there to come back to, she gave shape to his life, though he wondered if it would be more interesting to stay in the wilderness. 'And I'm glad to see you,' he said. 'That's all I came up for this time, as well.' To forestall her calling him a liar (though she never would) he said: 'This is a wonderful house you've got.'

'I suppose it is, but I'm used to it. We lived in a council house at Bilborough, before George had his accident, then we were able to get this place. I know it's big, but it wasn't when I had seven kids running around. One of my daughters has taken one of the rooms upstairs because she got a divorce not long ago, and had to have somewhere to live. If you can't go home again, where can you go? I sometimes think of getting a smaller place, but you can't beat a bit of space, can you?'

He had to agree. Maybe that was why he had left the two up and two down, and sharing a bed with Arthur and Derek. He stood by the large window, the glass so clean it might not have been there. 'Everything looks very tidy.'

159

'Oh, I don't have to look after it,' she laughed. 'I've got children and grandchildren for that. I don't have to lift a finger. How many have you got?'

He turned. 'Three, but I hardly know where they are, or what they are doing.'

She was amazed. 'How is that, then?'

'They like to lead their own lives. If they needed help, I'd hear from them.'

'It sounds rum to me. I thought families stuck together. What about grandchildren?'

'There could be one or two knocking around.'

'Don't you want to see them?'

'Now and again, I suppose.'

She drew back, as if her questioning might turn him into the unfeeling person she knew he couldn't really be. 'You're still as funny as ever. I never could make you out.'

'It's the same with myself, let me tell you.'

'That's not the way to go on,' she said kindly.

But he was angry at being judged. 'It's the way I am.'

'As long as it don't bother you. I like having my family near me, so's I can tell 'em what to do! They're a good lot, though, and don't need any telling.'

'Like when they fixed your birthday party?'

'That was a shock, I can tell you.'

'Your face looked a picture when you came up those stairs.'

'I'll bet it did. But I just couldn't believe it. Wasn't it good of them? They went to no end of trouble.'

'You deserved it, after all you've been through.'

'I only did what I had to do, though it was bad near the end when George kept saying all he wanted to do was die. He asked me over and over for stuff to kill himself, but I couldn't do a thing like that.'

160

He recalled talking about it with Arthur, who said: 'She should have left him at the beginning. He'd have been just as happy, though the few times I saw him he was a miserable bastard.'

'You wouldn't leave me if I was crippled like that, would you?' Avril said lightly.

'No, love, I'd stand by you to the end.'

'Well, then,' she said, 'how could Jenny leave him?'

'But she didn't even love him.'

'How do you know? She must have done.'

'Not by then,' Arthur insisted. 'Not with a real love. He'd have been just as unhappy with lots of young nurses looking after him.'

'That's where I'd put you,' she laughed, 'if you had an accident. You'd like it a lot better than being at home with me.'

Arthur kissed her. 'As long as you came to see me every day.'

'I'd do that,' she said, 'but I'd have to make my toy boy wait outside, wouldn't I?'

Jenny came back with his cup of tea. 'What are you going to do for the rest of the day?' he asked.

'I expect I'll do some knitting. Then read a bit. Cook myself some dinner. I like my days.'

She could keep them. Time to run. The tea scalded his throat because he couldn't get it down fast enough. There had to be more in life than talking to someone with no common bridge.

She claimed a kiss at the door, as if by right, which he took as valid so as to get away more quickly. The day palled as he drove into town via the long south wall of Wollaton Park, passed the White Hart where his grandfather had taken his beer as a farrier, over Abbey Bridge and onto the boulevard by the Grove Hotel at whose bar his mother and her second husband used to drink, every glum place getting a good wash from the rain.

He parked by the Castle, which Arthur had always wanted to blow up. It would be a shame to destroy the works of art, but seeing it ascend into the sky even appealed to him at the moment. From the town centre he went into the Lace Market, wanting to walk his feet bloody and have them match how he felt, doubling back among the gothico-elegant warehouses and silent factories on Broadway (mentioned in Pevsner) to a pub on Bridlesmith Gate, where he sat in a sweat and had two pints of lager.

He browsed in Dillons and bought a street map he didn't need, then had a big tasteless five quid lunch in a tastelessly decorated open plan pub. The vast space of Slab Square wasn't where he wanted to be, either, but he walked around it twice, bought a magazine at the top of Birdcage Walk and threw it away at the bottom, then did an almost running march back to the car.

He drove to Wollaton Park, couldn't be bothered to walk around the lake, stayed in the car and tried the *Guardian* crossword, rain sprinkling the windscreen, cigar smoke steaming up the inside and blocking visibility beyond, just as he wanted it, voices and engines blurred in the drizzle, thinking maybe the Hall would vanish as well, up the spout with everything, didn't know what he was doing here, if it weren't for Arthur and Avril (and Derek and Eileen) he'd slide down the M1 back to his snug hole in Highgate. He fell asleep, then woke up and set off for Arthur's.

Basford Crossing looming up, fuck the place, why had he come this way, with so many other routes? Remembered the time when they were going to Jenny's party in Arthur's car,

162

Avril done with her chemotherapy and all of them optimistic about her chances.

Two traffic islands, and on the beam to get through there was a queue and he wondered why, thinking it must be the rush hour, if ever there was one, or maybe the traffic lights were broken, glued on red. The car in front moved, and he kept close, as if to unnerve the bloke, then he shunted forward, and on the turn saw the gates of the crossing closed, lights on red.

A train through Basford Crossing? Electric, no smoke, but a train nevertheless, and not a ghost train because it came in a hurry, electric invisible power rushing it between open gates, no kids to howl, but where was it going, and what for?

The gates swung inwards, lights flicked to amber and then green, and he was beyond before red came back. A train using Basford Crossing was a sign of hope, that things would get better for everybody, regenerate the area. Up the hill and over the top, on his way to the refuge of Arthur's, he stuck two fingers out of the open window, and shot down the road at fifty.

TWELVE

The snout of Brian's car pointed up the road, houses at the top, and above them a painting of clouds that brought the idea of freedom to mind, an aching to be off, knowing that one day he would have to go through the Tunnel and, after a while of wandering in France, set the compass for any other place culled out of the atlas.

Arthur walked across the pavement. 'I saw you coming up the road. I've just got back from the hospital. I took Avril at four o'clock, and they kept her in. As soon as the doctor saw her this morning he got the hospital on his mobile and told them to send an ambulance. I sat with her in the ward till she went to sleep holding my hand. They doped her up to the eyeballs. I got back a few minutes ago, so you're just in time.' In the kitchen he pressed the kettle on. 'It's the best place for her. She wasn't keeping anything in her stomach. There's nothing else I can do.'

'I only wish I could help.'

He set down two mugs of tea, a shade of his old self returning: 'I was surprised to see you back so early. I said to Avril, "He's giving her the one-eyed spitting cobra. He'll start living with her, and stay in Nottingham like the rest of us." She was being tucked up by then, and burst out laughing. But I'll bet Jenny would be delighted, if you did.'

'We sat around, and talked, just nattered like old friends.'

'You won't tell me anything. I've got you weighed up. I know everything about you and always will. Want more tea?'

'I'll never stop pissing.'

'The place is only next to your bedroom door.'

'Pour me one. If I thought I'd got myself weighed up I'd be dead.'

'I don't know about that. If you've got yourself weighed up you're always spot on when it comes to weighing somebody else up.'

Such self-assurance was to be avoided, though his brothers only put on a simplicity of outlook to further their common humour. Upstairs, he looked along the shelves Arthur had carpentered, the top row tight with novels, others packed with travel and adventure books, atlases and maps, small encyclopaedias, date books and dictionaries found at car boot sales or Oxfam shops.

On the walls were framed pictures of Clifton Grove and Wollaton Hall and an antique map of the county he couldn't tell whether genuine or not. An enlarged photograph of their mother and her second husband Tom included Avril and Eileen, Derek and Arthur and himself, taken in a pub twenty years ago, the mother not dead nor Avril dying, pints on the table and cigars half smoked, shorts and cigarettes for the women.

Arthur's suits hung in the built-in wardrobe, shirts and underwear, ties and handkerchiefs folded and stacked in a chest of drawers. A chess set was laid on a table by the bed, a game Avril had learned from her father, and schooled Arthur in. Brian once found them in mid-match, each striving to avoid losing, or hoping for checkmate. He wondered whether Arthur would look at the board after Avril was dead, though his shirts would be as neatly folded in the drawers.

The central heating dulled him, so he hung his jacket over a chair and lay on the bed, recalling how he had a long time ago tried to become a novelist, but every proud-arsed bullshitting bowler-hatted toffee-nosed publisher with his rolled umbrella, idly indulging in his parasitical occupation for a so-called gentleman, had turned lily-white thumbs down on everything he wrote, Soviet Bloomsbury's censorship wanting none of him.

His furnished attic room had been at 13 Cockroach Villas near St Pancras Station, as if ever ready, at such failures, to lug his suitcase down the street and get on the Puffing Billy back to where he came from. Unable to look at another page of scribble one day, he humped a television set – black and white – back to his room from a stall in Camden Town. After using his know-how to still the ever rolling screen it was obvious, on seeing the staid crap displayed, that funny scenes from his pen would have a better chance of making money than novels nobody wanted.

The truth was, he thought, using the sink instead of walking down four flights of stairs, that talent couldn't be talent if it took so long to bring success, while the starvo humour of childhood and youth pattering in his brainbox for much of the day and night would make good entertainment on the goggle-box. To struggle at novel-writing, when cascades of money waited to overfill his pockets, hardly bore consideration.

In the sixties he'd had the good luck to meet Gordon Pike in a pub near the station. *The* Gordon Pike. The Great Gordon Pike. Gordon-fucking-Pike, mate. Well, nobody remembered him now, but why should they? Writers for television come and go, and so would he, which was why he thought it better to eat now and die later.

Where the money was, he had to be, and when fate took

the upper hand he was only too willing to dig a fur-lined grave and live with good wine, cigars and fifty quid meals till he popped his clogs. No one but a wool-head would do otherwise. Largeness of spirit meant letting fate take care of you, and only self-indulgence would give the best out of life. Seeing a rung on the golden ladder, he swung on and held tight, coming from too far away to let anyone push him off.

Gordon Pike hadn't had much schooling, the same for me, Brian said. Even dyslexics get into university these days, but then it was different, or maybe not so much, but a maverick had a chance. Pike, five years older, an air gunner in the war, had written concert party sketches to entertain every erk and bod at the Much Bindings and Little Wedlocks and Upper Mayhems he had flown from on his two tours of ops. Connections made got him into radio, and then writing for the box.

He made mattresses of money, but seemed about to descend into the melancholics' plughole when Brian met him at the bar, unwilling to get the train to his wife and four kids in St Albans after dragging his feet (in elastic sided boots) from the bed of a girlfriend on Marchmont Street. Pike sobbed on about the hard days of his childhood, not fashionable to do so, but Brian outlined, over the third pint, something of his underprivileged infancy.

Pike, having met a man who understood, went up manic by manic steps to thinking life might be worth going on with after all, and gave Brian his card, telling him to phone if he wanted advice about his scripts.

Brian's new acquaintance – the inert Pike, no less – spewed his way across St Pancras booking hall, but he got him into a train, then phoned the wife to say (no news to her) that hardworking dedicated Gordon would be needing assistance at the other end, and that she ought to be there, hoping she wouldn't turn on the big guns of justifiable invective when the poor misunderstood genius opened his bloodshot eyes in the morning and shot his fist into her long suffering face.

Brian's work was taken, sketches and short plays which, Pike said, were plugged into the hearts and minds (insofar as they had them) of the kind of people which those who ran the television business hadn't a fart's chance in a whirlwind of meeting, though they saw good money when they sniffed it. The light of magnanimity in Pike's eyes betrayed pride at being able to overcome his loathing of everyone in the world just this once. For Brian it was enough, because Pike was God, and he learned from him, then forgot all he had learned, and became himself, as far as a self could be found.

Material came with nothing like the effort of writing a novel. Television up to then had shown family entertainment of the drabbest kind, while as the sixties picked up steam you could write about the lowest of the low provided the decibel meters showed a high enough score of idiot laughter.

He moved by taxi from his room in Cockroach Villas to a flat in Highgate and then, able to believe his wealth wouldn't melt after waking from a good dream turning bad, a removal van took his accumulating chattels to a property in Chelsea. After waiting till Gordon Pike had conveniently killed himself, he sold his abilities to a company paying higher fees.

If he knew that the sixties were different from any other time it was only because he had read it in the newspapers, unable to believe any particular decade wasn't similar to those already lived. He was behind the time, detached from it, observing, unwilling to use drugs at parties where hooks could be hung on the stench of marijuana smoked by those of all ages. A certain amount of alcohol and a good cigar was enough for him.

Too old to show interest in those bearded charlatans who toned down their posh school accents to a proletarian mumble, he recalled how so many people claimed to have an engine-driver as a grandfather (instead of being descended from an Irish grandmother) that the country must at one time have been chock-a-block with puffing billies going around in circles.

No utopian nursery themes impressed him, though he wasn't so daft as not to notice any phenomena which might be useful in his trade. As the decade went on, better and better contracts came his way, as if being in opposition to the times made it easier to exploit his sense of humour.

During his marriage to Jane she showed him a barely comprehensible review in a weekly paper of a so-called play at the Roundhouse, a redundant engine shed in Chalk Farm made into a theatre. A troupe of actors in black tracksuits scrambled up and down a monkey climber in semi-darkness for over two hours, screaming insults at the audience, so that he regretted not having a few stones to hurl back. After the show he heard a man and his wife say they'd never enjoyed themselves so much.

His scorn brought on a quarrel that marriage could hardly sustain; either the actors' intention had succeeded, or he used the event to undo a relationship there was no further use for. The beginning of the end, they lost their sense of irony, and humour turned into malice.

'We never go out together,' Jane said when he wouldn't escort her to an Arts Lab. He was unable to understand, he said, how art could be produced in a place which carried out experiments on rats. Only individuals make works of art; and nothing but mechanical contrivances ever came from workshops.

Holding such comments back, or smiling to suggest that

170

they were harmless, maddened her when wanting an honest opinion on some 'happening'. 'You're getting to be like your grandfather.' She nodded at the old man's photograph pinned beyond his typewriter. 'And you're even beginning to dress the same' – seeing him in a suit and tie for a party, rather than jeans that reminded him of overalls at the factory.

She took him to the LSE on the night of a 'sit-in', where talk of peasant revolutions and working class uprisings seemed a more exciting game to the students than Monopoly or Scrabble. He talked with someone on whom more than twenty thousand pounds of education was being wasted by a shilling copy of *The Little Red Book*. He wanted to know if Brian didn't feel treacherous at having left his working class roots (as if he was an aspidistra!) instead of staying to *politicize* 'the masses' with his superior powers of understanding. Brian wanted to say fuck off and don't be such a daft prick, but politely told him that no rural worker or factory hand with a sense of humour would listen to the exhortations of a Chinese tyrant, and he saw their talk as no more than a middle-class ploy to keep the workers in their place – for which remarks he was called a racist.

As for sex in the sixties, it made little difference to him. From the age of fourteen the commodity had been free enough with what girls he had known, or with women whether married or not, though from the present talk he could well believe that anyone born in that decade (and surely in any other) would have cause to wonder who their real father was.

When Jane shouted, after he'd caught her out in a love affair: 'My womb is my own. I do what I like with it,' he knew that if such was the case she could use it with man, woman or beast for all he cared, though he had to agree when she added that life was too short to be faithful. If

171

he'd wanted loyalty from a woman he should have stayed with Jenny.

In the words of Tacitus they created a desolation and called it peace, yet often mustered sufficient affection to reopen the campaign, energy bubbling up like water in a desert when they thought the well had been sucked dry. Two intelligent and otherwise tolerant people could have continued living together, but it was a time more than any other when not to nod with the herd was taken as an heretical attack on a person's deepest beliefs, and being in love was not enough.

The spirit of the age decided they had no common ground, though out of pride he preferred to think that with tact, skill in love, and diplomacy, he might have kept the marriage going. In bed they invariably went off like two pieces of dynamite, and no lovemaking had been the same since. After the divorce, when she went back to working on a newspaper, he long recalled (and still did) her short dark hair, lithe almost androgynous body (except when she was pregnant) and sizzling lavatory cleaner wit on which he had sharpened much of his own.

Among people he worked with were those who enjoyed the artful self-indulgence of the decade, until the time of sending their children to schools where 'doing your own thing' was thought to be more important than spelling or the precision of arithmetic. Some didn't care, while others (who had more money, including himself) found places which still believed in education. Many were later to shake their heads at the increase of single mothers, at so-called football violence, and at unemployed youths 'shooting up' in underpasses, who were only doing in fact what they themselves had done in their flats and houses.

Meanwhile life in his home town had gone on as it always had. People such as those at Jenny's party lived in the same old way, impervious to influence, sceptical, independent or ignorant (or both), engrossed in themselves and their families, taking no guff from anyone, nor talking it either. They were rowdy, went boozing, worked hard when they had to (and they nearly always had to) but skived when they could get away with it, and turned violent at times out of boredom or lack of excitement, or anger at not being acknowledged as intelligent human beings, or because a worm of unknown compounds was eating at their livers. They were themselves, and if he were to ask Jenny whether she or any of her family had taken drugs she would look at him 'gone out', too surprised to be offended.

Because such people had always been his inspiration he went on earning, but should his brain turn to wet sand, and no more cheques skim through his letter box in the morning or at midday, he had enough money not to worry about the future, though working as long as he could would enable him to go on feeling younger than his age. As happy as he had ever been after a lifetime of thinking that something was wrong if he wasn't unhappy, he was guarding his time and freedom, having won the long struggle for autonomy.

He slept until Arthur called that supper was ready. 'So how about coming down, and getting stuck in?' he said at the second knock. 'The wine'll get cold if you don't.'

Among the spread was a slab of cheddar, cut by wire from a drumlike piece in the local market. Arthur stabbed through the cellophane packet of smoked fish and laid a fillet on each plate.

A bottle of red among the edibles radiated like Eddystone Lighthouse over plates and side plates, glasses, knives and forks, and napkins in metal rings. 'At least we eat well. I don't know why, but I can't remember what we used to eat as kids.'

Brian forked stuff onto his plate. 'The smells from the dinner centre come back to me now and again and make my mouth water.'

'You remember the two women who ran the place?' Arthur laughed as he poured the wine. 'The big fat one was Miss Carver, and her assistant was little Miss Bradley. Miss Carver used to hit us with a wooden spoon if we didn't keep quiet. I even saw her take a swipe at Miss Bradley when she did something wrong. Another time, she gave her a kiss while she was slicing the bread. You could tell what they were a mile off, but they were guardian angels to us. Sometimes we'd get custard and bananas for dessert, and I remember the hot milky cocoa they used to dish out. I don't see how anybody can have mental troubles if they've gone hungry. If I felt myself going mad all I'd have to do was think about the next meal.'

Brian clinked his brother's glass. 'I was looking at that family photograph in the bedroom, the one with Tom in it, taken about twenty years ago.'

Arthur found it impossible to mention Tom without laughing. 'A good thing mam married him though. He looked after her a lot better than Harold ever did.' Chain-smoking Tom, ten years younger, was the bloke she should have had from the beginning. In the war he drove tanks from Chilwell depot to loading ramps at one of the stations, and he'd had a good time taking ATS girls to the pubs in Nottingham, a smart quiff held down under a beret. After demob he never wore a hat again, mindful of his Brylcreemed sculpture to the end.

After his wife died from cancer he met Vera in the lounge of the Boulevard Hotel, and a few Sundays later took her to Skegness in his fifty pound banger. She felt safe with him because he never drove the old Austin faster than forty-five, nor ever did much more on the motorway: 'I've seen too

174

many pools of blood on the road,' he told her, walking on the sands after a fish and chip dinner. Then he popped the question, and she said yes.

He was thin and above middle height, lantern jawed, blue-eyed and jaunty, cool and dependable. They'd sit holding hands and looking at television, each with a fag on the smoulder, drinking mugs of strong sweet tea. Sometimes they'd go to the pub, and put back shorts or half pints, or both in rotation.

Tom was the caretaker of a large chapel just off Slab Square, a four-roomed flat going with the job. On Saturday night, trying to sleep, Brian would hear gangs of drunks coming out of the pubs, the crash of glass sounding like bars of contemporary music, and curses when they set on each other under the chapel wall four floors below, then the clatter of boots as the shaven headed, earringed posse of Nottingham Lambs fled before the screaming sirens.

On Saturday afternoon Tom checked the heating system of the chapel for Sunday morning, while Vera with bucket and cleaning rags wiped down the pews, helping him to get the work done so that they could go back to their snug living room, to put the kettle on and have a smoke.

'They were happy enough,' Arthur said. 'It was a charmed life. A shame Tom had to have that heart attack while he was up a ladder polishing the organ.'

'He was lucky to go so quick,' Brian said. 'He was only sixty-odd, but at least he didn't take up space in the hospital for more than a couple of days.'

Tom had been brought up by his mother, no father in the offing, and they had supposed him to be, though without prejudice, a bastard, but he told them the real story when the three brothers took him to the Trip and made him jolly with as much ale as he could sup, plus a neverending supply of fags.

175

His father Leo had worked at Chilwell factory during the Great War, and on Monday July 1st 1918 the sun scorched the vast area of camouflaged roofs. People sweated to meet their quotas, in halls storing seven hundred thousand high explosive shells. Out of ten thousand people hard at work four thousand were women, and between them they filled fifty thousand a day.

Tom's father hadn't been able to sleep the night before. A clear June sky kept the sunshine recorders working as much overtime as the men and women, focussing the sun's rays as it swung overhead from one horizon to the other. Blocks of ice were brought into the factory to cool the TNT, but the weather turned more sultry, and the atmosphere in the powder gallery was so oppressive that some found it hard to breathe.

They had been grumbling about the heat for weeks, and knew the machinery was overworked, but each shift vied with the other to turn out powder and fill more shells. The sticky TNT made the bearings overheat, some had been raised as dust to mix with the air, but work went on because the soldiers in France were suffering far worse.

On the First of July (another one, Arthur said) Leo walked out of the boiler house where he worked on maintenance, hoping for a cooling breeze, recalling how he had said to his mother at breakfast that he'd rather be up the Trent doing a spot of fishing in such weather. Standing on the concrete, he took his watch out at just after seven in the evening.

People in a cinema nearby were watching a film (silent, in those days) about an explosion, when the floor vibrated and dust started to fall from the ceiling. Eight tons of exploding TNT shook the ground as far away as Nottingham, breaking windows for miles around.

Leo took an orange from his pocket, then it vanished

176

from his hand and he was thrown across the path to the laboratory door, too stunned to know how he got there. The whole compound was falling apart, nothing but smoke and wreckage as everyone tried to reach the safety barriers. Unable to stand, a man whose right arm was a bloody mess of rags and bone put his left arm around Leo and dragged him towards safety.

Every kind of vehicle was used for getting the wounded to the hospital, Leo on a cart pulled by a brewery horse, one of a long procession of injured men and women on the road to Nottingham. Pools of blood formed between the cobblestones, groans and screams terrifying the horses as whips cracked to drive them on.

Leo's legs were amputated and he died ten days later, one of four hundred killed and wounded. A week later the plant was turning out shells again.

'A real killpig,' Arthur said. 'Tom worked there in the next war, but they didn't fill shells anymore. Even so, he nearly got blown up.'

'Maybe it runs in the family,' Brian said. On opening his eyes in the morning Tom had a few puffs while pulling on his trousers and shirt. He walked downstairs whistling a tune, and put the fag in his mouth to pull the door open. No sooner had he stepped into the room than a flash and a bang knocked him back, his eyebrows burnt and the fag blown from his lips.

'It must have been like a bomb going off,' Arthur said. 'I expect to mam it sounded like the biggest bang since the Blitz. Tom said he got over the shock in a couple of seconds, but mam swore it was at least five minutes before he could speak. She came down in her shimmy, and opened the doors and windows, while Tom went out to give the gas board blokes the worst bollocking they'd ever had. The man who came said it was a miracle he hadn't been killed, seeing as how big the leak was.'

'But you've got to sympathize,' Arthur went on. 'These days he would have counselling. Social workers would have been all over him. Any whiff of trouble and they're like flies on raw meat. But some people phone up for them, even if it's only a husband or wife walking out on a marriage. And the social workers think they've got to come in case anybody does themselves in.'

He blew a smoke ring towards the stove. 'I heard about a bloke who had a car accident, just a bang from somebody coming out of a side road, but he was so upset at his crunched up car he couldn't stop shaking, and took himself to bed with a cup of tea and a hot-water bottle. He wouldn't come down to go to work next morning, so his missis phoned the social services and asked 'em to send some counselling.

'A young woman came, just off her course. I suppose they told her at head office to go and practise on him. The man's missis sat downstairs waiting, but it seemed to be taking a long time, and when she went up to see how things were going she found 'em in bed together. There was fucking ructions. You could hear her screams all up and down the street, doors banging and cars stopping, even people switching off their tellies to come and see what the fuss was about.'

Brian stopped laughing to refill their glasses. 'You've got to be exaggerating.'

'Me? I never exaggerate, you know that. A bloke was going on about it at work. He lived two doors down and his wife heard it all. The social worker drove away in her natty little powder blue hatchback and nearly collided with someone turning into the street, so I expect she needed counselling when she got back to the office – before they gave her the sack. Anyway, the bloke she'd been to see went off to work the next day as happy as a bird because he'd pulled a young woman into bed. It all came out later that he hadn't needed counselling at all. He was a sly bleeder: he'd only stayed in bed knowing his wife would phone for one and that they'd send a young girl. They're like that round here. I'm sure his wife didn't have him counselled again, however much he needed it by the time she'd done with him. But social workers are the enemy number one. Most people are wary of them. Nearly every other house has an absconded kid hiding in the attic, and social workers come round in vans now and again trying to get them put into care, like Germans looking for Jews. But nobody gives them up.'

After a silence Brian said: 'I wonder where old Tom is now?'

'Probably sniffing around Chilwell, to find out what caused the explosion that killed his dad. No, he's well rotted in good earth, the only place after you kick the bucket. I suppose we like to think of people looking down on us after they're dead, and I must admit I sometimes wonder if Grandad Merton's keeping an eye on us. If he's up there at all, or down, I'm sure he's dressed in his best suit, with a dicky collar, a waistcoat and watch chain, and shining black boots. Old Nick favoured blacksmiths, so he'll be looking on everybody with contempt because they're moaning about the blazing fires. I can just see that gleam nobody could stand up against.'

His five daughters hated him, but he wanted to protect them from the dangers of a changing world. If he was hard it was because he had been born that way, working at nine in his father's forge, and never learning to read or write. His older brother George beat him around the shoulders with a steel bar for any small fault, but he grew to well over six feet tall, into the sort of man who imposed his will on others. Bringing up eight children on the earnings of a farrier hadn't been easy, but his three sons were also tall and fit and, like the five girls, lived well beyond three score and ten, though the credit for that was due even more to his wife Mary-Ann.

'I was in grandad's house at Christmas once,' Arthur said, 'and I noticed him looking at me as I tackled the plum pudding. He had his eye patch on. He had a smart black one to match his best suit, which grandma probably ironed for him. Anyway, his good eye made it seem as if he was about to laugh. "Don't eat your pudding too quick, you young bogger," he growled. Normally he liked to see you getting stuck into your food, so I suspected a trick. Then my teeth bit something hard, and I picked a silver threepenny bit out of my mouth. He'd got grandma to put it in for me, but he didn't laugh, just looked pleased when I sucked it clean and put it in my pocket.'

'He was good to us,' Brian said, 'but if any of Aunt Ada's kids came to his door he'd chase 'em away with a stick.'

'They were a thieving lot,' Arthur said. 'He thought people who got in trouble with the police were scum.'

The bottle being empty, Brian went to the front room for another. 'I read that a litre a day keeps you healthy.'

'I could do with a couple at a time like this. Grandad never said much, but I remember one Sunday dinner when I was slouched in my chair, he said: "Sit with your back straight at the table. And if you want summat ask for it, don't reach. And don't keep your hands on the table when you're not eating." So I had to behave, but I learned a lot from watching him. I expect he talked plenty in the pub with other men, though he'd have a lot to say, living in the area all his life. A few pints inside him and he'd be as talkative as anybody else. Not that he had much money to spend on ale, not on the old age pensions they got in those days. He worked his bollocks off all his life, then lived the last few years in poverty, like old people still do.'

Arthur clinked his glass. 'We'll drink to him. Aunt Ada said I took after him more than anybody else in the family. She said as long as I was alive Merton would be.' He speared the last segment of pie. 'Sure you won't have it?'

He laid two black Toscanos between their places, the last from a fat cylindrical box from Italy. 'I'm stuffed.'

'Me and Avril drove to Spain once.' He lit up, a noticeable relaxation of his features. 'We got to Bordeaux and it was hard to stop, but after Bilbao we found a hotel on the coast. It was cheap and the grub was marvellous. We couldn't speak any Spanish, but we got on so well with the people who ran it they couldn't do enough for us.'

He stood at the stove to make coffee. 'We took turns driving, but Avril did most of the navigation because I got us lost once in a French town. On the way back I wanted to drive around the Great War cemeteries in France, and see where the Nottinghamshire battalions got wiped out, but we only had a few quid left.'

'In the next year or two,' Brian said, 'I'll take both of you in my car. That's a promise.'

'I'll keep you to it,' Arthur said. 'I like travelling, and so does Avril. We went to Rimini on a coach ten years ago, but I'll never do that again. My legs were jammed against the seat in front, and I needed a few buckets of wine before I could straighten myself up. I had one though with every meal while I was there. I always feel good when I'm abroad.'

'You, me, and Avril together. We'll do it.'

Arthur knocked the ash from his cigar. 'You think so? I don't know. It's a bastard, isn't it?'

It was no use shirking the matter. 'You've got to prepare for the worst,' Brian said, 'yet hope for the best.

181

If I can't speak openly to you I can't do it with anybody.'

'There's nobody else I expect it from,' Arthur said. 'Or get it from, except Avril. She talks straight about it, and I talk to myself about it all the time, unless I'm saying it out loud to you. I'm always glad to see you for a couple of days.'

'When I'm not here, if there's anything I can do, give me a bell.' Not even God controlled life and death, so any support would be feeble, though better than nothing. He would have taken Arthur's pain had it been possible, but pain was greedy and never shared itself. He had known women survive cancer of the breast, and men who had beaten cancer of the colon if they caught it early, but no one had lived with cancer of the liver. Yet what if she started walking to Constantinople, eating nothing but garlic; or went by air to the alps of New Zealand and looked on scenery that would shame her illness away? He wanted the glint of mischief to miraculously reappear in her eyes, the colour of apples to shine in her cheeks, strength return to legs and arms, appetite reaffirm itself.

Arthur, a good-looking man who carried his age well, might marry again, easy to imagine, though he felt treacherous thinking so, as if impatient with her dying. 'When I get back to London I'll phone the hospital, but I'll call you first, to check that it's all right to talk to her.'

'That'd be best. She might be back here in a few days, but I know she'd like to hear from you. She thinks a lot of you. I told her the other day I'd kill her if she died, and she said: "Well, I'll have to come through, then, won't I? I wouldn't want you to kill me." He poured coffee without asking. 'The fact is, she civilized me. I settled down with her more than with any other woman. Everything that's good in me I learned from her, and it's a mystery to me why somebody who's so marvellous got cancer.'

'I've known more women recover from it than men,' Brian said. The nursery bricks of hope couldn't explain what lay at the core of illness, though science and a determination to defeat it were on Avril's side. 'People walk the streets who've been at death's door,' he said, to help Arthur's fragile optimism, which may not survive his putting out the light for sleep. 'Women have a way of fighting it men don't have. Maybe it's faith.'

'She's got that.'

'When we go to France we'll travel on minor roads and find nice little hotels in the evening. Whatever work I'm doing, I'll put it by. Tell Avril. It'll give her something to think about.'

There was no deceiving Arthur, though he was glad to hear of the plan. When Avril died it would be good to get him to France, after the year of mourning. On the other hand, all three might go, no one able to foretell the future.

THIRTEEN

When Brian told his father he was writing for television and making money at the game (real money: he raked in more in the first two years of his success than the old man had earned in a lifetime) Harold Seaton found the whole thing a mystery he hadn't a hope of making plain. The fact that one of his sons worked for a medium which had mesmerized him from its first appearance was unbelievable. 'You're so lucky, our Brian,' he said. 'You'll never have to work again.'

He smiled at the unforgettable comment, lucky indeed at not having to labour the way his father had (when not on the dole) with shovel and pickaxe. As a boy of twelve Seaton carried upholstered armchairs and sofas on his shoulders up flights of stairs. Nowadays such objects were moved by machines, or by two full bodied men, nobody treated as beasts of burden anymore, hernias or heart attacks or sprains bred out of common tolerance.

The weights he had shouldered in the factory at fourteen were now moved by forklift truck, though he didn't recall being unhappy, as he looked around his carpeted study with its shelves of books impossible to live without. In the early days in London he had humped them about in suitcases, but later they were boxed by expert packers who, as he checked that they were taken down and put back in the right order, made him feel guilty at not having to stretch his muscles like them.

Reference books on the lowest shelf saved searching for some arcane fact or other in the public library, while above were texts of playwrights from ancient days to the present, as well as biographies of actors and comedians, books on the theatre, cinema and television. A ladder was necessary to reach Burton's *The Anatomy of Melancholy*, *The Prince*, *The Crowd* by Gustav le Bon, Hobbes' *Leviathan* and Tom Paine's *The Rights of Man*. Even higher were shelves of Everyman and Oxford Classics: Melville (especially *The Confidence Man*), novels by Conrad, Dickens, and scores of others, into any of which he could retreat from whatever miseries he made for himself. Without such books he would know even less who he was, and he feared to take many from their places because after the first page he would be compelled to read the rest.

On a side table stood objects of comfort and reassurance: a prize statuette from the Fellows of Humour Society for the best comic writing of one year; a Craven 'A' cigarette tin from his service days; a coat of arms mug of his home town; and a photograph of the bust of Euripides from the National Museum in Naples.

He came into his room every morning after a shower, and a breakfast of orange juice, cereal, bacon, egg, sausage and tomato in the kitchen. Except for a quick lunch of salad and bread and cheese, and the occasional making of coffee, he worked till time for a three-course spread in the evening, which never took more than half an hour to get on the table: cold fish for a first course, then meat with vegetables, and fruit or tinned pudding to finish, with half or a bottle of wine to send it down. If he wanted to see faces he went to the Café Rouge, always full of interesting people, and young girls with good figures.

186

He saw a traffic warden ambling up the street, with so much technological machinery swinging from his stocky white-shirted figure he looked as if about to go into action in Vietnam. He glanced at every windscreen to make sure the car had the correct accreditation. Stopping by a vehicle, he began tapping into his computer and Brian, with a surge of loathing, fetched his high velocity air rifle from behind the clothes in the wardrobe.

The man was gleeful at having collared a victim only half an hour before parking restrictions came off for the evening, maybe some poor bloke passing a few minutes with his girlfriend before her husband came back from work. Break the rifle, push in a fat bellied lead slug with his thumb, snap it shut, silently open the window an inch, and aim at the man's neck. What a fucking surprise he would get. He would jump twenty feet, notebooks and clobber, flat copper's cap and two months' supply of little plastic envelopes winging across the pavement, as he screamed like a stuck pig. That would settle his nice white shirt. Paint it red. What a fuckface. Little Hitlerian bastard.

Not caring to waste the next few years in jail ('AGEING SCRIPTWRITER IN DISGRACEFUL SCENE') he slid the rifle back in its hiding place, though maybe serving time would give material for an updated version of *Porridge*. The man stuck his penalty notice in its neat little plastic envelope under the windscreen wiper, a smile on his pasty chops as if expecting people to clap from their windows, or jeer execrations, which he would like even more.

The tree-lined area was usually quiet, but tonight fireworks crackled as if a serious bout of street fighting had broken out, the odd thud suggesting one side or the other had got their hands on a trench mortar.

He dimmed the lights and stood by the window, red, green and orange bouquets flaring in every direction, hundreds of thousands of pounds' worth decorating the sky in loud continuous explosions, so much seeding of the clouds it was bound to deluge with rain in the morning, as after the Battle of Waterloo.

The multicoloured fire of primitive potlach went on and on, not so much to denigrate Guy Fawkes as to make him regret that the incompetent bastard couldn't come back and do the job properly. As if a thunderstorm also plied its mischief, he recalled scores of earsplitting rounds fired at German bombers during the war, and missiles in the piercing certainty of their descent as you sat in the shelter hoping your number wasn't chalked on the snout. Fireworks were harmless, joyful music to the heart, with no significance of death or wounds, rockets exploding in fairy colours, whistles going up instead of coming down.

He put on the light, and lit a cigar. The page of a penny exercise book (at least that was their price when he went to school) was half spent with dialogue, but at the end of a scene he wondered what could be done with the three dustmen, holiday luggage in the cab, and the stolen bank money concealed in the rubbish, which would be difficult to find when they got to France and wanted to pay the bill for their posh hotel at Le Touquet. In their panic they would throw the scummy detritus of England all over the neat *chaussée*.

Their vehicle, parked among the Volvos and BMWs and Mercedes, would bring even more laughs when they crunched a vintage Rolls (or maybe a Bentley) in the forecourt, and tried to pay the damage with bundles of pristine fifties, joking that they supposed the ink to be dry and Her Majesty's head the right way up.

188

At the moment their dustwagon, brand new GB plates back and front, was waiting to embark. They hoped their papers were in order, and a vinegar-faced emigration official provided amusing repartee when they said they were making the trip for charity, before being allowed on board.

A young woman hitch-hiker came with them to France, being promised Chanel Number One from the duty free and a day in Le Touquet. The plot was easy, but speech elusive, though it would come if he sat long enough before the lined page.

The driver of the wagon was an earringed and tattooed ex-jailbird ready for any foray into unfamiliar areas. His loudmouthed humour was laced with cunning, so the possibilities of surreal chitchat were limitless, especially since the gentlemanly (though even more ruthless) Rodney, known as the Admiral, an ex-public school boy with impeccably false credentials, stayed with them to be sure of getting his payout at the end. Such a putrid mishmash promised mayhem.

He ran his finger along the nearest bookshelf, as when rattling palings with a stick as a kid, wondering what books to glance at, restless as ever before writing the first quips. The lit match to light a cigar fell on the carpet. He picked it up, tamped the flame with his fingers, and sat down to strike another. His pen went over the page, ideas pushing into order, dialogue like back and forth balls at Wimbledon.

The phone sounded. It often did at this point, and the shock to his body brought a mouthful of curses. He recalled how Jane used to interrupt him twenty – no, thirty – times a day, and wondered whether that had been the cause of their divorce. If it hadn't, it fucking well should have been. Any further ideas went over and out like the carriages of the train toppling apart on the collapsing bridge over the River Tay. He snapped off the receiver. 'Yeh?'

189

'Hello, Brian, it's Arthur.'

He could tell something was wrong. Arthur wasn't talking from outer space: 'She's still in hospital, but they're sending her home, because there's nothing they can do. The doctor told me just now. Two months at the most. She knows it, and said she didn't want to die in hospital. I don't blame her. I saw them dying when I looked in a side ward once.'

'What a killpig. You're going to look after her on your own?'

'A nurse'll look in every day.'

'You must have been expecting this.'

'I have, but it's different when you know for sure.' His tone was level and restrained. 'There's nothing to be done. Not a thing.'

'I'll come up as soon as I can.'

'I don't mind if you can't.'

He wanted to be alone with Avril while she was dying. Or perhaps she couldn't bear anybody to see her. 'I'll phone tomorrow. I'm just sorry.'

'I know,' Arthur said.

He didn't want to end the talk abruptly, but there was nothing except pain from Arthur, and on his side no mood for the usual talk. The crows were out in such force they hid the sky, and neither could make their voices heard above the noise. Repeating what they had already said would only bring them against the same full stop. 'I'll call you,' Brian said, 'as soon as I know what time I'll get there. Anything I can do in the meantime, just pick up the phone.'

'Yeh, all right.'

'So long, then. Give my love to Avril.'

'She might not be able to take it in. She comes and goes, out of sleep doped up with painkillers.'

'Bye, then.'

'Bye.'

'Bye,' a declining syllable from both till each put down the phone.

His pen rolled aside, no more to be done. On his next visit he would stay with Derek and Eileen, because Arthur would want to be alone with Avril, no one to disturb their farewell silences or final pledges.

He tapped out the number. 'Have a word with Avril,' Arthur said, after their greetings. 'I've just made supper, and she's coming down in a few minutes to have hers with me.'

He didn't ask how she was, assuming there'd be nothing new. 'I'd love to.'

'I can't keep her in bed. She keeps getting dressed when she can. It's a terrible effort, and I have to help her, then get her downstairs. It breaks my heart, but she's determined to act normal.'

'Put her on, then.'

'Hello!' Her voice was weaker than when they had talked over the years, and he wondered whether such determination to stay alive would draw down a miracle, or whether a miracle was more likely when hope lost its hold and there was nothing left but to stick up two fingers – if you still had the strength – and tell fate to do its worst. 'I hear you're having supper downstairs.'

'The duchess has to eat some time.'

'What nice thing is he giving you?'

'Some chicken, he says.'

'I hope you enjoy it.'

The ever toneless laugh may now have had a grin to go with it. 'I eat what I can.'

'Don't let him get you drunk. You know what he's like.'

'Oh, I do. He's a devil. I have to watch every move. But that's why I love him.'

The pause called for a change of topic. 'I'd come up to see you, but my car got bumped into yesterday.'

'Not again. That car's always in the wars.'

'It wasn't my fault this time. It got hit by a bus at the traffic lights. The driver must have been asleep. He saw the lights go green before I did, and slammed into the back of me. He went a bit pale when I made him get down from his cab to have a look at the damage. He thought I was going to clock him one, but I kept my temper.'

'Were you all right?'

'I was, but the rear lights got crunched, and part of the bumper. I wouldn't like to drive up the motorway with no brake lights.'

'We'll be glad to see you. Arthur loves it when you're here. But I've got to go now. If I'm not at the table on time he'll shout at me!'

'You'll have to shout back, then.'

'Oh, I would if he did, but I've never had to. He's always been as gentle as a kitten with me.'

Nothing wrong, you might have thought, but nothing right either, because she had the courage to keep her worst fears to herself. He couldn't go back to his desk, everything he wrote would be a mockery of her condition, as she stood with grace against the odds before going into the dark.

Part Three

FOURTEEN

Brian hoped never to drive over Basford Crossing again, at least not for the purpose he was set on now. The people you think will be the last to die are too often the first, and even when you've expected it for so long there's no denying the shock. Many obituaries in the papers were about people younger than him, often with so few years they could be his children which, though not dispiriting, sometimes made him wonder how long his luck would last.

A glum and nondescript road over Sunrise Hill took him on to the dual carriageway and through more cheerful estates. He pulled in beyond the constabulary headquarters to look at the map and make sure he wouldn't miss the turnoff to the cemetery. Rejoining traffic, a hooter screamed at his near miss, but he was too set on his errand to curse back.

'It was a terrible way to go,' Arthur said on the phone. 'If I'd been able to get my hands on a gun I'd have put her away. Out of love I would have done it. She wanted me to, near the end, knowing she had to die, and suffering as she was. But there was nothing I could do. She was like an animal in pain, and life's no longer precious when it comes to that. But I didn't have a gun, and no poison either, so what could I do but watch? I helped her to the lavatory because she was too proud to do it in bed, and I wiped her – did everything I could. I kept on trying to get her to eat, but by then she'd stopped fighting to stay alive, and I could only wait for her to go. It's awful when you have to be glad that the person you love most in the world is dead.'

He filtered by traffic lights on to the main road, put on his blinkers and cruised so as not to miss the inlet. Even so, typical for him, who always took turnings too soon, he drove into a cul-de-sac of newish houses, noting a twitch of the curtains from someone wondering who the cheeky devil could be, straying into their haven to rob them of their happy savings. Maybe she was waiting for her fancyman, and was disappointed at his three point turn back to the main road. A hundred yards further on, the cemetery was clearly indicated.

Cars were parked opposite the chapel not much bigger than a mountain refuge hut. He embraced Eileen by the door. 'What a terrible time it is,' Derek said. 'I hoped it would never happen, and now it has.'

'It's a blessing she's gone, that's all I know.' Eileen looked grim and concerned. 'But I can't tell you how sorry I am for Arthur.' Pale and silent, she had nothing more to add, or let go of beyond tears. The weather wasn't too cold for January, not the usual pissing down funeral scene. He was pulled from his drowsiness after the drive from London on seeing Jenny's son Ronald holding the door open for her and his icily attractive wife Sylvia to get out.

'It's gone eleven, so the hearse is late.' Derek looked at his cold pipe, but decided it would be disrespectful to light up. 'They're usually punctual to the minute.'

'It should have left the house at half past ten,' Eileen said, 'and it's only ten minutes away, so there's no excuse.'

'In that case,' Brian nodded, 'I'll nip over and say hello to Jenny.'

Who smiled: 'I knew you'd be here. But isn't it awful for

poor Arthur? I didn't guess Avril was that badly when she came to my party. I know what it's like though, having someone die.'

She had dragged out her widow's weeds to get togged up in, a black that made her look much younger. He kissed her, and regretted that on shaking hands with Sylvia she too didn't put her face forward for a kiss, but stood apart even from Ronald, as if they'd had their usual early morning bicker. 'I'm glad you came,' Brian called to her.

'Couldn't not, could I?' She smiled, and he wondered how much wooing he would have to do, how much patience show, and persistence need, lies to tell and humour to spend before getting her to shed those clothes and come to bed where, once the sackcloth of reserve had gone, she would be as frisky as a Tasmanian kitten. 'Don't you find funerals just that little bit sexy?'

She looked stern, then laughed, the unusual sound bringing her husband across to find out what might be the matter.

Brian forestalled him. 'I'm glad to see you.'

Ronald, wearing the same suit as at the party, shook his hand. 'The lad needs support at a time like this. I've left a good chap in charge of the firm.'

Sylvia smiled as he shook her warm hand again, her eyes showing there was little call. 'I'm sorry about your brother's loss. Jenny wanted us to come, and in any case someone had to bring her.'

'She'll have to take up driving again,' he said. 'It'd be good for her to be free and mobile, though I expect you'd have to watch her when she went out on her own. She might meet a bloke and get married again.'

Sylvia was wondering how to reply, when the first car of the cortège came up the drive, heavy tyres crunching the gravel. Brian went with Derek and Eileen to greet Arthur.

He got out of the car and stood alone, straight-backed, head in the air, and stark with sorrow, as if he would remain through rain and snow in that stance for the rest of the winter until, recovering from his grief and realizing where he was, he would go home to as much of a normal life as could be made.

He looked around, knew he was by the chapel, that Avril's body lay in a long box in the car, and that everyone was here to see her put out of sight forever. Sorrow was the common feeling as they placed arms around each other, squeezed hands, put pressure at the shoulders, nothing too violent with Arthur in case he crumbled, all regretting that his misfortune could not be shared, so much bereftness beyond the power to placate.

Brian didn't know whether the ache in his heart and stomach was for Avril (who had been dead a fortnight because of the Christmas holidays) or for Arthur living in his vacuum of pain, or even because he was hungry after the drive from London. But he registered anguish for his brother who was trapped into a state he could hardly imagine, since he hadn't experienced it, and hoped he never would.

Four men from the burial firm slid the coffin out of the hearse, and pulled it on a fragile trolley into the chapel as if afterwards they would drag it to the South Pole like one of Captain Scott's crew. People filed in behind, and Brian took a place at the back from which to look at the ceremony.

Arthur sat at the front, next to Harold dressed in a suit like the other men; his hair was cut short. On the other side of Arthur was Melanie and Barry, then Avril's son Jonah, a slim man with a moustache, and now the foreman at an electrical components firm. Avril's daughter Rachel, who had come from London, sat by her brother, while behind were Jenny and her family, and a stocky elderly man Eileen pointed out as Oliver, Arthur's friend from his allotment days. A few other acquaintances almost filled the little chapel.

The minister (or whatever he was: Brian had never sorted out the titles or hierarchy of those in the church industry) was a tall, pale, balding man who said a few words about 'our sister Avril' as if he had known her all his life. Brian thought what a hypocrite, but he was only doing his job, and he supposed it comforted Arthur to hear Avril's name mentioned in a public place.

Passages were read from a softened down version of the Bible, too much mention of Jesus for Brian, though he supposed you had to expect it at a service for sending a dead body into the ground.

Everyone got back into their cars and drove a few hundred yards to the far end of the cemetery, lips of dull earth around an oblong hole, the box already in position. He had to remind himself that Avril's body lay inside. The wind blew colder, and clouds ran across the sky as if to bring news of rain before the ritual finished.

Arthur stood tall and dignified, his face looking raw, eyes as if unseeing, alone as only he could be. After the words 'ashes to ashes and dust to dust' (mud, more like it, not being in the desert for which the words were written) he picked up a handful of heavy soil from the spade given to him, and sent his last goodbye clattering onto the box. Others in turn did the same, the only part of the procedure that brought Brian close to tears. A vivid picture of Avril smiling and talking in her prime vanished when he stooped to lift a handful of soil from the ground, muttering farewell as he let it fall.

Arthur stood in the garden among the dead midwinter plants, staring as if to bring back all their colours after he and Avril had tended them into growth. Harold laid a hand around his

199

shoulders, and said something which made Arthur smile, and take his son's arm to come into the house.

Brian sipped his coffee, for the first time in years stirring sugar into it. Few people bothered with alcohol, as if it was out of place, but all were talking in the same old lingo, telling stories and reminiscing. He recalled a remark by Hannah Arendt that 'the homeland of the Jews is in their language', and being again among people he had grown up with, he realized that their idiom was his home base as well.

More people were at the house than had been at the funeral, because some neighbours had come in. Arthur looked as if a ponderous weight had been taken from his back now that the interment was over, but Brian realized that a year would need to elapse before he could be anything like himself.

Harold was telling them about driving to Calverton one winter's dusk, a northerly drizzle slewing against the windscreen of his white Mercedes van as he went over the Dorket Head crossroads. 'After so many houses on the edge of town you're suddenly on your own in the middle of nowhere. You all know where I mean. I went down the hill and the lane got narrower, or it seemed to, because there was hedges on either side. Then the drizzle changed to sleet, as if somebody was chucking it in buckets.'

To encourage him, a darkly clouded sky threw rain against the living room window. 'There's a sharp right hand bend, and after a few hundred yards another bend to the left. Then the lane goes down steep, through the wood.' He turned to Arthur: 'Then I saw her, as plain as I'm looking at you.'

Arthur nodded, and told him to get on with it.

'Are you sure you weren't sloshed?' Derek said.

'Not then I wasn't. I had to go slow, and put the main beams on. She came from the trees, right across my path. I couldn't believe it, but I had to, because she looked at me.

The fucking ponytail I wore in them days stood up on its hind leg. She had a white face, and big dark circles under her eyes. I thought she was going to do a header through the windscreen, she was that close. I shouted. Talk about panic, and I'm not like that. Screamed, more like it. I braked, and nearly hit a tree. Missed it by inches. Then I pressed on, but I was shaking like a leaf. I hadn't had anything to drink the night before either.'

'I can't believe in ghosts,' Ronald smiled

'So what was it?' Eileen said.

'Maybe she'd broken out of Mapperley Asylum,' Arthur suggested.

Harold's hands shook while lighting a cigarette. 'Say what you like. When I got to the village I delivered my packages. Then I had to go in the pub for a sit down and a drink, I was so shaken up. An old chokka at the bar asked why I was looking so white at the gills, and when I told him he laughed, his false teeth doing a dance from one side of his mouth to the other. "There's been a lot of accidents at that spot," he said, "but it's nothing to worry about. You've only seen the ghost. People do from time to time."

'Then he told me what happened about a hundred years ago. He said that just off the first bend of the lane was a place called Abbey House. The owners were abroad at the time, and the housekeeper was living in, with her twenty-year-old daughter. Anyway, on a winter's afternoon the mother took ill, didn't she? The girl put on her cloak and bonnet to go and get a doctor from the village.'

Everyone was quietly waiting to hear what happened next, as Harold, now knowing that he could take his time, reached the arm of a chair and shook ash from his cigarette. An increasing ferocity of rain reminded him to get on with it. 'She thought she'd take a short cut, down the fields and through the wood, and it was nearly dark when she got to the trees. She must have been wet through, because it was the worst afternoon you can imagine, and just as dark as it is today.

'Anyway, she went into the wood, but she never came out. She was found next day, or her body was. She had been raped and murdered. A shepherd found her, and they never got the one as did it. The old bloke told me all this in the pub. Funnily enough, he said, all the accidents at that spot had been to men drivers, never to women, though these days with everybody having long hair you'd think she'd make a mistake now and again. But she never did. He told me to be extra careful on the way back, because she'd be angry I'd got away, and might have another go. She wants to kill all the men she can. "Fuck that," I told him, "she ain't going to get another chance with me. She's blown it already. That was my lot." I drove the other way out of the village, went like a bat out of hell, flashing everybody in front to get to the A614. And I've never been that way since. I never will, either. I don't see why the daft bitch should want to do me in. It wasn't me as raped and killed her.'

Oliver stood by the mantelpiece to fill his cold pipe. 'Are you sure it wasn't an hallucination?'

'You bet I am. I wouldn't even go that way on a bright summer's day. I'm not a coward, but I was shit-scared. If she hadn't had such big mad eyes I might have fancied her, but she looked like trouble, so I didn't. I couldn't clear out fast enough. Anyway, it's you I love, ain't it, duck?' he said to Harriet.

She reached for his hand. 'And I love you. Luckily, I talked you into getting rid of that poncy long hair and buying a proper suit, not to mention pulling out that daft earring.'

'She nearly yanked my tab off over that.' He sounded in no way regretful. 'And I got a job as well, didn't I? I ain't had the sack yet, and I won't either.'

She was a tall girl, wearing slimline trousers and a green duffel coat, and Brian saw a resemblance between her and Avril that wouldn't be lost on Arthur. 'You'd better not get the push, either,' she said, 'or you've seen the last of me. I go to work, so you've got to. I don't need a house-husband yet. Not that I believe you ever saw that ghost. I've heard too many of your tales.'

'There you go, showing me up in public again.' He released her hand and straightened himself. 'If there's one thing I can't stand it's being called a liar. It ain't right. I tell everybody about the most terrifying experience of my life, and the one I love most says I didn't see it.'

'You're worse than Arthur.' Eileen helped Rachel to clear away cups and plates. 'I've never heard such a daft story.'

'I believe you: thousands wouldn't.'

He laughed. 'I don't care about the thousands. All I know is I'm telling the truth.'

'The place is on a hill that used to be an ancient camp,' Brian said. 'Or so it says on the map. Maybe there is something spooky about it.'

'I'm glad you believe me, Uncle Brian.' Harold reached for Harriet's hand. 'We've got to be off, though. I told the gaffer I'd do the afternoon shift, and he's starting to rely on me.' He embraced Arthur. 'You'll be all right, dad. We'll see you at the weekend, won't we, love?'

'I like your dad, even though he's wary about me because I'm a social worker.'

'Don't be so daft,' he said.

She kissed Arthur. 'We'll see you in a few days.'

'I thought Avril was marvellous,' Harold said. 'She was always good to me, and I'm dead sorry she's gone. She was one of the best. She was lovely and generous.'

Arthur, unable to speak, kissed his son, and let him go. He looked gravely after him, Brian noticed, as if he couldn't fully believe in Harold wearing a smart suit, and even regretted the lack of earrings, ponytail and jeans. Maybe Harold's settling down – if you could call it that – in some way disappointed Arthur, who saw him as ceasing to rebel against the toffee-nosed poxed-up loudmouthed swivel-eyed fuckpigs who had plagued him all his life and would continue to do so. It was no good thing when a bloke stopped wanting to dynamite the Houses of Parliament. Nor was it so good that Harold no longer looked as Avril had secretly liked to see him, a saddening factor because she couldn't see anybody from now on.

'It's like being in a submarine.' Arthur sat in the front seat, Derek's car smoothing its way through Burton Joyce and up the Trent Valley. 'Round here, the sky sucks water out of the river and spews it on the road.'

Brian, sitting behind with Eileen, thought he might create a character called Joyce Burton. She'd be a bit of a tartar, tall, statuesque, with red hair, and wearing little gold-rimmed glasses, an opinionated woman always convinced she was right, but causing mayhem wherever she poked her sharp nose, ending in bed with someone totally unsuitable at the end of each episode.

It was main beams on and all systems go, though plenty of cars came with panache and confidence from the other way. Derek turned on to a lane out of Thurgarton village, the car splashed as if trundling along a stream bed. 'What a rotten night,' Eileen said.

'It would be, today of all days,' Arthur said, in the gloom of the car. 'I'm glad the funeral's over.'

'We all are.' Derek swerved slightly, then righted. 'We'll be in a snug pub soon. It's quite close to the river.'

A car coming head on, no time or inclination to dip its beams, nearly drove them into the hedge. 'We could have been in the river just then,' Arthur said, everyone glad to hear him laugh. The all-enclosing dark after Bleasby was as if drifting through space. 'You'd better slow down. We don't want four more funerals. At least not for twenty years.'

'I'll be driving back,' Eileen said, as Derek slotted into a space at the car park. They ran through the rain into a comfortable lounge warmed by flame from real logs, a score of people at tables and by the bar; an aroma of meat and chips and mellow beer filling the air. 'Now we can warm our arses,' Derek said. 'Though let's get tanked up first.'

Brian stood by a table laid for supper, and let Eileen choose their seats. Arthur took his pew, as always without using his hands, looking straight before him, and when the pint came, elbow at an angle of ninety degrees, he lifted the rim to his mouth, and took the first long draught with movements, Brian recalled, exactly like those of his grandfather.

The pub was isolated in the Valley of the Trent, strong gusts across sodden meadows spattering rain to fill the dykes and runnels, driving swans into hiding and fish under wavelets on the river. 'I don't suppose the water ever comes over the lanes?' Brian said.

'If we do get stuck,' Arthur said, 'we'll be all right as long as the beer doesn't run out.' Avril had been with them last time, which he remembered, because his hand shook so much on lifting the glass for another go that he had to put it down.

'It'll be like that for a while.' Brian thought it better to mention than not. 'It'll take a good year to get over a blow like yours.' Eileen and Derek said comforting words as well, till diverted by a waitress asking what they wanted to eat.

No one had much to say during the meal. Brian went to the bar and replenished their pints, and Arthur was unable to finish his cutlets. 'It's the first time it's happened to me.'

Eileen put a hand on his shoulder. 'I wouldn't let it bother you.'

'Grandad Merton would have forgiven you,' Brian said.

'I expect he's looking down on us,' Arthur smiled.

'If he can he will,' Derek said.

'When I used to go to his house on Sunday morning,' Arthur recalled, 'grandma would set a place for my dinner. I once left something on my plate. It couldn't have been much, a bit of potato or some gristle. Grandad looked at it. He had his eye patch on, and the good eye glared as if it would burn right into me. So I swallowed what was left. He'd never let anybody leave a scrap of food on their plates.'

Brian remembered the copy of Mrs Beaton always on the sideboard. 'He didn't want you to insult grandma's cooking.'

'He needn't have bothered. Everything she brought to the table was good to eat.'

'I hope she's listening,' Eileen said.

He tampered with what remained of his meal. 'I never know what to think about that.'

Brian knew that right now he was wondering about Avril. 'Nobody does.'

'It's hard to imagine she isn't still looking.' Eileen had picked up Brian's thoughts, which she knew Arthur wanted to hear.

'Have one of these.' Derek pushed his case across, the top section off, five cigars like a magazine of ammunition waiting to be slotted into a rifle. Tears were in Arthur's eyes as he pulled one out, as if only a bullet for himself would soothe the anguish. Derek peeled off the cellophane, lit it, and put it into his hand. Laughter from the bar, but nothing to be done except stay calm and help their brother to endure. Every tortuous minute of the year to come would, at a quick calculation, need over half a million before the worst of the pain wore off.

His face was fluid of feature, uncertain in its age, and in a feat of control his hand was rigorously coaxed to normal. He looked into the distance as if hoping to get some comfort, not seeing the bar, or tables at which people were eating, or the farmer-like man who stopped on coming from the gents to stroke a big docile dog blocking his way. He turned back to them and gestured an apology for his weakness, as if to say I won't embarrass you anymore. Let's just carry on as if you didn't see anything.

'It's still throwing it down.' Derek glanced at the windows. 'I think February filldyke's got here in January. We might have to swim back.'

Arthur smiled, as if to face such mortal peril would be a pleasure. But whatever the weather, they were safe and warm and fed, and between puffs at his cigar he tackled the pint Brian set before him, listened to their chaff, returned some of it, and looked at the pretty waitress when they paid the bill, of forty-seven pounds made up to fifty because she had been so charming.

A waiter brought the receipt. 'I thought I'd let you know there's water on the lanes, so look out for it on the way back. A chap just came in and told us.'

They got into their coats. 'We'll take care,' Derek said.

Eileen coasted through the shallow floods, and even on the main road drove carefully under the rain, mindful that Arthur above all had to go on living.

FIFTEEN

Brian said to Jenny: 'Let's go to Matlock. The weather's miserable, but we'll be all right in the car.'

'Do you mean it?' – as if unable to believe he could suggest something so pleasant.

Every decision could be the wrong one, but he'd opened his mouth and it would be cruel to dim the light in her eyes, though in the old days she wouldn't have been shocked if he did. 'I wouldn't say it if I didn't.'

'I'd love to. I haven't been since I nearly went on the bike with you.'

'I was sorry about that,' he said, as if it was yesterday.

She didn't want him to be sorry. 'But I got to Matlock in the end, because you took me a month later on the train.'

He'd hoped she'd remember. 'Did I?'

'You know you did.'

'Now I do.'

'George always had to go the other way on his travels, to Skegness or Mablethorpe. He loved the sea.'

He hadn't come to hear about dead George. 'We'll get there by one, and have something to eat. You won't need to cook dinner today.'

She gathered the cups and saucers. 'Eunice was coming to see me, so I'd better phone and tell her I'm going out.' Laughter from the kitchen: 'I'm not letting on where he's taking me. Don't worry, he'll bring me back. You think we're going to run away together? I should say not. See you tomorrow, then. I'll tell you all about it.' Another laugh. 'Or I might not. I'll see you then, then.'

He held the umbrella over her to the car, and threw a couple of cardboard boxes into the back so that she could sit down. 'Which way do we go?' she wanted to know.

'We make for Cinderhill, get onto the A610, and head for Ambergate, through Langley Mill and Ripley.'

'I love them names.'

He turned for the main road, feeling strange having her by his side in a car, the girl he had so intimately known turned into an unfamiliar old woman. What he wanted he couldn't say, nor knew why he was taking her to Matlock, but there was no turning back, so he decided to enjoy it.

'I remember struggling up all the hills. It was so hard I didn't even feel good when it came to freewheeling down.'

Less traffic after the motorway turnoff, rain still splashing the windscreen. 'Do you want a cigarette?'

'I don't smoke, as a rule, though I will today. It's nice to puff on a fag now and again.'

He passed the packet. 'Light one for me as well.'

'George smoked a hundred a day sometimes. But you can understand that, can't you?'

He certainly could. 'I usually smoke cigars, though not too many.' The rain stopped as he drove up the gentle slope into Derbyshire, usually the opposite. 'Do you ever think of getting behind the wheel again?'

'Sometimes. I've got a licence, but a few years ago I had a near miss coming back from Skegness, and I haven't been brave enough to drive since.'

'You'd enjoy it, now there's less to look after. You won't have anymore near misses.'

'I might try next summer, roam around a bit.' Both at their ease, he was taking this old age pensioner out for the day. They were the same age, but he couldn't believe it, because there was no retirement for him, nor any pension either, since he had never bothered with stamps, though a private scheme was there to be milked if he stopped earning. 'What happened to you after we split up?'

She needed time to think, as he weaved through Langley Mill and went towards Ripley. 'It's going a long way back. Too far, maybe. We were different people then, weren't we?'

He shouldn't have asked. She might think he'd only brought her for that reason, and was taking advantage. 'True, yet we're still the same people. It's just that such a lot's happened to us.'

'We don't look the same,' she laughed. 'Anyway, about a year later, I had an affair, as they call it now, and I got pregnant. The man didn't want to know. He told me to get rid of it, and when I said I couldn't do such a thing he ran away. He was married, though I didn't know at the time. Gordon was his name.'

'It would be.' Yet he didn't want to denigrate someone she must have loved.

'He was a draughtsman. He got a job near Bristol, and took his family because he didn't want his wife to find out.'

'You didn't think of chasing her up and telling her?'

'There wasn't any point. He wouldn't have come back. I had the baby. You've met her. It's Eunice, and she's fifty now.'

'She wrote to me about the surprise party.'

'A couple of years later I met George, and when he said he loved me, and I told him about Eunice, he said it didn't matter. He would take her in, and she would be all right with him. And she was. He looked on her like one of his own, and

211

when I had six more she just blended in. So you can see how I had to care for him after the accident. Not that I thought I wouldn't, though I did sometimes wonder how long it was going to go on, mostly for his sake, especially near the end. Well, you would, wouldn't you?'

You would indeed. He thought about the tolerance and mutual affection between himself and the women he had been with, where it had always been a gamble as to who would flee first. Such signs as had been in the offing were mistaken for those of undying love which, as he well knew, never ran smooth.

'I feel a lot better now,' she said, 'even if the weather isn't very good. It's nice to come out, a real change from being stuck in the house.' She touched his arm as he overtook a gravel lorry on a few yards of dual carriageway. 'I never thought you would be driving me around in a car.'

'Nor did I.' He followed the white arrows, and got in front of the enormous lorry just before the road became a single lane, the perfect end if they were killed at the same moment, both so maimed they'd be shovelled into plastic bags rather than coffins, at least not divided in their deaths.

She pointed. 'You can see blue sky and a bit of sun over there.'

'I got God on the blower this morning and asked Him to make the weather good for us.'

'Did you know by then that you were going to take me out?'

'I thought about it, and hoped you wouldn't tell me to get lost.'

'Well, I didn't, did I?'

He never knew whether he was more alive while thinking, or while talking, but now he was glad to be talking as he threaded four traffic islands to get around Ripley, where he had once abandoned her.

212

'I know that after you left me,' she said, 'you married Pauline Bates, and when you came out of the air force you left her and your little boy, and went off to France.'

He began the winding descent to Ambergate, knowing it hadn't been like that. Pauline had told him to go, and he went. She had been seeing someone else while he was abroad, but to explain would sound like dodging whatever responsibility had been his.

'I met her one day while I was shopping, and she told me about it. Things don't often work, do they?'

'No use going into whose fault it was.' They went under the train bridge and on to Ambergate junction, the Hurt Arms Hotel facing the road like a sentinel, as it had done for more than a century. A furniture centre and a Little Chef on the opposite corner were recent additions. There was more traffic on the trunk route to Matlock, a road in the old days empty except for the odd army lorry.

'I didn't hear any more of you,' she said, 'till we met at the station when I was going to visit George in Sheffield. And when I called on your mother she told me you were working for television.'

The grey stone walls of Derbyshire gave a homely air, woods beyond Whatstandwell sleeving the road. He was reluctant to ask, in case she thought him wanting to tear her heart out and hold it up to the light: 'When we split up all those years ago, how long was it before you forgot me?'

'I had other things to think about. We were just kids, weren't we?'

He was glad the question hadn't disturbed her, as a similar one wouldn't have bothered him. 'Yes, but you were the first woman I had, and I did think about you now and again,' which was no lie, otherwise why was he driving her to Matlock?

213

'I've had lots of time to think,' she said, 'about how it might have worked for us but didn't.'

Traffic lights held them on red before the turning into Cromford. 'We'll have lunch at a pub here. They serve a good meal.' He parked by the kerb, and held her arm across a road in heavy use by gravel lorries.

'Is it a long way?' She took his hand as in the old days. 'I can't walk far.'

'It's just up this narrow street.'

'My legs feel like columns of lead. Maybe I should have them chopped off, then I wouldn't have to drag them everywhere. Even if I'd wanted to run away from George I wouldn't have got very far on legs like these.'

'You got a long way from me, though, didn't you?' Banter had always been used, either to find out what each other truly wanted, or what they actually meant to say. Sometimes it was used to irritate, at other times to amuse. More often than not if served its purpose, though not sufficiently to keep them together so many years ago.

'Yes,' she said, 'but you didn't chase me very far. When I said I wouldn't want to see you again you didn't even argue. I don't think I knew my mind. I did want to see you again. I cried myself to sleep that night.'

'I've never been one to do the right thing at the right time, either then or since.' Hardly an apology, but he hoped she picked up his enduring regret.

'Nor me, if it comes to that.' He held the door of the low eighteenth-century Boat Inn and followed her into the long ceilinged room with its beams and plain tables, an untended juke box facing the bar, and a few books arranged on the window sills. She took in everything with hardly a glance, he noticed. 'I suppose if we had done what you call the right thing we'd never have met up again like this, with you taking me out,' she said. 'I feel a real old fogey sometimes, but at others I don't feel a day over eighteen, especially – and I've got to say it – now that George has gone.' They laid their coats along a spare seat. 'It's nice and warm in here.'

Former girlfriends had found it quaint and picturesque. The place never changed. 'I'll go for the drinks, while you look at the menu.'

'What are you having?'

'A tomato juice: I'm driving.'

'Get me a gin and tonic, then. It's like being on holiday.'

A rugged farmer of the region standing at the bar remarked in a friendly voice that the weather wasn't much to write home about. 'But you and your wife will be all right in here.'

Brian wanted to say she wasn't his wife and never would have been. 'Yes, it's a snug place, right enough.'

He took the drinks back. 'Your tomato juice looks cold,' she said. 'You haven't even got Worcester in it.'

'That bloke at the bar thought you were my daughter.'

'A likely story.'

'Well, what are you going to have to eat?'

'Roast beef and all the trimmings.'

'Me too.' The young woman who took their orders had pale and pleasing features, a slender figure, and though not for him he recalled, while following her progress back to the bar, that a virgin was put into King David's bed to hold him back from dying.

'Do you know her?'

'I've seen her before. Knock that back, and I'll get you another.'

'Are you plying me with alcohol?'

'I wouldn't get far with a couple of those.'

'I don't want to do anything foolish.'

Maybe she had when she first got pregnant. 'I can't see that happening.'

'Nor me,' she laughed. 'Whatever I did that was daft in my life didn't need drink to make me do it. Perhaps if I had been drunk I wouldn't have been so stupid.'

'That goes for us all.'

'You never know why you do anything, but when you've done it you're stuck. I often wish I could turn the clock back.'

'After I left you,' he said, 'I got married to Pauline because she was pregnant. A shotgun wedding, though no one needed to point the barrel at me.'

'The one who got me pregnant ran away.'

'It might have been worse if he'd stayed behind.'

'I loved him enough for it not to matter. But you did the right thing by Pauline.'

'And look where it got me. Maybe I should have bolted as well. It wouldn't have been any worse for either of us.'

'You did right, because if you'd got me pregnant we would have stayed together. And what would have happened then?'

'Who can tell?'

'You can imagine, though. You can dream. I wouldn't have married George, would I? You and me might still be married.'

As far into sincerity as he'd ever strayed, he was nevertheless glad to see the large platters set before them. 'It's possible.'

She unwrapped the cutlery from its paper napkin. 'I like to think so.'

'And so do I.'

'Rain always makes me hungry, and I love Yorkshire pudding.' She took a bit of this and a scoop of that, but such a laden platter dulled his appetite. He established a bridgehead, and reduced the greens, the peas and carrots, the roast potatoes, Yorkshire pudding, and occasional reinforcement of the meat as if on a military campaign.

'I like eating something I don't have to cook.' She gazed along the opposite line of tables. 'I dreamed a lot during all those years caring for George.'

'What about?'

'One thing and another.'

'That's not saying much.'

'It's harder to remember day dreams than night dreams. They helped me to keep going, and while I was dreaming I just wasn't there. I was somewhere else. I would dream that George wasn't George, that he had two legs and was somebody else, and could walk wherever he liked. After we bumped into each other on the station platform I dreamed that George wasn't George, and that the somebody he was was you. The best thing that ever happened to me was that I met you before getting on that train.'

'I can see how hard things were.'

'You can't. Nobody can, though I could never say so. I can now it's all over, but I couldn't at the time. You can never complain. People don't want to hear, and you can't blame them, because neither do I.'

He would never see such a smile again, brought on by understanding her more than he ever had or that anyone ever could, a smile meant for him alone, which came as lightning burrowing into his flesh for evermore.

He leaned across to wipe the tears on her cheeks with the fresh handkerchief always in his lapel pocket. She deserved a place in the Official History of the World, an impossible paragraph to write since too many would be competing for space.

Her distress burned into him, to put out the tears before they could flow from his eyes, a connection he had no option but to allow, even if he was destroyed as he deserved. Her generous and friendly smile was shaped by long endurance, was offered to what in him was able to receive it, telling him that he couldn't have stayed long with a person of such quality, would have been no more use to her than George, an emotional rather than an actual cripple, who would have released her sooner because at least he had legs. 'You did more than was expected.'

'Your mother was nice to me when I went to see her. She laid out a good tea while I talked my heart out. I didn't call often, because I couldn't always get somebody to sit with George, but it was good to get rid of what was on my mind. It was the pressure of having to care for him every minute of the day and night, so I had to talk about it, though maybe I didn't think there was all that much pressure at the time.'

'What sort of dessert would you like?' He picked up the menu card. 'There's hot apple pie and custard. Then we can have a cup of coffee.'

'I don't think I could eat a pudding. Well, maybe I will,' as if it was a novelty to have a decision made for her. 'I can't let you eat on your own.'

When the waitress brought his coffee, and one with milk for her, she said: 'I don't know how you can drink it black, and with no sugar.'

'The dessert sweetened it.'

'Is it to keep thin?'

'I don't need to.'

'I can see that. But I've got a sweet tooth.'

'You don't get fat, either,' he said. 'Maybe it's because of our early years in the factories. When we've done we'll have a look around Matlock Bath.'

'It might bring back memories,' she said lightly. 'We came on the train. And you said you didn't remember!'

'I do now. I took you rowing on the river.'

'You nearly got us caught in the weir.'

'I wanted to give you some excitement. I also remember when I came on the bike, and you were so tired I left you in Ripley. I've never liked that place since.'

'You can't blame Ripley. I wasn't well. I was having my period.'

'You should have told me.'

'You might have guessed. Anyway, I didn't want to spoil it for you. On the way home I had an icecream in Eastwood. I went to bed with a hot-water bottle in the afternoon because my back ached.'

He wondered why they'd waited so long to talk openly. They used to chat like two monkeys, yet conveyed nothing important. He held up her coat, as he always did. An odour of rain on the cloth reminded him of former days. 'That was cheap,' she said, as he paid the bill.

To spend more at the best hotel might have been as exotic an experience to her as the Boat Inn was for his girlfriend from London, though her remark only meant what it said, no troubling reverberations. He saw how relaxed life would have been with her, instead of the eternal confrontations with other women. After a few years, however, she might have turned just as vitriolic, out of self-preservation – though decades of George's bad temper hadn't crushed her.

He parked by the parade of cafés, and shops selling the eternal fishing tackle, and souvenirs for trippers, technicolored gewgaws for the mantelshelf, or the scrapheap soon enough.

'Byron thought this place was as beautiful as anywhere in Switzerland,' he said, seeing her gaze at the wooded cliffs.

'I've never been there, so I wouldn't know. I suppose you have, though?'

'A couple of times. Ruskin said the valley was ruined by too many trippers.'

'People have got to have somewhere to go. And there aren't many here at the moment.'

'Things are closed up until spring, so I can't take you on the river.'

'It's too cold for that,' she said. 'You can do it another time.'

He couldn't think when that would be, there being little more to know about her, or that he could know about her, wondering what the connection was between them, as if they'd lived too long, and should stop being curious about what they had done in the misty days of long ago. They had been through too much to need the disturbance, yet he couldn't avoid an inexplicable fondness for his first love, and for himself as he might have been, as if bringing her on the jaunt had turned him back into a feckless youth.

A coat pocket warmed her hand, his damp from closing the car door as they left the main road and walked a cobbled track towards the Heights of Abraham. 'You get a wonderful view from there,' the gradient no trouble for him, taking her arm as if to help her. 'And there's a café at the top.'

'I can't make it.' She stopped. 'Well, I could by tomorrow morning.' Mist moved between the houses, plumes of coal smoke bending from the chimneys. 'It's starting to rain, and I've left my umbrella in the car. You go up, and I'll wait by the road.'

All of life's anguish had taught him that she was too old a friend to be abandoned a second time and in the rain. 'There's a comfortable place in the town where we can have a pot of tea.'

'I do feel good,' she said, when he had ordered from the waitress. 'And being with you makes it even better.'

'Do you ever think of the future?'

'Why should I?' She poured his tea.

'I don't know if you don't know. I thought everybody did from time to time.'

'I go on living, so what do I want to think about the future for?'

'Don't you dream of doing something now that you're free?'

'I don't know what you mean by free. But I'll never get married again, that's for sure.'

'I didn't mean that.'

'I didn't think you was asking me,' she laughed. 'You mean like going on a world cruise? I wouldn't want to even if I could afford it. I've got enough to live on, and there's my family to think about.'

'I met a few at the party. And Ronald and Sylvia were at Avril's funeral.'

'Yes, Ronald didn't like the way you looked at Sylvia.'

'I thought she was interesting.'

'I'm only joking. He said what a nice chap you were, and how different he would have been if we'd had him. But my family keeps me up to the mark, so what more do I want?'

Hard to imagine. The comfort and security of helping the species along had never been part of his purpose, plenty of others to take care of that, and any good people the world couldn't do without would soon be replaced.

She drank her tea halfway down the cup. 'Yes, I've been lucky with my family.'

'You weren't with George.'

'No, but it balances out. I used to wonder if it did, but I see now that it does.' She smiled. 'I've never talked to anyone like this before.'

'You used to call on my mother.'

'It wasn't the same.'

'It's because I'm asking you.'

'I wouldn't answer if I didn't want to.'

She wasn't telling anything he couldn't already know, but he needed to find out what had kept her going with George, what were her thoughts after tucking him into his special bed at night and she was on her own in the dark, what had been in her mind when, with his cripple's petulance, he had struck her as quick as a cobra across the face on her leaning down with a weary tenderness to see to him. He wanted to get to those sacred springs and learn more about her noble qualities because she had been his first love. By himself he could only put together clues, never sure how close he was to understanding.

By knowing his brothers as well as he knew himself, by listening to their families and friends, by all he heard from people in the pubs, by using the packed experience of his childhood and youth – because wherever he had lived and however much he had changed – he still belonged with them and could therefore understand Jenny without the need to rake her soul over the coals of past suffering. First love had put him in sympathy with everything to do with her, because they had been through a courtship that was still accessible to both.

If Pauline or Jane had been crushed in a motor accident would he have spent his life looking after them? Such sacrifice would hardly have been expected. After the shock habit took over and you lived from day to day, crushed with pity, life changing until accustomed to the routine of living without hope.

In a restaurant he always placed the woman so that she could see on to the street, then he would watch her features as she observed whoever went by. He smiled on knowing she was about to say:

'A penny for your thoughts.'

'I haven't got any.'

She looked towards the window, as if a friend might look in and see her with her first love. 'That's what you always said.'

'Was it? All right, I'll tell you.'

'You said that, as well, after I said "That's what you always say." I can't believe it.'

'I told you people don't change. But I was thinking about you. Who else, on such a day?'

'You've got to tell me, then.'

'I was wondering how much I really knew you.'

'And how much do you think you do?'

He had nothing to lose by lying, but how much of a lie it would turn out to be he would never know. 'More than anyone else. And you know me more than anybody else you know.'

'I think you're daft. I don't think there's all that much to know about me.' She stopped her amusement from turning into a laugh. 'Somebody with more thought in their head wouldn't have done what I did. In any case I'm not hard to know, so you wouldn't be claiming much.'

'I make my living by putting words into people's mouths.'

'You're lucky, being able to do that. And clever, I suppose. Not everybody can. If we'd been married you'd have got fed up with me in no time.'

'Not if you'd had half a dozen kids.' He would have made sure she didn't, though it would have been cruel leaving her with no family.

She was enjoying the game. 'If you could know all about me that easily, you would. You'd have packed me in and gone off on your own, or with somebody else.'

'I told you you knew everything about me.'

'Well, I'm not that dense.'

'I never thought you were.'

'George often did, but I suppose he had a right to.'

223

'Nobody with a head on their shoulders would say such a thing.'

'He wouldn't wear anything when we were in bed together, and then he grumbled when I got pregnant. But I suppose every man would.'

'It sounds unreasonable.'

'I couldn't tell him that.'

'Why not?'

'He might have clocked me. He did now and again, though there wasn't too much of it. I wouldn't have put up with that. We got along all right, and I liked him most of the time. He was a cheerful sort, before his accident.' She looked as if at last interested in someone walking along the pavement. 'You don't say much about yourself. Your life's been a mix-up, according to what your mother said.'

He could just see them, having a head to head natter. 'I'll get us another pot of tea, and some cake.'

'I had that big dinner, but the kids tell me I never get fat because I burn it all up inside.'

'The same with me. I eat like a horse, and never put weight on.' He signalled the waitress. 'We'll have a proper tea, with scones and honey.'

'I'll have jam with mine. Honey's too sweet.'

'You want to know about me?' The spread was laid before them. 'So do I. I always have. I only know what happened, and never what any of it meant. I don't think I have the sort of answers you want. Things happened too fast for me to learn much. Yet I knew very well what was going on but was too idle and self-centred to be able to learn, or to control myself. Bismarck said it was better to learn from other people's mistakes, but I never could.'

'It sounds sensible. Not that I think anybody else ever could, either.' She leaned forward to touch his hand, a

224

motherly gesture he could have done without. 'You got on all right, though, by the look of it.'

He certainly had. As Arthur reminded him, he had clothes on his back, all the food he wanted, a roof over his head, a car to drive around in, and he could spend without thinking too much about it. Some of his life had been difficult, but to tell her would be meaningless. 'There's not much I can say. You know me well enough as it is.'

'I don't think I do, otherwise we wouldn't be talking like two separate people. I don't know anything about your life. I can't imagine it, even if you tell me. We're strangers, though that's what makes it nice being with you, because you don't want to put one over on me. And if I'd really known you early on you might not have left me. I'd have been able to stop you.'

'Why didn't you? You knew me well enough. We split up. I married Pauline, which was a disaster. Later on, I had a few affairs, and then met an interesting and pleasant woman, as I thought, who came from Lichfield, though when I met her in London you wouldn't have known. We were married for twelve years, till I read a bundle of my wife's letters, and realized there was more than a chance my daughter wasn't my own. When I tackled her about it she said her womb was her own to do what she liked with. So I left her. I'd brought the girl up as well. She was eleven when I lit off, but I kept sending her money to go through university.'

'It was good to do that for her. Our Eunice wasn't George's, but he treated her like one of his own. I have to say that for him.'

'Maybe I shouldn't have let my first marriage go. We'd both had affairs, so neither of us could complain, though we fought like cat and dog about them. It livened our existences, and kept us together longer than it should. But to bring a kid into

225

the family that she knew couldn't be mine didn't endear me to her. After that I had a few years on my own, and had what girlfriends I wanted.'

'I expect they grow on trees in London.'

He smiled. 'Trees for men to hang themselves on. I got married again, and the couple of kids we had were surely mine. That lasted until two years ago, when she went off to become an art historian.'

'You wouldn't get married again, would you?'

'No. I've done enough damage already.'

'I like being on my own,' she said. 'Life's good now, I don't mind admitting. Eunice said the other day: "You've earned your peace, mam." "Perhaps I have," I told her, "but if I looked at it that way it wouldn't be worth having gone through so much trouble."'

He went to the toilet, and paid at the desk before returning to the table. 'I'd like to dock at Arthur's before it gets dark.'

'I'm ready, though there'll be plenty of daylight left.'

The way back was always shorter, traffic lights open at the Cromford turn-off, and no wait at the Whatstandwell bridge. He drove on dipped beams through the rain to Ambergate. 'The River Amber joins the Derwent here, so I suppose that's how the place gets its name.'

'You learned a lot,' she said.

'Facts are easy. You get them out of any book. But knowing something useful is quite different.'

'Can you make jam?'

'I'd burn it.'

'Can you knit?'

'Only knots.'

'Can you cook?'

'Enough to stop myself starving.'

'I know a few things you don't know, then.'

226

They laughed. 'You certainly do,' he said. He drove over the Erewash and along the dual carriageway back into Nottinghamshire, an area so familiar from childhood and youth it seemed he'd never been away. He certainly had no other place to come back to, yet knew that if he stayed more than three days a panic to travel overwhelmed him, to move and keep on going, especially in winter when dusk dimmed the countryside as if all life on the planet was draining away. He only belonged when in the kitchen with Arthur, or at Derek's and Eileen's, lights on and curtains drawn, bottles on the table and the smell of dinner cooking, talk crackling like squibs on Bonfire Night.

An enormous greyblack cloud reared in front. 'I'd like another fag, duck,' she said. 'It's nice to have one in the car.'

'It's not fashionable to smoke.' He passed the usual two, and she lit one for him.

'I never was fashionable, was I?'

'Nor me,' he said.

'Not many people are. Not round here they aren't. They just do what they want to do.'

A girlfriend once said that smoking defined the social class you belonged to. If you smoked, she said, you were working class. He replied that if such was the case he would join a cigar club, except that he never joined anything, being of no class at all, which shut her up. He made the affair so difficult that she broke off the relationship, a more kindly system which let her think she had abandoned him.

He had done the same with Jenny early on, proving that you never change, only perfect the most advantageous techniques to live by.

He parked by the house. 'I'll see you inside.' The rain had stopped, daylight still, even a glisten of sun from behind a cloud. A small grey bird flew like a fighter plane by the chimney. He noted its marks and colours, then realized that Avril wouldn't be able to tell him what it was.

He followed her into the living room, noticing that the plaster birds had been taken away, the wall blank. 'I've had a wonderful day,' she said, 'but I always feel good when I get back home.'

He saw again the face of an old woman in her well lit room. 'It was a real pleasure being in Matlock with you.'

'Will you stay for a cup of tea?'

'No, thanks a lot. I want to see that Arthur's getting on all right.'

'I was ever so sorry about that. He must be having a rotten time. You'd better go, then, or he'll be worried about you. Don't forget to give him my love.' She took his hand, out of regret for happiness lost, or for one she'd never had but felt some sign of today. 'Come and see me any time you like.'

'I will. I call on Arthur more often now that Avril's dead.'

'I'm sure he appreciates it. You're a good brother, anyway.'

'I can't be anything else.' Which he supposed couldn't be entirely true.

'I'll phone Eunice and let her know I'm back.'

'We don't want her to think I've hauled you off to Gretna Green!'

'She'd love to hear that, I expect.'

Hard to say whether he went to her or she to him, but they stood in the middle of the room for a kiss which had all the passion of their early meetings. The only excuse he could find for not getting her to the floor and fucking her was that the scorched infant he suddenly turned into wouldn't allow him to get a hard on, and when one came he saw panic on her face in case he tried. It was equally hard to know who broke away first, their pressing lips no more, after all, than a sign of days long gone.

SIXTEEN

Near the end of May he was on his way to see Arthur for the fifth time since the funeral. On the phone every few days, Brian never had much to say but Arthur always made sure there was something, even if only to prove he was coming out of the slough and back into daylight. And if he wasn't he would never admit it.

'She still seems to be in the house. I think of something, and get up to tell her, then I find she's not there. The thing is, we did everything together. I saw Oliver the other day and he offered to bring some apples in the autumn, but I told him not to bother. I'll never be able to cut up apples again. There's a few jars in the deep-freeze, but I'll eat them when I can. It'd be a shame to let them rot.'

He steered into the inner lane so as not to miss the A606 turn-off. When he was pole-axed by the flu Arthur advised him to get some antibiotics. 'You're not as young as you used to be. I always have a jab before the winter, and then I don't get the flu. So make sure the doctor gives you one next year, or I'll thump you!'

He had written letters, sent him books and magazines. 'Reading a lot takes my mind off things,' Arthur said, 'so it's good you keep feeding me interesting stuff.'

'If I enjoy it I know you will.'

'I finished *A Scrap of Time*, and now I'm about a third

through *Dreadnought*. That'll keep me going a few weeks. The trouble is it's hard to sleep. In the day things aren't so bad, but when it gets dark and I draw the curtains, that's when it hits me.'

'I'm sorry to hear it.'

'Not much to be done.'

'We can only hope things'll get better.'

'They're OK already. I took all the curtains down yesterday, and during the night I put 'em in the washing machine. It don't cost so much electricity if you do it then. This morning I hung 'em out in the garden, and they got dry just before it rained. Now I'm hanging 'em back at the windows. Last night when I was making supper I spilled frozen peas all over the floor. I thought fuck it,' he laughed, 'I can't be bothered to pick 'em up one by one on my hands and knees, so I just hoovered them up. It worked a treat. The vacuum cleaner had mushy peas for supper!'

'Do you eat a hot meal every day?'

'You bet I do. I can look after myself.'

Traffic was slack when he turned off the Great Arterial, a restful drive between woods and fields to the large car park by Rutland Water. He slotted in a pound coin and put his ticket under the windscreen for a half-hour's relaxation before going on to Nottingham, then descended the curving macadam track to a toilet complex. The sombre bark of a chainsaw from the trees stabbed at the silence, a rural noise never heard by Virgil.

At one o'clock it was time for a chorizo sandwich, and to broach the flask of black coffee cooling by the brake handle so that it wouldn't scald his lips. Through the trees that looked as if they had been scraped and sanded a tug-boat cruised to some anchorage he couldn't see, the opposite shore green except for a field of yellow rape whose freshness was gone, richer pastures squaring it in. Fat crows by the shore enjoyed their morsels as much as he relished his sandwiches.

On previous visits he had taken Arthur to Matlock, where he had never been with Avril, so he couldn't be reminded of her. They ate an ample platter of good Derbyshire lamb at the Boat Inn, such a meal that Arthur didn't need to cook for them in the evening. After a cold supper he slotted in a video about the Jews of Paris at Drancy concentration camp. 'Why didn't they get every single fucking German after the war who'd been responsible and make them pay for what they'd done?' Arthur said. 'I wouldn't have rested if I'd survived. I'd have got them one by one, given them the pasting of their lives, then shot them in both feet and left them bleeding to death. Hanging would have been too good.'

Next day they called on Jenny, and Arthur remarked on how much better she looked than at the funeral, especially her legs, which were not so swollen because she had, as they were told, seen the doctor and been given pills.

A son, daughter and two young children were there, but Jenny sitting as if even now subdued by having looked after George for so many years. 'But then, she's always been a quiet person,' Arthur said, 'and difficult to know.'

The steamboat wandered like a lost soul, as if not knowing where to berth. Black at the base, superstructure white, nobody was on the top deck due to a chill wind. They sat in the saloon, bored but comfortable, till the captain made up his mind and edged his vessel towards the jetty close to the car park.

A woman stood between the trees looking at the water. He named her Edith Weston, after the nearby village. Tallish and slim, she wore dark slacks, a windcheater, a white blouse, and had short hair. He noted well cared for teeth and a fresh complexion when she walked to a small maroon car parked

231

in the next row. Seeming pleased with herself after gazing at the water (though the wind had been sharp, and she had no more time to spare) she sat in the car and looked at a magazine through rimless gold-sided glasses, sipping from a can and nibbling a bar of chocolate. He imagined shapely legs when she took off her slacks and showed the whitest cotton knickers.

On looking again she was no longer there, had finished her snack and driven away, though on what errand, whether to husband or lover or business, he couldn't say, Edith Weston gone forever and leaving a pain at his heart she would never know about.

Stories came out of imaginary confrontations, mental wanderings into realms more pleasant than the one he was in when alone. Encounters turned violent when he sensed assaults on his dignity: 'What did you say? Who the fuck do you think you are?' – in his earlier life no need to curb the forked lightning of his fists.

Interior pictorial activity reinforced his cool Merton aspect. Verbal slambacks, laced with rehearsed slanders that no so-called civilized opponent could equal (once he was forced into speech) defended psychic territory valid to himself, the significance of an event not obvious until even twenty years had gone by, when he would realize too late the damage that had been done.

He drove to the main road, and in Oakham got into the wrong lane for Melton Mowbray. Someone behind flashed him on his way, as he himself had often done, and halfway up the hill he realized that it must have been Edith Weston, but because she had turned in another direction he couldn't pursue her to give thanks, and chat to her, cajole her phone number, find a way to see her again, arrange a clandestine weekend in some remote hotel in East Anglia.

The rolling wolds of Rutland and Leicestershire were familiar from cycling trips on Sundays, his body still sluggish after sessions with Jenny on Saturday night, and his spirit renewing before Monday morning's start in the factory. He turned onto the Fosse Way so as to outflank Nottingham from the east, make the familiar indirect approach to Arthur's.

Ever since he'd had a car, whether married or not, whether he had a girlfriend or was living by himself on Vinegar Hill, he kept material in the boot with the notion of driving away at half a day's notice, and living on the road for as long as life and money lasted – a motorized tramp, no less.

He would drive to Rumania or Russia, or perhaps not to Rumania and Russia till he had done with Spain and Portugal, taking in Italy and Sicily before Rumania and Bulgaria, then into the Ukraine and Russia, to see if he could drive to Siberia and Turkestan, with enough fluid cash in his account, and his little leather satchel or credit cards. The more inches on the map, the greater the chance of getting away from himself. His passport was always up to date, though he occasionally panicked that it might not be, and pulled into the next layby or petrol station to fumble through his wallet.

The inventory of equipment and supplies was such that Lepporello would have run out of foolscap, and on boring stretches of mainroad or motorway he ticked each item, knowing that in one box was a highway atlas of Europe, with Blue Guides for civilized places and Lonely Planets for the rough. Treating the car as his desert island, there was a King James' Bible, the single volume Shakespeare, a dictionary, Herbert Read's poetry and prose anthology for soldiers in World War Two called *The Knapsack*, and the stubby little *SAS Survival Guide*.

He'd make sure there was a radio with short wave and

plenty of spare batteries, in case he felt a pang to know whether the world was still going, or even to hear the current equivalent of the Goon Show, should he be so lucky, which would be little different to the news.

A supply of Partagas cigars would create a satisfying cloud of solo bonhomie in the evening, or send mosquitoes away coughing fit to die if they strayed too close. (Mustn't forget half a dozen boxes of matches.) The serpentine tubes of a water purifying kit, which he didn't know how to use but hoped would serve him well when he stopped at dusk by a scum surfaced pond to make safe liquid for a brew up was also carried.

Once a year he put up the Marechal bivouac tent and crawled in with a flashlight to be certain the moths hadn't got their incisors into its canvas, a tent he had used years ago on taking his children camping in the New Forest. A safari bed that fitted inside would also go in the car.

A pocket barometer would warn of foul weather, and combine as an altimeter to tell the height of Dracula's castle while exploring the Carpathian Alps, though scientific observations wouldn't distract him long enough for a vampire bat to lock on to his throat because he'd wear a woollen scarf and a string of fresh garlic around his neck.

A compass was necessary in case he had to abandon the car and make his way over desolate moors, or go through a ride-less fairy tale forest, and beam onto the nearest small town where a snug hostelry smelling of delicious roast meat (a nubile young serving girl to welcome him in the doorway) would glow from all windows in the main square.

Should he cross a desert other than the one in himself a thermometer would measure the heat of his heart before it burst. A pair of binoculars would pick out distant figures homing towards him with malign intent, or would scan the

234

heavenly meadows of a Shangri-La he'd always hoped to make real from his dreams.

With an electronic calculator and pamphlet of mathematical formulae he would reckon how far he had travelled after going round and round in the same circle, during hours of loneliness when he would wonder why the hell he was where he was. Or he could actuarially predict the time remaining which he had to live, or tell how much money was left for his self-indulgent wanderings, and even how many miles and kilometres back to Calais. Otherwise the calculator could pass the hours (having finished the Bible three times and Shakespeare twice) while stranded by flood or snowfall in some outlandish candle-lit flea-bitten caravanserai of the Balkans.

A camping stove slotted neatly into its metal container would fry bacon-egg-sausage in the peace that may or may not pass the hallmark of understanding in the tent at evening, followed by coffee and powdered milk under a storm lamp to read by when on his last nightstop before the Coast of Bohemia. Or he could use the signalling attachment should he be stricken by a strangulating hernia, a massive cardiac arrest, snake bite or broken limb.

For sustenance in emergencies, if all shops were shut or empty, and there was no room at the inn when he wanted a bath, he stored (apart from soap) half a dozen tins of sardines and anchovies, cans of baked beans and corned beef, steam puddings and a tin of pineapple chunks, some marmalade, packets of soup, a jar of Mrs Ellswood's gherkins – and a Leatherman tool to get everything open. Every so often he took the supplies into his flat to check the sell-by dates, to replace any that had elapsed or were about to.

Eating-irons and a tin plate were wrapped in a tea towel, with a metal mug, a small kettle, a teapot, and a mess-tin kit picked up from Laurence Corner. Rolled blankets, sheets and a sleeping bag, a spare sweater, oilskin trousers, wellingtons (green) and a long cape, would keep him warm and dry in the worst of weather.

Tangled jump leads would help to rescue anyone whose car battery was spent, preferably a young woman with the magic of Edith Weston (maybe the very woman herself) stranded by the roadside, and his expertise would be so appreciated that she would accept his offer of dinner at the next town, and they would spend the night having delicious sex in bed.

On the other hand the jump leads might be useful in the frosts of Transylvania, or the damps of the Danube Delta, should his own car be as uncooperative in coming to life as a dead dog, and he shivering for an hour before a motorist stopped and transferred enough power to get him back on the road.

A toolkit, already stowed, included an axe sharpened by Arthur, in case he ran out of camping gas and needed to chop wood for a fire on which to cook his supper and keep the wolves away if stranded in a forest. An entrenching tool would dig the wheels out of sand or snow, or be used for self-defence against violent peasants when he slaughtered a gaggle of poultry driving through a village or, slithering along a road of grey mud, hit and killed a grey donkey.

Cartons of cigarettes from the duty free were to hand out as gifts in repayment for minor favours when money would be insulting or the local currency worthless. A brace of full whisky bottles lodged in a box would raise the spirits, toast a meeting, repay hospitality, or get him quietly sozzled over supper before zipping up the entrance to his tent and saying goodnight to the world and himself, the entrenching tool at his feet in case animal or human marauder thought to disturb him.

Or maybe his car would be the only one in the main square of some Moldavian backwater and, within locked doors of the car, he would make his way through both bottles in good old English being-abroad style, then stagger out blind drunk for a bit of mayhem among the local riff-raff or gilded youth, a seventy-year-old in the lock-up putting the town into *The Guinness Book of Records.*

Fitting into two or three cardboard boxes, such supplies took up little space in the ample back of his estate, the list endlessly checked, a hand-held tape recorder-notebook on the spare seat should anything need to be added.

He could set out for the mainland and support himself on the road for as many months as he cared to take, with the assurance that if the world ended while on his travels there was enough material on board to begin civilization all over again. With such foresight, why hadn't he so far done it? One day he surely would, become one of the landboat people in a vehicle that might crash but not sink.

SEVENTEEN

Beyond Saxondale Crossing Brian turned left for Lowdham, over the River Trent yet again, a glance at wide and placid water, dull grey today, always a sign of getting home whichever of the four bridges he went over.

He walked through drizzle to the front door and shouted in his roughest voice: 'I've come to collect the rent!'

'Mam isn't in,' Arthur bawled, 'so fuck off, and see if you can do better next door.' He was no longer the pitprop he'd been as a young man, but still straightbacked and alert, more middle-aged than elderly, an aspect helped by short hair and a clean shave.

They embraced in the hallway. 'You look so well I thought I'd come to the wrong house.'

'Well, it's no use crying, is it? It's funny, though, I still imagine her voice in the next room, that she's dozing over her sewing machine, or I'm waiting for her to come back from the supermarket.'

'It's not half a year yet, don't forget.'

Arthur turned to six-year-old Philip who sat at the table in the clean kitchen. 'He's Mary and Jonah's lad. Aren't you, young boggerlugs?' He lifted him off the chair, held him to the light. 'Look at him! A bleddy great cannonball with curly hair on top!'

'Put me down, grandad. And don't swear. I'm not a boggerlugs.'

'They dumped him on me, to go shopping, but they should be back soon.'

Brian, unseen, closed a pound coin into each hand, and held both towards Philip, back at the table with his book. 'There's a pound in one of these hands, and if you guess which one it's in, you can keep it.'

Philip stood, a finger moving over one and then the other as if his future depended on the choice.

'Don't take all day,' Arthur said, 'or he'll put it back and spend it in the pub tonight.'

Philip touched a knuckle, then smiled at his luck, and cried out with pleasure when Brian opened the other hand as well. He put the two pounds in his pocket. 'Now you can finish telling me that story, grandad.'

Arthur pulled him onto his knee. 'But where were we?'

'That monster-man was going up the dark staircase.'

'So he was. He was following this little woolly haired six-year-old nipper called Sabbut Handley up the mildewed slippery steps, and daft young Sabbut didn't know Boris the Frankenstein was only a few steps behind as he went higher up the tower. He didn't hear him, though if you ask me, the little bogger had no sense poking his button nose where he shouldn't have done. Boris put a foot down every time Sabbut did, so the poor lad didn't hear that somebody was right behind.'

'Well, he wouldn't, would he, grandad?'

'No, he wouldn't, but then he soon wished he had heard him, because when he got to the top of the tower lightning was flashing all over the mountains, and thunder was booming like big guns in a war, and he felt bits of icy rain coming at his daft little face.'

He lowered his voice to an ominous growl, Philip's face turning paler with, Brian thought, simulated fright. 'A hand went around his neck, and young Sabbut didn't know whose it was. He was just about to say "Hey, what the bleddy hell do you think you're up to?" when he heard a scream from Boris, because Boris hadn't heard somebody coming up behind *him*, and putting a foot down everytime *he* did.

'The man behind Boris was little Sabbut's father, who'd come out looking for him. His father was a champion heavyweight boxer, and he gave Boris a terrible pasting, the biggest fight you ever saw, blood all over the place. He went hurtling over the wall, and hit the boulders a hundred feet below. It looked like he'd broken every bone in his body, because he just lay there moaning, though I don't suppose we've heard the last of him.

'Mr Handley lifted careless little Sabbut on to his shoulders, and took him back to the cottage they lived in, where they had cream buns for tea, sitting by a blazing fire. Sabbut's mam was ever so glad to see them safe and sound. And that's the end.'

'Oh, grandad, that was smashing. Tell me another story. I want another.'

Arthur kissed the top of his head. 'I'll think one up for next time. I've got to mash the tea now, or Brian'll die of thirst.'

Philip's lips went down, then he smiled. 'When mam and dad come I'll go back home and play with the computer.'

'Are you on e-mail yet?' Brian asked.

'No, but dad says he's going to fix it all up for my birthday. I'll only believe it when I see it, though.'

'He always keeps his promises, don't he?' Arthur said. 'Dads always do.'

'Well, I've still got to see it, haven't I?'

Arthur swung him. 'You're the sharpest little sharpshit, and I don't know what we're going to do with you.'

241

'Chop me up for firewood!' he screamed.

He set him on a chair and turned to Brian. 'He'll be all right, won't he?'

'I'm glad to see he's reading.'

'He always is. Can't keep him away from it.' The bell sounded, and Arthur let in Jonah and Mary, both in too much of a hurry to wait for the offered tea. 'We won't be able to get Philip in the car,' Jonah said. 'It's jammed with shopping. You'll have to stay with Arthur.'

'Oh yes! He can tuck me up like last time, and tell me another story.'

'Then again,' Jonah winked, 'we might tie him on the luggage rack, if you can find a bit of old rope.'

Mary took Philip's hand. 'Let's get you home. We bought some cupcakes for tea, so's we won't have to stop at a cob shop.' He went out on his father's shoulders, the exodus leaving Brian and Arthur to a few minutes of silence at the table till Brian asked how things went at the local elections.

'Labour lost this seat, I suppose because only twenty-nine percent bothered to vote.'

'Why was that?'

'I didn't, for a start. I'm sure it's this bombing of Yugoslavia. I just can't believe it. They should have spent all the billions dropping TVs and washing machines, then the people would have stopped killing each other to get at them. Or they could drop a million mobile phones so's people could start talking. That Blair's a real prat. Bombing hospitals and orphanages – it's cruel. And all they can do at home is cut benefits for the disabled. A lot of people round here say they won't vote Labour again.'

'In London we get the Euro elections soon,' Brian said, 'but I won't vote, for the same reason.'

'I never will again, not for anybody,' Arthur said. 'I

can't stand Blair and Cook and Robertson yammering about NATO winning the war when they've never heard the whistle of a bomb. The fuckpigs started it in my name, and spout about how right they are, but I just want to live in peace and have a good time like everybody else, as far as fucking miseries like that will let me. All the rest is propaganda.'

A bottle of supermarket Bordeaux stood by the usual lavish supper when Brian came down from an hour's sleep. 'I phoned Derek and Eileen,' Arthur said, 'and they're picking us up in an hour to go to The Five Ways for a drink. Meanwhile, eat some of this. You must be clambed after driving up from London.' He loaded both plates. 'I heard a few rumbles of thunder while you were upstairs, but it might blow over.'

As if to deny it, a clatter sounded from close by. 'I didn't hear a thing. I go right down, and wake up as if there's a clock inside me.'

'I wish I could. The doctor offered me some tablets, but I didn't bother. It's better than a few months ago, but I don't sleep in the afternoon in case it stops me getting under at night. I sometimes read till one o'clock.' The window was covered by a flash, and the rooftops seemed to explode. 'At least there's nothing lethal at the end of it, like on those Serbs and refugees.'

Brian took a swig of wine, rain as if driving against the house from all directions, ripples of light cutting out the battleship grey sky, followed by shattering blows of thunder. Arthur went upstairs to make sure every window was shut.

'It's going like the First Day of the Somme,' Brian said.

Sulphur tanged the air, and a flash and immediate blast put the lights out. 'That's done it.' Arthur walked through the gloom and took out a packet of candles from the cabinet

243

to put into holders, but a minute later the lights came on. 'On the Somme every flash could have had your number on it. At least we've got a million to one chance. Let God do His worst, is what I say. Come on, we're nearly at the end of the bottle. We'll split what's left.'

Slaps and hugs over, they got into the car, and Derek drove them to The Five Ways. The storm had grumbled its way north but the streets were still empty, so that in ten minutes they were in their favourite music-free drinking place close to the City Hospital – where many in the family had died, though if any recalled sad times (and Brian knew they did) none mentioned them.

The appetizing smell of freshly drawn ale greeted them at the entrance to the lounge, Derek doing a quick march to a table for four. 'They must have kept it for us,' Arthur said.

Young men and women, maybe nurses who worked at the hospital and lived close, talked and drank at tables not packed against one another. The publican, a slim man in his fifties, dressed in a suit and wearing glasses, thin hair combed back, came to offer his hand to Brian, which he shook as if they were old friends, though he hadn't been in for weeks, while the barmaid pumped up pints of Mansfield and fixed the shandy for Eileen.

Built in the early thirties, some of the rooms were under a preservation order so couldn't be altered, the walls of the room covered with drawings of past customers, done by local artists. Such faces were dead and gone, but alive in their small frames and looking (if they could) at what was now poignantly missed.

'There was a lot of protest when the company said it was going to make alterations,' the publican said, 'and now they can't do it, which makes me happy as well as the clientele. It would have been a shame to tart up a nice place like this.'

Arthur was telling a story about Stan the shop steward at a factory he once worked at. 'He was red hot, old Stan was, always calling meetings. Anything wrong, or supposed to be, and he'd go from one machine to another getting us to drop tools and gather around him for a half-hour talk. He called the gaffers blind, and we cheered him all the way. The management didn't know what to do about it. They were going off their heads, specially if he got us to drop tools when there was a rush order on, which there nearly always was. They didn't know what to do. Stan was a real demon, and there was hardly ever a dull day.

'Well, I suppose the gaffers put their heads together at the board meeting, or they must have had a bottle of whisky on the table that day, because one of the directors had a brainwave. They decided to promote Stan, and the next Monday morning he turns up, not at half past seven, but at half past nine. He was wearing a suit, with a collar and tie. The little white tip of an ironed handkerchief peeked out of his lapel pocket, his thick fair hair went back in waves, and his shoes shone like black glass. He walked across the shop floor with his nose in the air and a clipboard under his arm, not saying a word to any of us. We couldn't believe it. The cunning bastards had found him a job in the office, and doubled his wages. He got a salary now. In other words, they bought him off, and it paid 'em to do it.

'But it was no job at all. He'd got nothing to do. They sat him at a desk and gave him a writing pad, a box of paperclips and a set of coloured biros. Maybe they told an office tart to sit on his knee now and again, but all the time they must have been laughing at him behind his back. They'd post something on the sly to a branch in Birmingham, and send him in the company car to fetch it back, saying it was urgent, just to make him think he was useful and might get promoted one day. Or they sent him to a firm as their representative, telling him to collect some obsolete spare parts in the boot.

'We teased him unmercifully whenever he had to walk through the shop. "Hey up, Stan! How are you?" we'd shout. "Have they put your rate up lately? Where are you going, then, Stan? Are you going to buy the directors' condoms? When are you coming back to work with us? We ain't had a meeting for a while. We're just longing to down tools."

'He didn't know where to put his face. We ragged him so much he got to be the fastest walker in the factory. Not that we could blame him. I suppose most of the others would have fallen for it as well.'

Derek took a long drink. 'So what happens to a bloke like that?'

'Wait till I tell you. Every story has an ending. The firm went bankrupt six months later, and Stan was out on his arse. He got no golden handshake, either. Firms were closing down all over the place in Thatcher's time. I got another job, and so did a lot of the others, but Stan was known as a firebrand, and one of the blokes I met on the street told me he'd seen him drawing the dole. Stan didn't know where to put his face. He was counting his money as he walked to where he'd parked his car.

'He wasn't on the dole for long, though. I was in town one day and saw him coming down the steps of the council house with a briefcase under his arm, dressed even smarter than when he'd worked in the factory office. I waved to him, and he waved back, but he didn't stop to talk. I haven't seen him since. He'll probably be Lord Mayor one day, as long as he's not Labour. Come on, sup up. I get thirsty talking so much.' No second telling, since no jar had far to go, and he stood up to go for their refills.

'He doesn't seem too bad now,' Eileen said.

Derek passed the cigars. 'He's getting over it, but there's still a fair way to go.'

'You wouldn't know, though.' Brian puffed on his cigar. 'None of us would show what was going on inside.'

'That's the best way.'

'I'm not sure about that,' Eileen said.

Derek smoothed the froth from his moustache. 'That's Arthur's way, and it's working. They don't need to send him a social worker for counselling.'

'Not unless she's got good tits and nice legs,' Brian said, creating sufficient laughter for Arthur to think what a merry lot they were as he laid the jars down: 'I bought four packets of pork scratchings, so get stuck in. I saw 'em behind the bar, and remembered how mam used to love 'em, but I can't eat 'em in case they break my teeth.'

Brian put one in his mouth, and softened it with a gulp of beer. 'I haven't tasted them for donkey's years.'

'My dad took 'em down the pit in his lunch box,' Eileen said. 'He said they made him work better.'

'They used to be spread out on a big tray,' Brian recalled, 'at La Roche's the pork butchers on Ilkeston Road. Mam often sent me to get some, and told me not to eat any on the way back, but I could never resist a pick.'

Arthur lifted his jar. 'Let's drink to her.' Glasses were emptied and taken by Derek for another filling.

'I remember when I went with her in the ambulance, after she had that last heart attack,' Arthur said, when Derek came back. 'I was sitting holding her hand because she was frightened. Well, who wouldn't be? But the ambulance bloke told me to get away from her, and sit on the other side, because it was against regulations. My fucking blood went up. He was a big bloke and thought he could put one over on me, but I told him to shut his trap or I'd punch his head in. I stayed where I was. He could see I was doing her some good, but he wanted to show his authority.

'After I'd seen mam tucked up in bed I went outside looking for that ambulance man. I was going to give him a right fucking pasting, but luckily for him I couldn't find him. He'd probably gone on another trip to try barking at somebody who'd cringe and do what he said. I'd been going to smash him in the ambulance, but didn't want to upset mam. If I had knocked him about a bit they'd have needed an ambulance for him.'

'The world's full of 'em,' Derek said. 'Somebody's got to keep 'em in their place, or the scabby Hitlers would be all over us.'

Eileen turned to Brian. 'How long are you up for this time?'

'Until Sunday morning. Then I'll slide back to London.' He would bypass the Smoke and head for France on the Shuttle, go travelling for as long as he could stand being by himself. Or maybe he'd put it off till Arthur was right again. They'd go together, and what a trip that would be! 'I'll see you and Derek before I go. Tomorrow I'm taking Arthur to Matlock. It's our favourite run.'

'And on the way back,' Arthur said, 'we'll call and see how Jenny is.'

The waiter came in and laid platters of food on each table, legs of chicken, small sandwiches, meat balls, bits of kebab. 'What's all this?' Derek wanted to know.

'It's from a wedding party in the back room,' the publican said. 'There was too much food, and all this is the leftovers. They told us to spread it among the clients.'

Hands went out, picking things to eat. 'It looks good,' Eileen said. 'I wish I was hungry, that's all.'

'If you don't eat it it's going in the bin, and it'll be a shame if it does.'

'Who do we have to thank for it?'

'It was the bridegroom's idea. Here he is.'

A slim six foot man in his early twenties, with short fair hair, grey eyes, and wearing a T-shirt and jeans, stood smiling at the door, to be thanked and shaken hands with by everyone in the room, congratulated, wished happiness and a long life.

'It was time for me to get spliced,' he said, 'because she's five months pregnant. So eat the grub up if you can. It was too much for us. If we sent it to Yugoslavia it'd be rancid before it got there. I'll get back to my wife now though, because she's a bit tired. It's time to take her home and tuck her up.'

'Which is where we ought to go.' Eileen stood. 'I'm starting to yawn.'

'You aren't five months pregnant, are you, duck?'

She turned to Derek and kissed him. 'I sometimes wish I could be, but I've got to drive you lot home, and it's lucky I have, otherwise who knows where we'd end up?'

Pot after pot of tea at Arthur's kept them talking till the middle of the night, and Eileen knew that when they left Arthur would have no trouble falling asleep. If it meant that Brian wouldn't get his wake-up mug of coffee at eight o'clock he would surely look on it as the best news of the day, as would the rest of them when they heard about it.